MW00641758

THE DEAD CANNOT HIDE

A VISCOUNT WARE MYSTERY #2

J. L. BUCK

CAMEL PRESS

KENMORE, WA

CAMEL PRESS

A Camel Press book published by Epicenter Press

Epicenter Press
6524 NE 181st St.
Suite 2
Kenmore, WA 98028

For more information go to:
www.Camelpress.com
www.Coffeetownpress.com
www.Epicenterpress.com

Author's website: janetlbuck.com

This is a work of fiction. Names, characters, places, brands, media, and incidents are the product of the author's imagination or are used fictitiously.

The Dead Cannot Hide
2023 © J. L. Buck

Library of Congress Control Number: 2022936123

ISBN: 9781684920631 (trade paper)
ISBN: 9781684920648 (ebook)

Printed in the United States of America

Dedication:

To Kath Marsh, my critique partner, whom I cannot thank enough for remaining with me and inspiring me throughout the earlier fantasy novels and into the historical mysteries.

Chapter One

London, July 1812

Lucien Grey, Viscount Ware, doffed his hat to a gentleman on a passing phaeton and stepped up to the front entrance of the Salcott London mansion. The time was exactly half four. The summons from his grandmother Augusta, the Dowager Countess Salcott, had arrived hours earlier, but he had put off his call until the Earl would be in session at the House of Lords. Lucien had every hope of avoiding a quarrel with his father.

The viscount and Salcott had been at odds...well, all of Lucien's life really. The less they saw of one another, the better they got on—especially now. When his father's worst beliefs about his only surviving son had proven false last winter, Salcott's resulting embarrassment had made him more intractable than ever.

And Lucien was in no mood to be polite or tolerant. The War Office at Whitehall was in disarray, and in recent weeks, Lord Rothe had laden Lucien and his fellow intelligence agent Andrew Sherbourne with too many private, clandestine assignments—some frivolous or even foolhardy.

Lucien rapped the knocker twice, keen to get out of the stifling July heat. The door opened promptly, and the elderly butler, a family retainer since Lucien's childhood, greeted him with a smile. "Your lordship."

"Good afternoon, Jeffers. You look in the pink of health," Lucien said, stepping inside. "I trust the gout is not giving you too much trouble?"

"Not bad, my lord. Just now and again." The butler bowed, showing proper deference overlaid with the familiarity of long acquaintance. Only in the last few years had he given up referring to the viscount as Master Lucien. Jeffers' hair was showing significant white now, but age had neither slowed his step nor dulled the alertness in his eyes.

Lucien handed him his hat. "Is the dowager countess receiving?"

"She is, my lord, and will be as delighted to see you as I am. As the Smythes left not more than ten minutes ago, she is still in the drawing room."

"Excellent. I shall announce myself."

"Very good, my lord."

Lucien smoothed his hair, straightened his cuffs, and made his way across the marble hallway, hoping his grandmother's summons wasn't just another opportunity to lecture him. Despite her blatant manipulation to get whatever she wanted, he was quite fond of the old lady and admired her strong-minded spirit. He had no wish to offend her, but any attempt to press him regarding Salcott or his duties to the family name would sorely try his patience.

Frankly, he was tired. A respite from both family and political intrigue was in order.

In the six months since a French spy had been unearthed inside Whitehall, the Home Office and its War Office division had moved from one crisis to another. The war with Napoleon continued to swing back and forth, giving the populace little to cheer about. Discontent, even revolution, was whispered loudly on the streets. In the midst of it all, Prime Minister Spencer Perceval was assassinated in the very heart of Westminster by a madman, and a month later, War Secretary Jenkinson, the 2nd Earl of Liverpool, was appointed Prime Minister and his former position filled by Henry Bathurst, 3rd Earl of Bathurst. As if those events had not caused sufficient upheaval in the upper levels of British government, sixteen days ago, on June 18, America had declared war on Great Britain.

Fortunately, Lord Rothe, the man Lucien reported to in Prinny's secret spy unit, had remained unscathed by the turmoil and still enjoyed a favored position with the Prince Regent. But even that had its downside. As the prince grew less trustful of others, he had relied more often on the Marquess of Rothe and his aristocratic spies to solve the least little problem that annoyed him, including indiscreet scrapes and scandals among his friends or other members of the haute ton that were a potential threat to Prinny's peace of mind or the smooth conduct of government. Rothe, in turn, had reached out to Lucien and Sherbourne more often than not. They had been putting out political fires way too often.

Upon reaching the drawing room, Lucien found his grandmother absorbed in a book, a pair of spectacles perched on the bridge of her nose, her back straight, not a white curl out of place. She was still a grand lady, aging with indomitable elegance. As he strode toward her, she looked up, hastily put her novel and glasses on the table, and held out both hands. "Lucien! I had begun to wonder if you were coming. I have waited all day, naughty boy." Despite the scold, her eyes twinkled as he bowed and took her hands, leaning down to kiss her cheek.

"I beg pardon for my tardiness, Grandmama. I did not realize your request was urgent."

"Fustian. We both know why you dallied until this hour, but rest assured, I did not ask you here to box your ears. Do take a seat, my boy. You look fagged. Shall I ring for fresh tea?"

"Not for me. I feel the want of something stronger." Crossing to the sideboard, he picked up a crystal decanter of port, pulled out the stopper, and turned, cocking his head. "Will you join me?"

The dowager's eyes gleamed. "Need you ask? Surely you did not think I would leave you to drink alone."

He chuckled, handed her a half-filled glass, and settled into a wing-backed chair. After taking a reviving swallow of the excellent port, he picked up the conversation again. "I am surprised to find you in London. I thought you were permanently settled these last few years in the dower house at Salcott."

"Oh, I am. Very comfortably, I might add. Country life suits me at my age, and I would not normally travel so far, but I had business with my London solicitors. They could have come to me, of course, but I also wished to speak with you."

"I gathered that." He leaned forward and studied her face, a flash of unease bringing a frown. "Is something wrong? You are not ill?"

"Do I look ill?" The dowager appeared startled. "On second thought, do not answer that. I am afraid what your answer might be."

"Nonsense. You are as beautiful as ever."

"Now who is talking nonsense?" she said with a smile. "I am well, Lucien, as well as one can be at seventy." Her mood visibly shifted as she pursed her lips. "However, I shall not deny I am disquieted. I came to town because I need your help."

"You shall have it. What can I do for you?"

"A girl from our village, a young woman, I should say...Lucy Drayton is missing." The dowager's hand fluttered in the air. "Oh, I doubt you know her. She must be twenty...or one and twenty by now. Her great-aunt, a dear lady, and I are close acquaintances. Lucy's mother married beneath herself, you see, and the child was brought up in the impoverished but gentle home of an estate agent." She stopped abruptly as though realizing she had drifted off course. "Well, never mind all that, the long and short of it is at her age and still unmarried, Lucy took a position as governess in a respectable household near London. That was a year ago. Her family had one letter, telling them she had arrived safely, but nothing since."

"What makes you think she is missing? She may be busy, involved in her new life."

His grandmother shook her head. "She was ever a polite and considerate child. Her family and I agree Lucy would write and not worry them in this way. Something has happened to her, Lucien. I want you to find her, and if she is not well situated, I hope you can bring her home."

Lucien tapped his fingers on the chair arm. Young servant girls, even governesses, went missing in London all the time, swallowed by a city that could be heartless. Some were later found to have run off with young men; others turned off their positions for a variety of reasons, including accusations of loose morals, disappeared into the seedier parts of town, surviving in any manner they could. Finding her might not be easy, especially if she didn't want to be found. "What does her employer say?"

"Not enough. That is what makes it so concerning." The dowager's frown deepened, exaggerating the age wrinkles around her mouth. "The family wrote to Mr. Harwick, twice, but received no response. Three weeks ago, Lucy's cousin David made the trip to Harwick House and was told she had left without notice late last autumn. And yet nobody told her family...not even Lucy. Is that not strange?"

"I do not disagree, but it is not alarming." He went on, condensing his earlier thoughts. "Girls are let go or lured away by false promises and end up with lives they won't divulge to friends and relatives. She may not thank me for finding her."

"No need to mince words, Lucien. You mean she may be working in a brothel."

"Well, there are other possibilities, but yes, that is one."

"Very doubtful." The dowager spoke with decisiveness. "I know the girl. But *if* she has sunk that low, her family will want to help her. They at least need to know whether she is alive or dead. Will you look into it?"

Lucien smiled. As though he could say no. She knew he would not refuse her. "For you, anything. I shall do what I can. As you know, Lord Rothe has priority on much of my time." The dowager was one of the few who had known, even during his four years of seeming frivolity in the ballrooms and courts on the Continent, that he worked as an agent for the Crown. He had sworn her to secrecy, and she had kept her pledge. Family ties notwithstanding, he owed her. He unfolded his long length and stood. "Speaking of Rothe, I have an appointment with his lordship that I must keep."

"Must you go so soon? Yes, of course, you do." She sighed and gave him an earnest look. "Thank you, my boy. The Draytons— and I, of course—shall be eternally grateful for anything you can discover. I shall not detain you longer, for I know how important your work is, but I hope to see you soon with news of her. I shall remain in London at least another week or two."

"If today's meeting goes as expected, I may be able to look into this right away." Rothe's message had implied he and Sherbourne might be getting a break from assignments. If so, he would be at leisure to do what he could for the Drayton family.

"Oh, excellent."

"No promises the answers will be what you want," he cautioned. "But I shall do my best to learn the truth." He kissed her cheek good-bye and walked toward the door.

The old woman sighed audibly this time. "Oh, Lucien, I am sorry to vex you, but I cannot let you leave without urging you to speak with your father. I mean truly talk with him. I know he should have had faith in you, trusted your character...but now that he knows of your secret work for the Crown, I am convinced he wants to make amends."

Lucien had stiffened the moment she sighed. Now he turned. "You know our differences go back well before my years in the war. Discovering I have not been the care-for-nothing rake he thought I was changes nothing. He will ever hold me responsible for the death of my mother."

"Oh, Lucien, no..."

"It is no matter, truly. I understand. But that does not make it easier."

"No one is to blame for your mother dying in childbirth, least of all the babe. She was always delicate. These things happen in life."

"Try telling that to my father." He saw the pain in her eyes and wondered if it was a reflection of his own. It was not as though this was an easy or new conversation.

"My darling boy, he knows... deep in his heart he has always known, but he could not get past his grief. Theirs was a true love match, and, well... When he finally began to recover, I think he felt it was too late and pride stood in his way."

Lucien shrugged. "It *is* too late. My father and I will never have a normal father-son relationship. Too many bitter years of misunderstandings are behind us."

"I cannot accept that as true, dear boy, but if it is, could you not make something new? A friendship, perhaps. Surely it is not too late for that."

"You make it sound as though we are uncivil. I strive to always show proper respect." Lucien sounded defensive to his own ears and cut himself off. "I must go, or I will be late."

She gave a resigned nod. "Yes, I am sorry. I do not mean to plague you."

"I know." Lucien's face softened. "Just as I know the distance between my father and me causes you grief, but it is a lost cause. You must accept it, Grandmama. I have." He turned back toward the door. "I shall let you know what I learn of Lucy Drayton's fate."

• • •

When Lucien arrived at Whitehall, Andrew Sherbourne, second son of Baron Sherbourne, was lounging in the archway to St. James Park that connected the War Offices on the left and the Horse Guards on the right. A gust of breeze coming off the Thames River caught Sherbourne's auburn hair as he straightened and came forward to meet Lucien. They climbed the stairs to the second floor together.

"I am hopeful he has nothing for us," Sherry said.

"About time. Was this not supposed to be infrequent missions according to our original bargain?" Lucien said, asperity slipping into his tone.

"Rothe does not appear to remember it that way."

As they reached the Marquess of Rothe's outer office filled with the desks of his clerks and under-ministers, the man's personal secretary, Mr. Sloane, stepped forward. He nodded and waved them toward an open door behind him. "If you please, my lords. He is expecting you."

Jeremy, Lord Rothe, elegantly clad in his preferred shade of gray, perhaps to match the silver streaks in his dark hair, stood by the window staring at the archway courtyard below. As ever, he was precise in fashion and demeanor. He turned and smiled.

"Come in, gentlemen. I believe I have welcome news for you."

And indeed, he did. With Prinny gone to Bath for the next month, the confusion and conspiracies that swirled around the Crown had gone with him, giving the War Office and every associated department in London a chance to concentrate on the wars Britain was fighting on the Continent and in America. Since Lucien and Sherry by choice confined their endeavors to the foreign threats within the homeland, it meant they could return to their own pursuits...at least for a while.

"I have nothing for you...well, as long as this latest turn-up is resolved." Rothe lifted a questioning brow.

"It is, sir." Lucien and Sherry gave him the details surrounding the quashed scandal involving the Exchequer of the Treasury. "The woman in question saw the wisdom of returning to the Continent," Lucien finished.

"Thank God. It could have gotten ugly."

Lucien said nothing. He disliked rescuing the minister from such a sordid entanglement with the wife of a foreign diplomat, especially one with suspicious sympathies for "Boney." Intervention had been necessary, but did it need to be him and Sherbourne? He was relieved it was over.

"Well done, as usual," Rothe said. "I must leave you now. I have a meeting with Prime Minister Jenkinson to discuss Lord Southway's Bill of Opposition, and I must not keep him waiting. He takes Louisa to visit the Market and then the theatre one evening every week and today is the day."

Lucien smiled. Lord Liverpool's closeness to his wife, considered eccentric by some, was well known in political circles and among the haute ton. He was not surprised the new Prime Minister still made time in his busy schedule for an evening with her.

"But you, gentlemen," Rothe continued, "are officially on holiday as of now. Enjoy it while you can."

Until you call us back for the next crisis, Lucien silently added. Because of their unofficial status, he and Sherbourne always had the option of saying no, but it hadn't happened yet.

As they exited the building minutes later, Sherry said, "I leave for the country in the morning. Mother has been urging me to visit. I daresay she is missing Father, and I hope to cheer her while he is delayed by this long session of the House of Lords. And you—any plans?"

"A visit to Ware Hall if time permits. My estate manager has been after me for months to see the new improvements for myself. But first, I have a small matter to solve for my grandmother. A village girl from home has disappeared. She came to London as a governess, and no one has heard from her in nearly a year."

Sherry gave a short grunt. "A story likely to have a poor ending."

"Indeed. I warned her, but she tasked me to look into it. So, I shall. Just enough mystery to ward off boredom." He shared a wry look with Sherry, knowing his fellow agent understood how quickly one could go from bone tired to craving the next action.

"I should be back in three or four days, if you need help."

"Good lord, I hope it does not take that long. Give my respects to the baroness."

They parted at the road. Lucien's redheaded groom Finn brought the curricle forward, the high-bred chestnuts prancing at the promise of activity. Lucien took the reins, waited for Finn to climb on behind, then loosened the hold on his team. They broke into a brisk trot.

A weary smile lifted the corners of Lucien's mouth. He was looking forward to a few days to unwind—a morning sparring at Gentleman Jackson's on Bond Street and a leisurely ride to Ware Hall by early next week. But first, a visit to Harwick House, a mere two or three miles outside of London, locate Miss Drayton, or at least discover her fate, and report back to the dowager countess.

His smile broadened. Tomorrow night he was engaged for Mrs. Harrigan's soiree, where he had every hope of seeing the lovely Lady Anne again.

· · ·

Lucien arrived at Harwick House by horseback around one o'clock the following afternoon. He had sent a messenger ahead informing them of his intention to call and found Mr. and Mrs. Harwick waiting in the drawing room of the rambling old mansion. Still an imposing structure, nevertheless, the set of old stone buildings covered with vines had lost much of its elegance, inside and out. Even the furnishings could use a large influx of funds.

Given their lack of cooperation with the Draytons, Lucien had been uncertain what to expect from the resident family, but the couple seemed sociable enough when he was announced by a footman. Mr. Harwick, a tall, hawk-nosed man in his late thirties, stood by the fireplace, one hand smoothing a trim mustache. His wife, a rather plain woman with a casual, almost careless air about her, was seated before a freshly laid tea tray.

"My lord Ware." Mr. Harwick came forward to greet him. "I don't believe I have had the pleasure before today. I am Joshua Harwick, and this is my wife, Beatrice. Welcome to Harwick House, although I am sorry it was such a hopeless errand that brought you here."

Lucien bowed to Mrs. Harwick before turning back to her husband. "Hopeless? Have you had news of Lucy Drayton's fate since you spoke with her cousin?"

"No, no. It's just that…well, we know so little. I confess the whole thing was rather upsetting, having her run off like that. She left us in rather a difficult situation regarding the children. But pardon my manners. Let us be seated."

"May I pour you a cup of tea, my lord?" Mrs. Harwick's voice was as colorless as her demeanor, and she was already pouring as she spoke. An odd woman. She appeared to have little interest in what his answer might be.

"That would be nice. Thank you," he murmured, seating himself on a burgundy sofa across from her. Mr. Harwick came to join them, sitting beside his wife.

They chatted about Lucien's ride to their home, the dry weather, and Lucien finally set down his teacup. "Would you tell me what you know of Miss Drayton? How did she come to be your governess?"

"Through a London agency," Harwick said. "They sent us three names. She sounded the most promising, and she did very well in the beginning. But as the weeks passed, she became...I don't know what to call it. Less satisfied, I suppose."

"Ungrateful, I would say," Mrs. Harwick spoke up. "Nothing was good enough. She had been here no more than three months and wanted leave to go home. I found her crying in her room one afternoon instead of upstairs with the children where she was supposed to be."

"She simply wasn't happy," Mr. Harwick said, cutting off his wife's complaints. "When she turned up missing—"

"When was that?" Lucien interjected.

"It was November. I don't recall the exact date, do you my dear?" When his wife shook her head, he went on. "It has been so long now. Middle of the month, I would say."

"Did she tell anyone she was leaving? Or where she intended to go?"

"No, it was all most strange. After supper she put the children to bed and went to her room as usual. In the morning, she was gone. I assumed—we all did—that she had given into her yearning for home and returned to her family. We did not suspect anything different until her father's letter arrived."

"So, you did receive his letter? Or letters, I should say?" Lucien looked from one to the other.

"Um, well, yes. I know of one, possibly two," Harwick said. "By that time, we had a new governess and so much time had passed..." His voice dwindled off.

"Is that why you didn't reply?" Lucien persisted.

"I am sure I must have written, but really, it had nothing to do with us," Mrs. Harwick said when her husband appeared at a loss. "Wherever she had gone, it had been months before."

"We had nothing to offer the family," her husband added.

Except the courtesy of a response. He didn't for a minute believe Mrs. Harwick had written, and their answers so far had been far from adequate.

"Did she leave anything behind? A note? Any of her belongings?"

"Nothing."

The consistent chorus of replies heightened Lucien's suspicion that they had rehearsed this meeting. Were they hiding something or fearful their carelessness in the matter would come to light? "I assume she didn't use your coach or borrow a horse, so how did she get away? Are you saying she left on foot carrying all her belongings?"

"I see no other explanation." Harwick raised his palms in a gesture signifying his lack of knowledge. "She may have walked to London. It is not far."

Lucien lifted a brow. No, not far, but he tried to imagine a young woman walking three or more miles carrying a band box and dragging a trunk, the items her family reported she had brought from home. He let the silence lengthen without comment, and Mrs. Harwick filled it by offering more tea.

"No thank you. Did Lucy make friends while she was here? Someone she might have told her plans?"

"She and Bethy got along, I guess," Mrs. Harwick offered. "The girl kept to herself. She spoke of a sweetheart back home. Perhaps she ran off to join him."

Strange, he thought. His grandmother had not mentioned a young man.

"Do you recall his name?"

"Heavens, no." She looked at her husband. "Something common, was it not?"

He shrugged. "I don't recall hearing it."

"I believe he lived on a farm," Beatrice Harwick offered.

"There is your answer, Ware. If you can locate this farmer boy, perhaps he can help you." Harwick stood, marking an end to their conversation.

Lucien rose unhurriedly. "While I am here, may I see her room? I would also like to speak with Bethy and to your current governess. I would not want the Drayton family to think I had not made every effort."

"Why the governess?" Harwick demanded. "She never met Lucy. As for the room, Miss Stoddard has been living in there for months. There is nothing of Lucy's to see."

"Even so, I would prefer a brief look to observe how she might have gotten out of the house without being seen. I understand that Miss Stoddard will have no direct knowledge of Lucy, but she may have heard something from the other servants or in the village that was never reported to you."

"Unlikely, but very well. As you wish," Harwick said, giving in with ill grace. He turned to his wife. "If you could locate the two women, I shall show his lordship to Miss Stoddard's room."

Lucien's visit to Lucy's former lodging was, in fact, helpful; not the space itself, but the attic location and the narrow servants' stairs raised even more questions about the story he'd heard—in particular, the undetected removal of Lucy's belongings.

Although Lucien expressed his desire to conduct the interviews in private, the Harwicks insisted on sitting in, claiming it would be improper to leave the women without a chaperone, and they paid close attention to every question. To his surprise, Bethy, no more than sixteen but bright-eyed and spunky, ignored the presence of her employers and talked to him without hesitation.

"Sure, Lucy talked about Ned from back home, but he were just a good friend. She wouldn't've went off with him."

"Did she tell you she was leaving?"

"Nary a word. It weren't like her. I think she were taken, nabbed by some passing stranger."

Harwick cleared his throat, perhaps a warning to her, but said nothing.

"Why would you say that?" Lucien asked.

"'Cause she wouldn't run away, and it's all I can think of." She shrugged. "I just know somethin' happened to her."

Yes, me too, Lucien thought, but I doubt it was a random stranger. "Mr. Harwick thought she vanished in mid-November. Would you agree that time is about right?"

"It was November 18. I'm sure of it. My little sister's birthday was the seventeenth, the day before, and I spent the night at home with her. When I come back the next morning, Lucy was gone."

Miss Stoddard was not so forthcoming. She shifted her feet, denied hearing anything, and her gaze often flitted toward her employers.

"You found nothing in her room that indicated where she might of gone?"

"Oh, no, sir. I would have told the master or mistress." Her voice cracked with nervousness, and Lucien wondered if the Harwicks were that hard on the staff or if she was just that meek. In either case, her reticence could scarcely have anything to do with a young woman she had never met.

Lucien thanked the Harwicks and took formal leave. While collecting his horse from the stables, he seized the opportunity to question the garrulous head groom, who introduced himself as Thom, and Jack, a bashful stable-man in his thirties.

"Not a sight of her leaving." Thom turned and appealed to the stable-man grooming a bay gelding. "What say, Jack?"

Jack glanced up, his face twisted with surprise at being addressed, and shook his head of shaggy black hair. He mumbled, "No, sur," and returned to his vigorous brushing.

"Strange doings, it was." Thom scratched his head. "I'da heard if someone had come to fetch her up." He shrugged. "How does a girly just disappear like that?"

Excellent question.

As Lucien swung onto his stallion's back and settled for the ride to town, his brow wrinkled in frustration. He had been told a pack of lies. Why, he didn't know, but one thing for sure, Lucy had not dragged a large trunk from the attic floor down the servants stairs by herself; and certainly not in the quiet of night without someone hearing a loud thump, thump on the wooden steps.

Chapter Two

Lady Anne Elizabeth Ashburn, daughter of the Earl of Chadley, frowned at her reflection in the looking glass. Why did that curl insist on standing out like a twig on a bush? "Just pin it up with the rest, Jenny."

"Now, milady, leave it to me. When I'm finished, Lord Ware won't be admiring anyone but you tonight." Her lady's maid met her gaze in the looking glass with humor in her eyes.

"Truly, Jenny, you should not say such things," Anne admonished softly, but there was no proper reprimand in her voice. In the space of six months, Jenny had earned her mistress's confidence and had gone from temporary housemaid to abigail. The two young women were as close to friends as mistress and servant could be, and Anne had perhaps revealed more of her interest in the viscount than she had intended.

For in truth, she did like him. His tall, confident figure, fashionably tousled black hair, and, yes, those compelling gray eyes that seemed to know your every thought and found most of them amusing...well, he was devilishly attractive. How could she not admire him? Despite his somewhat wild reputation, she had seen another side of him last winter. Anne inhaled a deep breath, recalling those harrowing yet exciting days marked by murder, blackmail, and a secret spy code.

"How does this suit, milady?"

Anne raised her gaze to the looking glass and stared at her blue eyes surrounded by a flattering coiffure. "Oh, Jenny, you've done it. It is perfect. You are a wonder." Anne's fair curls were piled high on her head with two allowed to dangle down each cheek. She smiled and jumped up, her blue and white gown swishing around her feet. "My white gloves and shawl, and I shall be ready."

• • •

The clock in the hall chimed half eleven. Anne's hopes for the evening were fading fast. While her friend Miss Margret Barnett was talking about the latest scandal involving a certain married lady, Anne stole another glance toward the doors of the crowded drawing room. Where was he? Would Lord Ware miss yet another social event? Perhaps he was not as interested in her as she had thought.

Since her return to London in April with her younger cousin Georgina and her Great-Aunt Meg for Anne and Georgina's first social season—soon to be two and twenty, Anne would have been on the shelf for sure if not presented this year—Anne had been happy to renew her brief acquaintance with the viscount. It wasn't that she lacked for other admirers or indeed past marriage proposals, but no one had been just right or engaged her thoughts the way he did. She had thought their friendship might blossom... well, he *had* sought her company at soirees and society dinners and danced with her at balls. Yes, he had missed many of the season's events, but that was the fault of Lord Rothe and his mysterious errands, was it not? Recent walks in Hyde Park and two carriage rides had given her reason to anticipate Lord Ware's company at some point this evening. They were at least good friends.

"Oh, my." Anne clutched Margret's arm and pulled her back to avoid collision with a laughing gentleman from a circle of young sprigs. "Such a lively crowd."

"Pardon my clumsiness, ladies." The red-faced, young man who'd come close to stepping on their toes hastily bowed. "I hope no harm was done."

Anne smiled at him as she and Margret skirted around the merry-makers. "None at all. A near miss, but we are fine." From their excessive hilarity, she suspected they had dipped rather deeply into the host's expensive champagne.

Mrs. Harrigan's soiree was a crushing success by London standards but not so over-crowded that Anne and Margret couldn't move between rooms, stopping now and then to observe those in attendance, particularly those who had figured in the latest on-dits, or to briefly join a variety of activities from card games to dancing. Other guests, including her great-aunt Meg, preferred to spent their time chatting with friends while occasionally listening to the harp music that played in the background. Auntie appeared to be well-established for the evening with a circle of like-minded matrons.

Anne paused to watch her younger cousin Georgina dancing a quadrille with her betrothed Lord John Bennington. The limited space on the dance floor made the steps more difficult, but none of the couples seemed to mind.

Margret followed her gaze and smiled. "They make a fetching couple, do they not?"

"Very much so. I am pleased to see them so happy in one another's company." Only a few months ago, her young and impulsive cousin had put the engagement in jeopardy by a childish indiscretion. "I think she has settled a bit during the season. She will turn eighteen next month, and they are planning an early October wedding before it gets too cold."

"She will be a lovely bride."

"Which you shall see for yourself. Georgina has your name on the guest list."

Margret grinned, showing her rosy cheeks. "What fun we shall have! Where is it to be?"

"At his parents' home near Doncaster, last I heard. It is to be an entire week of games and parties. Naturally the men will be hunting." Anne lightly fanned herself with a handkerchief in one hand. As the rooms continued to fill, the air was becoming warm and stuffy despite the open windows. "Can you believe this heat?"

Margret suddenly nudged her and whispered, "Your Lord Ware just arrived."

"Hardly *my* Lord Ware," Anne whispered back, but she felt her cheeks grow warmer. Why was it the viscount invariably disturbed her composure in this manner? He wasn't the only handsome man in the room. She refused to turn and look. Let him come to her. She had seen little enough of him the past few weeks.

"Oh dear. I must have a moment," Margret said, pulling her to a stop. "I have something in my shoe." Margret shuffled her feet for a few moments. "There. I think it was just a wrinkle, and it is gone now. Oh, no. I've lost my slipper. Anne...?"

"Good evening, Lady Anne, Miss Barnett."

Both Anne and Margret turned toward the viscount's familiar voice behind them. Margret continued to search with one foot for her lost slipper.

"How charming you both look," Lord Ware continued. "May I join the company of two such beautiful ladies?"

"Indeed you may, my lord." Anne smiled at him. Upon seeing another man approaching, she added by way of warning to Margret, "I see Miss Barnett's beau headed this way, so you will not have both of us to yourself for long."

Margret stifled a shriek and renewed her efforts to recover the elusive shoe. "Mind your tongue, Anne. Beau indeed," Margret said under her breath, then she turned a beguiling look on Captain John Wycliff. "Good evening, Captain."

"My lady." He bowed, his eyes twinkling, and took her hand. "If you would consider putting on your shoes, would you join me in a turn about the room? I thought a lemonade might be nice."

Margret's eyes widened. "Unfair, sir, to expose my dilemma like that." She turned her back on him, facing Anne, lifted the front of her skirt a few inches to locate the missing shoe, and slipped her foot inside. Once she'd smoothed her skirt, she turned back around. "How could any girl resist such a gallant offer?" she mocked, yet a faint gurgle in her voice betrayed her suppressed laughter.

"Will you join us?" Wycliff asked glancing at Anne and Ware as he took Margret's arm.

"Maybe later," Ware said smoothly.

Wycliff nodded as he led Margret away through the crowd.

"Having you all to myself is no hardship," Lord Ware whispered close to her ear when they were alone. "We have had few chances for private conversation in recent weeks."

Anne felt her cheeks flush again, and she looked away. "It has indeed been a busy season for both of us. I have not seen Lord Sherbourne for a while either. Is he otherwise engaged?"

Lord Ware accepted her deflection, but she saw a hint of amusement in his gaze. "Sherry is rusticating at home for a few days. The baroness has been a trifle out of sorts."

"I hope it is nothing serious," Anne said earnestly. She had only met Baroness Sherbourne once but had liked her very much—a gentle and considerate lady.

"Sherry didn't think so. She has not said as much, but he felt she was blue-deviled from missing the baron. This session of parliament has been excessively long."

"Oh, of course. And the dreadful heat is so oppressive," Anne said, searching for her lace fan in her reticule and raising it to cool her cheeks. "It is nearly unbearable."

"Shall we step out on the balcony? I cannot promise it will be cool, but there was a light breeze when I arrived."

"That sounds wonderful." She placed her hand on his arm, and they strolled across the room, exiting through the open French doors.

Anne placed a gloved hand on the rail of the large balcony and looked out over the dark landscape. Several other couples were taking advantage of what relief the night could offer and talked softly in the relative solitude. A gentle wind caressed her cheek, and she drew in the pleasant mixture of fragrances drifting up from the gardens below. A night bird's call made her smile. Lord Ware was silent too, as they stood there under a star-filled sky, absorbing the companionship of the moment.

"Better?" he asked after a while. "You were looking a bit flushed."

"Much better, thank you." She turned her head to look at him, searching for something to say. "You missed Lady Woodley's dinner party last week. It was quite a lively evening. There was a great deal of talk regarding the colonies. Lords Farber and Southway became quite angry, close to exchanging blows."

"So I heard. I'm not sorry to miss another quarrel. They are becoming all too frequent, but I do regret not seeing you…and Miss Barnett, and your lovely young cousin, of course. Rothe is my only excuse. He has kept us steadily occupied until yesterday." Lord Ware turned on his devastating smile. "I am happy to say I am unfettered at the moment."

"Rare indeed." Anne returned his smile. She had known about his secret involvement with Lord Rothe and the War Office since a series of incidents last Christmastide. She also knew better than to ask for details. Instead, she asked, "How soon will you become bored?"

He chuckled. "Think you know me, do you? I dare say you are right. But my grandmother has given me a small task, so I don't envision suffering from ennui for at least the next few days. By then, I suppose Lord Rothe will have summoned us again."

"Your grandmother? Did you not tell me she was living in the country at Salcott Hall?"

"At the estate's dower house, yes. She is in London for a visit. Says she came to see her solicitors, but I believe it was her tender heart that brought her here—she would deny that, mind you. In any event, a young village girl, the relative of a friend of the dowager countess, is missing."

"Missing? Oh, dear. I hope she has not come to harm." Anne cocked her head. "Young, you say. How young? Are you free to tell me about it? Surely this cannot be one of your many secrets."

A gleam of humor chased his frown away. "No secret at all. If you are truly interested, I shall tell you all about it.

"You know I am. That insatiable curiosity of mine." She gave him a playful look. "Perhaps I can even help you solve it."

His smile broadened. "A lady's perspective would be of great benefit, I am certain, and simply discussing it should not place your life in jeopardy this time."

"How ho-hum."

"Yes, probably not worth the effort."

"Enough," she declared. "You have succeeded in whetting my interest."

"Then I shall not tease you further. In short, a young woman came to London a year ago to be a governess and her family has heard nothing beyond she had arrived. I visited the former employer today. After hearing his story, I agree that Grandmama and the girl's family have reason for concern."

"A mystery?" Anne turned to face him, keen to hear the rest, and lowered her voice. "What was the story?"

"That she left in the middle of the night without telling anyone, even her friends, and without anyone seeing her."

"It does sound unlikely. Do you think she came to harm?"

"Let us not get ahead of ourselves," he cautioned. "Other explanations are more likely."

She tipped her head. "Such as?"

"She took a better position, or she ran away with a man."

Without telling her friend? Doubtful. Young women tended to tell their friends everything. "Was the employer someone I know?"

"I doubt it. Although their home is just outside town, Joshua and Beatrice Harwick do not move in London society."

"Here you are," Margret's voice interrupted. She and Capt. Wycliff joined them on the balcony. "My goodness, it is warm inside." She was fanning herself somewhat vigorously with a dainty yellow fan. "We tried dancing, but it is just too stuffy in that crowded room." She turned to Lord Ware. "Did I hear you mentioned the name Harwick? Could it be the Harwicks from Blinker's Marsh?"

His brows lifted. "Why yes, I visited them today. Are you acquainted?"

"Well, yes, in a way. They are our nearest neighbors...although not at all sociable. I'm surprised you would know them." Her eyes lit with interest. But that was Margret. Ever looking for a bit of gossip. Not that Anne faulted her. A shared unquenchable curiosity was beyond doubt the reason she and Margret had become such bosom friends so swiftly.

"I don't, not really," Lucien hedged. "We only met this morning."

"I cannot imagine what you would have in common." Margret

tipped her head, giving him a speculative look. Clearly she expected him to say something more.

Anne tugged on Lord Ware's arm. "May I? She might know something that would shed light on the matter."

Lord Ware laughed, shaking his head at Anne and Margret's eager faces. "I see why you two are friends. Of course, tell her."

Captain Wycliff cleared his throat. "I was about to go for punch for the ladies, but now you have me curious too."

"Stay, by all means. I daresay refreshments can wait a little longer."

"Well…" Anne lowered her voice conspiratorially. "Lord Ware is working on a mystery. The disappearance of the Harwicks' governess."

Margret gasped, putting her fingers over her open mouth. "Miss Stoddard is missing? Good heavens, I had not heard." She dropped her hand. "When did this happen?"

"No, not Miss Stoddard," Lord Ware corrected. "The previous governess, Lucy Drayton."

"Lucy Drayton?" Margret frowned and repeated the name again. "Oh, yes. I remember now. I never met her because she was there only a few weeks, but I heard she was suddenly called home. I didn't realize she was missing." She looked up at Lord Ware, her eyes narrowed. "Do you suspect something is wrong at Harwick House?"

"I wouldn't say so, not yet. Everything appeared to be in order during my visit this morning. Although, I cannot help but wonder… The story they told of Miss Drayton's departure was odd, at best. The facts don't seem to fit."

Anne gave him a steady look. "Perhaps you should tell us everything. We might be able to help, and surely Margret and her family should be made aware of potential danger in the neighborhood."

"Now Lady Anne, you go too far. No one said anything about danger. Miss Drayton may have simply left Harwick House by her own choice."

"Of course." Anne nodded. "But what if… What can it harm to tell us?" she coaxed.

"I can only imagine." He gave a wry grin. "Since I have already pricked your curiosity, I suppose it would be cruel to withhold the tale now." He described his visit to Harwick House in detail, what the couple and their servants had to say, and pointed out his concerns about the bulky trunk and Lucy's unknown means of travel.

Anne wasn't the only one hanging on every word. Margret's intense stare and Capt. Wycliff's probing questions revealed their own keen interest.

"So she just vanished one night," Margret said. "How does that happen?" She dropped her voice to an ominous whisper. "Tell me, truly, Lord Ware, do you believe she was murdered? Or abducted?"

Three pairs of eyes flashed to his face, awaiting the answer.

"Too early for that. Several other explanations come to mind." His eyes turned grave. "Some of those are not fit topics of discussion in the company of ladies."

Despite her country upbringing, Anne was not a sheltered miss. Maybe she had not witnessed as much of life as others, but she had heard and read a great deal. She could think of two or three possibilities of the variety that ladies were not supposed to know. "I might agree, except, as you pointed out, nothing explains the trunk."

His gaze met hers. "Not yet. Much still needs to be done."

"Such as question their staff when the Harwicks are not around," Margret said. "Oh, you don't suppose our servants know anything? Servants do gossip. I can ask." She gave a little laugh and clapped her hands. "I have the most marvelous idea. Mama is holding a houseparty next week, starting Wednesday. You must come, Lord Ware. Dearest Anne and Capt. Wycliff are already invited, and it would be wonderful if you could join us. Then we can all assist you in discovering what happened to Lucy."

Anne stifled a laugh at the viscount's look of dismay. He recovered quickly and declared himself delighted to accept the invitation, but he had clearly not expected ongoing *assistance* with his inquiry.

Despite Lord Ware's reservations, Anne was pleased with developments. Conversations with Lord Ware were never boring, and she had missed his company. To add the intrigue of a real-life riddle to solve...well, to be sure, this houseparty had all the markings of being a lively one, perhaps the best she'd ever attended.

Not long afterward, Lord Ware and Wycliff escorted the ladies back to the drawing room where they chatted over refreshments until the men took their leave and headed for the card room. Anne went with Margret to tell her mother about the extra houseguest. Lady Barnett was of course most pleased to add such a distinguished person to the guest list. By some strange unspoken agreement, neither Margret nor Anne mentioned his investigation or the missing governess.

Chapter Three

Lucien halted his curricle at the front doors of the Barnetts' imposing red brick manor, stepped down, and flipped the reins to Finn. Taking his bag from the back, he paused and took in the white stone entrance set off by faux columns and an elaborate overhead fanlight. Sir George might not be of noble lineage, but he was certainly landed gentry of considerable means. The door opened before Lucien had a chance to knock. The diligent butler, a middle-aged, slightly pudgy man, bowed his head in welcome.

"I am Viscount Ware," Lucien offered. "I believe I am expected."

"Certainly, my lord. Allow Joseph to take your bag. The others are in the drawing room."

"Thank you." Lucien surrendered his bag to the tall, lanky footman, although he could just as easily have carried it. "I would prefer to freshen up first, if I may. It was rather a dusty drive."

"As you wish, my lord." The butler signaled to Joseph, and Lucien was shown to a second-floor bedchamber, a medium size room with dark, masculine furnishings and windows overlooking a well-tended lawn with a large stand of shade trees and a glimpse of a pond in the distance.

Declining further services, Lucien put his clothes and personal items away and brushed his jacket. He'd left his valet at home. During his years spying for England on the Continent, he'd made numerous hasty trips where a valet would only have added to the risks. Consequently, it was no great inconvenience to do for himself. Talbot bemoaned the practice as beneath a viscount's station, but Lucien had persisted in the habit, particularly when his primary goal was business rather than social and he traveled light.

After changing and washing off the road dust, he descended to the lower level and followed the patterned rugs runners down the hall to the drawing room. Sir and Lady Barnett and Miss Barnett—his host in knee breeches, the ladies in afternoon tea gowns of blue and yellow, respectively— were standing near the door to greet each guest.

"Lord Ware, you came," Miss Barnett exclaimed. "I wasn't sure as Anne has told me how often you are called away for one thing or another. These are my parents."

He inclined his head toward the middle-aged couple. "Sir George, Lady Barnett, thank you for allowing me to join your house party."

"We are delighted to have you," Lady Barnett returned.

Her husband gave a nod of agreement. "Ware. A pleasure."

Lucien turned a smile on Miss Barnett. "You should not have doubted me. I would not dare miss your party."

"I think you would dare anything," she retorted, "but I am very glad you're here."

"As am I." He excused himself some moments later as another guest arrived. He spotted Lady Anne looking lovely as usual in a white gown with green trim. Five other guests were getting acquainted or re-acquainted as the case may be, counting the older gentleman just behind him. A small party indeed, although in later conversation with Lady Anne and Miss Barnett, he discovered three additional guests had yet to arrive.

"We will be fourteen in all, counting family," Miss Barnett said. "The majority are older friends of my parents, but there are six of us of a younger set." She lowered her voice discreetly, "I am not sure Miss Grant and Viscount Pemberton will pay us much heed. They are recently affianced, and it appears to be a love match. I suspect they accepted our invitation to get away from prying family eyes for a few days." She nudged her chin toward a couple in the far corner, deep in conversation. "It is perfect really. That should leave the rest of us free to follow our own *particular pursuits*."

Lucien did not miss the implication, and he stifled a sigh. Miss Barnett had not abandoned her interest in the missing governess. She appeared to see his inquiry as a diverting lark for the duration of the weekend. He was not opposed to talking it over with the ladies, but in light of the unexpected risks Lady Anne had faced last winter, he was reluctant to involve them in any significant way.

Perhaps it had been a mistake to share Lucy Drayton's story, but then he wouldn't have been invited for the house party, giving him easy access to the neighborhood. And, truly, he had no compelling reason to exclude them. With Capt. Wycliff available to amuse Miss Barnett and hopefully keep her out of harm's way, Lucien would enjoy sharing the puzzle with Lady Anne. Her keen mind and extraordinary gift of recollection were certain to be useful and would add perspective.

"I look forward to lively discussions, Miss Barnett," Lucien conceded.

"Then we should begin," she said brightly. "As soon as I find Captain Wycliff. I think he is talking grouse hunting with Mr. Stewart." She hurried away across the room.

"Is it truthfully acceptable to you?" Lady Anne asked when they were alone. She gave him a pert smile. "I have good reason to know you do not welcome others meddling in your cases. Or was it just me?"

Lucien chuckled. "Most assuredly not. But this matter is unofficial, a favor for my grandmother." He hesitated a moment. "I confess I had hoped Miss Barnett would not show such keen interest. Lucy's disappearance may be a tragic event with answers unfit for a lady's ears. Or, to the contrary, it may have a simple explanation, a huge disappointment for those seeking diversion."

"Honestly, my lord. I thought you would know by now that not all ladies are as delicate or frivolous as men frequently believe."

"I am very much aware, and yet I would spare you either distaste or boredom."

"Well, I am looking forward to solving the mystery…a much more intriguing pursuit for the days ahead than Speculation or Spillikins."

Lucien lifted a brow. "That is not saying much." He had not played either game since childhood and would not be looking forward to evening activities if they were a sample of what he could expect.

Lady Anne laughed softly. "If you could see your face. No, my lord, neither game is part of the planned entertainment. From what Margret has said, you will find a variety of evening activities from dancing to charades, and I expect at least one table available for Faro or Whist."

"You relieve my mind, my lady. I had thought it might be necessary to take refuge in the library each evening."

This light-hearted discourse was interrupted by Miss Barnett returning with the Captain on her arm. "Now, that we are all here," she said, "let us retire to the garden, and I'll tell you what I've already learned about Lucy."

Heaven help us. Lucien feared he had under-estimated the captain's ability to curb Miss Barnett's enthusiasm.

Once they had gathered at the far end of the rose garden, Miss Barnett poured out her sleuthing activities of the last few days. "I asked our upper servants and the cook what they knew of Lucy. Not much really. Only two had met her, and most had heard she ran away because she wasn't happy at Harwick House. And our housekeeper repeated tales I've heard forever about strange noises in the woods, a monster in the bog. Local legends, you know the sort of thing. However," she paused dramatically, "my abigail, Suzy, had tea with Miss Drayton one day in Blinker's Marsh. Suzy thought her a sensible girl who would not have left without giving notice, not unless something bad had happened to frighten her... or she hadn't left on her own. One other suggestion I heard and wondered about—could she have had an accident, fallen in a ditch or some other mishap?"

"I suppose it is possible," the captain said slowly. "But only if she already intended to leave. Otherwise, she wouldn't take her trunk on an evening walk. Now if she was sneaking away in the dark... Surely someone would have found her by now."

Miss Barnett shrugged. "Maybe not. They were so certain she had gone home to Sussex that I doubt they looked beyond the house and stables."

"Perhaps we should start with a wider search," Lady Anne said, appealing to her companions. "The fields, woods, ditches along the roads. And the marsh."

"Oh. Well, yes, that sounds reasonable." Miss Barnett looked less certain than before. "We would be searching for her body, would we not?"

Capt. Wycliff gave Lucien a troubled look. "The ladies should not be exposed to anything so distasteful."

"Absolutely not." Lucien turned to Lady Anne. "When we talked about this, I had in mind sharing ideas, discussing the possibilities, not looking for corpses under bushes."

"It would not exactly be a body by now, would it?" Lady Anne asked as though seeking a dodge that would make it more acceptable. "More a pile of bones?"

"And that makes it better?" Lucien suppressed an urge to laugh.

"I had not really thought about finding a body or in what condition it might be." Miss Barnett shivered, clearly thinking about it now. She seemed torn between the excitement of the hunt and fear of what she might see.

"A body would not bother me," Lady Anne declared. "At least I don't think so. But you did not answer me, Lord Ware. Would it not be bones by now?"

"Probably." Lucien did not elaborate. He had seen bodies on the battlefield in various stages of decay. None of them were pleasant.

"I suggest we end this discussion and leave the inquiry to Lord Ware," Captain Wycliff said. "The day is far too nice for such gruesome thoughts."

"Are you backing out of the investigation?" Miss Barnett demanded, confronting him with a look of disapproval. Wycliff's hesitation seemed to stiffen her resolve. "I'm surprised at you, Captain."

"Do you honestly want to continue?"

"Why not? The idea of finding a body just took me by surprise, is all. I shall not sleep easy until we discover what happened to the poor girl. Are you going to help us or not?"

The captain sighed. "As you wish. I shall not attempt to dissuade you from participating in this venture, as long as you agree to one condition. If there is searching for a body to be done, Lord Ware and I will do it."

Miss Barnett's lips pursed in a willful gesture, then she suddenly relented. "I agree. I have no interest in poking under bushes or dragging the streams."

"Nor do I," Anne said.

The captain beamed in approval, but Lucien studied the women's faces with suspicion. They had given in too quickly, and Miss Barnett had been rather specific about what they would not do. A specificity that allowed a lot of room for their inventive minds. He frowned at Lady Anne, but she avoided his gaze. Would they dare to launch an investigation on their own? Of course, they would. But he'd be wasting his time to ask. They would only deny it, and he might give them ideas they didn't yet have. And in truth, after all this time, it was doubtful the ladies would discover anything that could get them into trouble.

He and Wycliff could search the countryside on horseback and talk with neighbors and tenants along the way. With any luck someone saw Lucy leave or would remember a young woman with a large trunk. The sooner he solved this matter, the better. The ladies would then be forced to find a more appropriate amusement for the duration of the houseparty.

• • •

The following morning, Lucien rose before eight and joined other early risers for a horseback ride before the heat of the day. He drew in a deep breath of fresh country air, free of the odor of human refuse that so often permeated parts of London during the summer heat. After the first couple of miles, he veered away from the other riders to begin his search of ravines or ditches where a body might go unnoticed. He hadn't gone far before Captain Wycliff caught up with him.

"Sorry, I was late this morning. Miss Barnett and I had a bit of a row last night. I guess I didn't sleep well. Are we really going to search for the girl's body?" he asked, settling his horse to a trot beside Lucien.

"Well, I am, but I don't expect you to join me if you would rather not. I hope to cover quite a bit of territory by horseback without the necessity of fighting my way through brush on foot."

"I'm here to help," Wycliff said. "Anything to keep the ladies from getting involved. I saw my share of dead bodies in the war and would not wish that on Miss Barnett and Lady Anne. They have no idea what it is like."

"You may be right," he said, although he knew full well that Lady Anne had seen a corpse before. "Lady Anne is made of sterner stuff than you think, and unless I miss my guess, so is Miss Barnett, but it would not be a pleasant experience. I'm also keeping an eye out for an abandoned trunk, which might be easier to spot."

"What would that tell you?"

"If there's not a body close by, I'm not sure," Lucien said urging his horse into a gallop. "If it belonged to Lucy, it would be our first tangible evidence what direction she may have gone...and a great source of speculation."

Despite criss-crossing several times, looking in gullies and ditches, behind hedges, fences, and stone walls, they found neither body nor trunk and returned to the manor at midday. The family and many of the guests were sitting in the garden, drinking lemonade and tea.

"Where have you been all morning?" Miss Barnett demanded as soon as she and Lady Anne got them alone. "Were you making inquiries without us?"

"Hush, Margret," Wycliff urged. "We do not want to be overheard saying anything that would arouse suspicion."

"So that *is* what you've been doing. What did you find?" she demanded with a definite pout.

"I shall tell you nothing, if you continue in that tone."

Miss Barnett dropped her gaze and subsided, and Lucien began to hope Wycliff might actually have some influence over the young woman.

"Will you tell us if we ask nicely?" Lady Anne smiled, taking up where her friend had left off.

"We learned nothing," Lucien said. "But I had a very pleasant ride. It has been a while since I've had the opportunity to get out of London and enjoy the freedom of the countryside."

Lady Anne eyed him doubtfully as though wondering if he was keeping secrets.

"Upon my honor," he said. "We saw nothing except birds, hares, and one fox."

"Oh, well, then I guess we missed nothing." Miss Barnett sniffed. "Next time it would be polite to be included."

"That was not our agreement," Wycliff reminded her.

The subject was dropped after that and amiability was soon restored. They joined the rest of the houseparty for a pleasant couple of hours chatting about horses, politics, or coming social events and strolling in the gardens.

Lucien grew restless and slipped away, stopping in the kitchen for a bit of bread and cheese, skipping afternoon tea to ride out again. He felt no remorse for going alone. He'd avoided any promises to Miss Barnett's entreaties, and Captain Wycliff was available to keep the women entertained. Lucien would cover more ground by himself.

Ranging farther afield this time, he stopped at farmhouses and the closest estate on the far side of the Harwicks' property. As he feared, memories had faded over so many months, but everyone he questioned was fairly certain they had not seen a young woman on foot last November and definitely not one dragging a trunk. Lucien turned his stallion toward Barnett Park, having eliminated a large section of the countryside without finding a trace of Lucy.

Rain started to fall when he was less than a mile from the

stable. After leaving his horse with Finn, he hurried into the house and toward the stairs to change his wet clothes before dinner.

"Lord Ware," the butler stopped him as his foot landed on the second step. "A letter came while you were out."

"Ah, thank you." Lucien glanced at it. An unknown hand. It must be the reply to his letter to Lucy's cousin, David Drayton. He had asked Drayton to write him here. Lucien put it in his pocket and climbed the stairs before Miss Barnett or Lady Anne spotted him. He was wet and dirty and needed to change. And, in truth, he wanted to read the letter alone. Once inside his room, he stripped off his wet coat and unfolded the message.

Lucien read rapidly, nodding a time or two. The Harwicks had told Drayton the same vague story Lucien had heard. What he hadn't realized was Lucy's cousin had taken his inquiry so far as to question people in the village, but unfortunately, his efforts had yielded nothing Lucien did not already know.

Perplexed, he shook his head. It made no sense. How could an inexperienced country girl vanish with all her belongings, including a heavy trunk, and leave no trace behind? Obviously, she couldn't. She'd had help. A friend had assisted her in getting away and provided transportation—a good friend who knew how to keep his or her tongue. Or she'd been abducted or harmed and carried away.

He went back to reading the post. Lucien had asked Drayton to speak with Ned, the alleged sweetheart, but Drayton already knew all about him.

They were close friends, not sweethearts, Drayton wrote, *but confided most everything. Ned went to the family last March, expressing his concern he hadn't heard from her since October, and that's when I approached the Harwicks.*

So, another possibility scratched off.

The last part of Drayton's letter addressed Lucien's questions about Lucy's belongings. Her mother confirmed she had brought one trunk, a small bag, and a hat box when she left for the Harwicks. All of which were now missing.

Lucien set the letter on the table and went to the wardrobe to select dry clothes. Tomorrow was time enough to show the note to Lady Anne and the others. Nothing more could be done tonight, and he intended to put the inquiry aside for a few hours and enjoy an evening of good company and Sir George's excellent port.

• • •

Despite the loud thunder and the heavy summer rain that beat on Lucien's window overnight waking him twice, he met Captain Wycliff on time for their arranged early morning ride. Although intended as a pleasure jaunt, their path led through a nearby ravine where they watched for anything unusual. At one point, Lucien dismounted to explore a suspicious piece of clothing, but it was a torn and shredded man's coat, probably lost years ago.

When they returned to the manor an hour later at a brisk gallop, a hearty buffet was laid. Lucien and Wycliff had nearly finished their repast when Lady Anne and Miss Barnett arrived in the morning room. Lucien set down his coffee, and he and Wycliff rose.

"Good-morning," Lady Anne said. "Oh, please be seated and finish your coffee. If the wonderful aromas are any indication of what awaits us at the buffet, it may take a while to make our choices." Her glance took in their riding apparel. "I see you have already been out for a ride. Without us, once again. Did you see anything interesting?"

"Only birds and beautiful countryside," the captain replied.

"We were not gone long," Lucien added. "Mostly I went to clear my head. We had rather a stormy night."

The ladies made their selections from the breakfast sideboard, and Miss Barnett sat next to the captain. Lady Anne hesitated only a moment before setting her plate next to Lucien. The footman immediately filled her cup with hot chocolate.

"Thank you, Bertram. You remembered my sweet tooth."

The young man nodded with pleasure at her praise. "Yes, my lady. I do my best."

She returned his smile and turned to her companions. "I hear we are taking afternoon tea at four beside the pond," she said. "The servants were leaving to find a spot and start set up as Margret and I were coming down the hall."

"So early?" Lucien asked.

"Well, they had tables and chairs. I suppose it takes a while."

"Is the pond not on Harwick property?" Wycliff asked.

"We share the pond," Miss Barnett said. "The property line runs down the middle of the marsh. In truth, it can only be called a pond during wet years. It is fed by the narrow stream that zigzags across both our properties. As children we looked forward to the rainy seasons so that we could go swimming in the heat and have enough ice for skating in the winter."

"I saw the gleam of water from my window," Lucien said. "I assume this was a wet year, even before last night."

"Yes, I would say so. The pond has been low, but the overnight rain will have helped. And what a change from last summer when the edges were nothing but cracked mud, and the main pond area was just a shallow marsh. The ducks returned this spring." She turned to Lady Anne. "We shall have to take old bread to feed them."

"A good idea. What shall we do between now and teatime?" Lady Anne's eyes twinkled at Lucien. "When we met on the stairs, Margret suggested a game of shuttlecock."

"I see," he replied. "Perhaps I might tempt you with a morning walk instead. I received a letter last night from Lucy's cousin. Nothing that explains her absence, but I thought it might be of interest to all of you. While you finish breakfast, the captain and I will have an opportunity to change out of our riding clothes and then meet you in the garden. If you wish, of course."

"Really, my lord Ware, you are such a tease. Why can you not tell us about it now?" Miss Barnett demanded.

"And risk being overheard? I prefer the inquiry remain a private matter as long as possible."

• • •

The ladies must have hurried through breakfast, because Lucien and the captain arrived in the garden to find them already waiting, seated on one of the stone benches.

"Did you bring the letter?" Miss Barnett demanded as Lucien and Wycliff approached. "We have been speculating over why he wrote and what he had to say."

Lucien grinned and retrieved it from his pocket. "I had written to David Drayton, asking him about his visit with the Harwicks and about Ned, the alleged sweetheart from home. This is his prompt reply." He handed it to Lady Anne.

Miss Barnett scooted close to her as Lady Anne unfolded it and began to read in a low-pitched voice. "Dear Viscount—" She broke off as an older couple approached and stopped at another bench nearby. She stood and said pleasantly, "Shall we walk? There are some lovely flowers at the end of the north path."

When they gathered again away from other guests, she finished reading the letter aloud and returned it to Lucien. "It is sad she never made it home. Her family and friends clearly miss her. Does this letter help us?"

"Well, I think it confirms that somebody is lying," Miss Barnett said with conviction. "Lucy could not have carried all that baggage away by herself."

"Just so," Wycliff agreed. "But the truth need not be sinister. The servants may have shared her belongings among themselves or given them away after she left. They might not want to admit it to us."

"Surely someone would have told by now," Lady Anne said protested. "They might have kept quiet in the beginning, but now that her relatives are alarmed and it is obvious people are looking for her, would they not own up to it?"

Lucien frowned. "The Harwicks and the servants are all telling the same story. Would such a group work together to cover such a petty theft?"

"I don't think it has anything to do with the clothing. They are concealing something else, and the servants have been told to lie by their master or mistress." Miss Barnett gave a decisive flip of her hand.

"And what is important enough to keep up the charade?" Wycliff asked.

"Is it not obvious?" Lady Anne murmured.

Wycliff raised a brow. "Not to me."

"Don't be obtuse," Miss Barnett admonished him. "Someone at Harwick House knows exactly what happened to her, and they don't want us to figure it out."

"I daresay you are correct," Lucien said.

Wycliff did not look convinced, but further discussion was interrupted by sounds of distant shouting. They all turned to look, and Lucien shielded his eyes against the bright sun with one hand.

"I say," the captain exclaimed, "what has caused the uproar?"

"It's the servants down by the pond," Miss Barnett exclaimed.

Two of the footmen were racing across the field to the house, shouting for Sir George. Realizing something was terribly wrong, Lucien hurried to meet them, Wycliff by his side. As the footmen drew closer, Lucien could see their expressions of shock and fear, then he noticed the rest of the servants were streaming behind them, abandoning the chairs and tables they had been arranging. Lucien, Wycliff, and two other gentlemen guests broke into a run.

"What has happened?" Lucien demanded, upon nearing the two footmen in the lead. "Is someone injured?"

The older of the two footmen sucked in a ragged breath and gasped, "Somebody's dead."

Chapter Four

The younger footman's gaze darted around as though searching for safety as he blurted his own disjointed response. "Terrible to see, m'lord. Women screamin' and cryin'. Never seen nothin' like it."

"Slow down and get a hold of yourself," Lucien said firmly, gripping the young man's arm to steady him. "Who is dead? How did it happen?"

The footman's eyes widened. "Bog monster maybe."

Lucien looked at the older of the two, hoping for a better account, but saw no help there—his eyes were round as wheels, and he was gasping for breath, winded from his erratic flight or too overcome to speak.

"Are you sure the person is dead?" Captain Wycliff demanded.

Furious nodding from both men. "Oh, yes, sir. It's bones. Well, mostly. I saw the skull and the waxy, stringy stuff—"

"That's enough," Lucien interrupted, uncomfortably aware of the growing crowd around them. "The details can wait until later."

The young footman glanced over the viscount's shoulder at the ladies and gentlemen who had gathered from the house and gardens and took a steadying breath. "Uh, yes, the ladies... Sorry, my lord."

"Not to mind," Lucien said. "Report this to your master, then perhaps a pint of ale in the kitchen, my good man. The captain and I will go to the pond and wait for the constables." He glanced over his shoulder, saw Lady Anne and Miss Barnett on the verge of joining him, and strode toward them shaking his head. "Please go inside, ladies. I promise we shall tell you what we find, but it is nothing you need to see. Keep everyone at the manor, if you can, until the constables take charge."

Lady Anne and Miss Barnett agreed without protest. They had been close enough to hear what the footman said, and he saw the questions in their eyes. They too were wondering if this discovery would end the search for Lucy Drayton.

Lucien, Captain Wycliff, and two other men headed toward the pond, striding rapidly through the sun-parched field not yet revived by the recent rain. They passed the other fleeing servants, many pausing long enough to voice their fear or morbid interest in the ghastly find. Lucien had a good idea what he would find at the scene, and he felt a twinge of reluctance as he slogged through the shallow water to an area of broken reeds and marsh grass at the pond's northern edge. His nostrils flared, but the only odor was a mixture of the earthy scent of sludge and the pungent odor of stale water. Then he saw it. Despite the servants' forewarnings, he grimaced at the gruesome remains. Water, weather, animal and insect life had all left their mark.

Someone behind Lucien sucked in a noisy breath.

The skull had split open, the upper half sitting like a cap. The eye sockets— empty except for oozing mud—stared at him mournfully. Slender finger bones and one skeletal foot stuck out of the mire, nearly hidden among the water grass. Last night's rain rushing across toward the pond had exposed and washed the bones white so that the servants noticed them.

Remnants of clothing, shredded by time and the elements, were stained nearly black by sludge and decay, but small patches of ruffles suggested the garment belonged to a female. Lucien spotted what could be a garment bag about five feet away, no sign of a band box or trunk.

He exchanged a look with Captain Wycliff, then turned to the two men behind them. "A young governess from the neighboring manor went missing last November. In addition to a bag, not unlike that one," he pointed, "she also had a bandbox and trunk. Let us spread out and see what else can be found. It might help confirm who this is."

The gravity of the situation was attested to by neither man

demanding further details. They simply started looking. Ten minutes later, the shout came. "Over here. It's a trunk."

Lucien waded along the edge of the pond to the trunk's location. He'd barely reached it when two constables came running down the hill. A third, older constable strode behind them at a slower pace. The younger men were yelling and waving their hands. "Get out of there! Get away from the body! Leave things alone."

The situation deteriorated from there. Once Lucien and his fellow guests had given the constables the information they had regarding the skeleton and who it might be, senior Constable Jones made it clear in plain language that he wanted them to leave. When Lucien offered to stay and help, Jones's eyes narrowed, and he looked the viscount up and down.

"Pardon me manners, but this ain't no business for you, sir. Reckon we can handle a small mishap like this without help from the Quality. Now, I'd be right pleased if you'd be on your way. I'll be sure to let Sir George know what we discover when I have time." His tone was more offensive than his words. The heavy-set constable was so puffed up with his own consequence that Lucien might have been amused under other circumstances.

Small mishap? So that is how it was going to be. The constable had already decided to write it off as an accident. Very convenient for someone. However, Lucien had seen all he needed for the moment, and he shrugged, offering no protest. If he hurried, he might have time to find and question the servant who found the body before the witness's memory was befuddled by Constable Jones' suggestive bullying.

Lucien nodded to the captain. "Shall we go? There is nothing more for us here."

"Aye. He is welcome to the poor creature," Wycliff said. "I'm thankful it is not my job to recover it."

"A difficult task, to be sure. If they don't destroy the bones in digging them up, a medical man might still be able to tell us something."

"It has to be Lucy, do you not agree?"

"I would lay a good wager on it. And her death was no mishap as the constable suggested. The body had been buried."

• • •

Although the guests and servants had retreated to and stayed within the house, Lucien spotted several faces at the windows as he and the captain approached. They made it to the side door without being accosted by anyone, wiped their boots and parted to clean off the mud and change before seeing the ladies.

Instead of going straight to his room, Lucien slipped into the servants' hall. Shocked faces, even anxiety, met him.

"Pardon the intrusion, but I wish to speak with whomever made the discovery at the pond."

"Of course, my lord," the housekeeper said, visibly relaxing that his unexpected appearance was not bringing further bad news. "That would be Rube Thrup, one of the stable lads."

"Thank you. I apologize again for the interruption."

"No apology needed, my lord." The matronly woman was being magnanimous. It was quite a disruption in the servants' routine to have a guest enter their quarters. He quickly removed himself and made his way to the horse yards.

Rube Thrup, no more than a boy in his late teens, was sitting on a harness box. The other staff who'd been questioning him faded away upon Lucien's approach. The lad was noticeably shaken and Lucien crouched beside him.

"Can you tell me how you came to find it?" Lucien asked.

"Nearly tripped over it, m'lord. So shocked I was, I almost fell." His face blanched at the thought of sprawling on top of the skeleton.

"Why were you in that particular spot?"

"We'd been told to clean up the area, and I saw somethin' white in the grass. Thought it might be a dead bird at first or somethin' else that would bother the guests. So I went to take a look, and… there *it* was."

"You were right. It certainly would have upset the ladies," Lucien said dryly. "Good work, lad."

Rube ducked his head. "Thank you, m'lord, but weren't nothin'."

"Did you touch or move anything?"

"Oh, no, sir." The lad gave him a horrified look. "Got away quick as a fox and yelled for the footmen."

Lucien nodded, eyeing him. "You seem an observant lad. Were you working here last November?" When he nodded, Lucien continued, "Did you see anything unusual near the pond about that time or remember anybody saying they had?"

Rube screwed up his face. "That's a long time ago, m'lord. Nothin' particular, 'cept there weren't enough ice for skatin' last winter. Pond din't fill till the spring rains. No reason to go down there, I guess."

As suspected, the remains must have been buried when the area was only marshland, the water level too low to form a decent pond. The muddy ground would have made it easy to dig a shallow grave. Perhaps the murderer had hoped the pond would completely fill and hide the body under water for years.

Or the killer may have acted on impulse, choosing the closest place to be rid of a corpse.

After praising Rube once again for his bravery, Lucien returned to the house. This time he left his muddy boots in the boot room, knowing someone would clean and polish them. Not to his valet's satisfaction, of course—nothing ever was unless Talbot did it himself—but perhaps his exacting valet would never know how badly Lucien had abused them. After all, Talbot was at Hays Mews and wouldn't see the boots for several days. By that time, he *might* not notice. Lucien sighed; not a chance. Talbot would know.

He took the back servants stairs to avoid being seen without his boots and rang for bath water. He smelled like the pond.

Forty-five minutes later, Lucien strolled into the drawing room for afternoon tea, only to be directed by the footman to the salon on the far side of the house.

"The mistress thought the view superior," the man explained.

Ah, yes, fields of wildflowers and hedgerows. Lucien gave a nod of understanding. His hosts hoped to distract their guests from thoughts of the unsavory investigation by keeping it out of sight. Before departing from the drawing room, he took a quick look out the windows. Three or four figures were visible at the pond in the general area of the remains. It might take hours to recover the entire skeleton. Nevertheless, he anticipated Constable Jones or one of his men soon would arrive to question everyone…or at least try.

Lucien smiled grimly, Sir George might have run them off. Polite society had very little tolerance for being questioned by anyone, much less officers of the law. Jones might well take the easy route and confine his efforts to Harwick's household, a less elevated personage than Sir George and closer to the inquiry, considering the probable identity of the bones.

Captain Wycliff was already in the salon—not surprising as Lucien had been delayed by his conversation with Rube, the stable boy—and the ladies had heard what the captain deemed proper for their ears. Lucien felt no obligation to fill in the gory details.

"Was it very bad?" Lady Anne asked him when the four of them found a moment alone.

"It was grim," Lucien conceded, exchanging a look with Wycliff. "And before you ask, I have little doubt it is Lucy Drayton. We found a trunk not too far away."

"The captain told us. He also mentioned how odious the constable behaved."

"He's always that rude," Miss Barnett said with disgust. "Father has little regard for him."

"I guess our inquiry is over," Lady Anne said. "The mystery has been solved."

Lucien lifted a brow. "Nothing has changed for me. I promised to find out what happened to the young woman, and I will see that is done. If the constables can discover how she ended up in the pond, that will be excellent. Since I doubt that will happen, or that they will even try, I shall continue with my own investigation."

"Can we still help?" Miss Barnett asked.

"Given the unpleasant turn of events, I think not," Lucien said.

His response was met by protests from both ladies, but as expected, Captain Wycliff heartily approved his decision. "It is too dangerous. If this was murder—and how can there be doubt? —the madman is still out there. This little game has become too perilous."

"It was not a game," Miss Barnett denied stoutly. "Was it, Anne? We knew Lucy was in trouble, and we wanted to find her. Of course, we hoped to rescue her and didn't think she'd be dead, not truly." She turned to face Lucien. "I'm glad you shall ignore Constable Jones. He would never find the scoundrel or see he was punished." She heaved a sigh. "Oh, this is so horrid. I don't understand why anyone would kill her. Cannot we still help, Lord Ware? At least continue to talk over your progress and sort through possible motives?" She hurried on as though confident of his acquiescence. "What terrible thing could Lucy have done for someone to want to kill her?"

Lucien was grateful Miss Barnett was being sensible about the need to limit the ladies' participation, but his gaze lingered on Lady Anne's face. He very much feared she would not be put off so easily.

"Maybe nothing, at least deliberately," Lady Anne mused in response to Miss Barnett's question. "Murder is dreadful...and unthinkable to most of us. But if one were inclined to violence, I suppose there could be several reasons. She may have unwittingly seen or heard something she should not."

"But what? Ooh, I can think of another reason. What if Mr. Harwick seduced Lucy and she was in a delicate condition?" Margret said in a hushed voice. "Would he not try to silence her to protect his reputation?"

"And perhaps you read too many novels, my dear friend," Anne said in the same undertone, quirking an eyebrow at Miss Barnett. "Do you know anything of Mr. Harwick's character to make him such a villain?"

"Well, no, but..."

Capt. Wycliff laughed. "Rather fanciful and melodramatic, Miss Barnett. More likely a disagreement that ended in violence. It could even be an accident that someone tried to conceal."

"Why would they hide an accident?"

Lucien was content to let them speculate while he pondered how to get a look at the bones or at least the doctor's report. A bashed skull or broken long bones might indicate the cause of death. Constable Jones would never give him the information, but Bow Street would…if Jones requested the runners' assistance. However, that was not likely. Too many country constables resented what they perceived as interference from London, and Lucien strongly suspected Jones was among them.

An appeal to Rothe would get him access, but he was loath to reveal his connections with Whitehall. He preferred to poke around discreetly another day or two, be a little more sure of the facts, especially the victim's identity, before bringing outside pressure on the constabulary.

Chapter Five

Late the following morning, Lucien found his host alone in the manor's comfortable study, furnished with leather chairs, dark woodwork, and a marble fireplace that commanded an entire wall. A gentleman's room. Sir George sat at a table glaring at what appeared to be estate books when Lucien tapped on the open door.

"Pardon the interruption, sir, but if I might have a word?"

"By all means, Lord Ware. Do join me. These confounded books are putting me in a sour mood. I cannot make head nor tail of my steward writing." He slammed the open book closed and stood, offering Lucien a hand. "I suppose you wish to talk about this sad business at the pond." He gestured toward one of the chairs and seated himself again.

"I do," Lucien admitted. "And I must confess I accepted the kindly invitation to your house party under what might be considered false colors. I came here looking for Lucy Drayton."

Sir George's brows arched in surprise. "You have nothing to confess. Margret was very excited and couldn't keep the secret. She told us all about it. Your inquiry seemed harmless enough, but I did not anticipate it would expose what appears to be a murder."

"Nor did I, or I would never have told the ladies about it."

"I appreciate that." Sir George cocked his head. "The remains are those of the governess, I presume?"

"Not confirmed, but I am proceeding on that theory."

"Then you are continuing your inquiry?"

"Yes, sir. Whether or not the remains prove to be hers, I hope to discover exactly what happened to Lucy Drayton, including who was involved."

"What about my daughter and Lady Anne?" Sir George asked, a frown crossing his face. "With the discovery at the pond, surely they should no longer be involved."

"I completely agree. Captain Wycliff and I are doing our best to convince them their participation in this matter is over."

Sir George gave a reluctant laugh. "I have not known Lady Anne that long, however, I know my daughter well. Margret is a good daughter, but she is headstrong. I doubt if you succeed in putting her off for long, but I would appreciate it if you keep trying."

"You can count on it. A murder inquiry is no pastime for the ladies." Lucien could almost hear Lady Anne's indignant reaction. "I will do what I can to divert them, but I have been acquainted with Lady Anne for several months. She and Miss Barnett are a well-matched pair. It would not surprise me if they are making plans for their own investigation. If that is the way of it, I would prefer to have them under my eye."

Sir George nodded slowly. "I suspect that is true. Ah, well, I *know* it is, but I shall hold you to it that you will attempt to dissuade them."

"Absolutely. Now, if I might ask you a few questions related to my inquiry?"

Sir George waved a casual hand. "Whatever you need. But if you are inquiring about the residents of Harwick House, I barely know them. They have been in residence four or five years but keep to themselves. I doubt if I saw this Lucy Drayton. You might ask our servants."

Lucien smiled. "I believe your daughter has already questioned them."

"Has she, by Jove?" Sir George chuckled, before his expression sobered. "Well, there you are. She may have the bit in her mouth over this and will not be deterred short of locking her in her room."

Feeling the less said along those lines, the better, Lucien moved on. "If the Harwicks don't socialize in the neighborhood, what about houseguests? Do they entertain?"

"Not large parties, but they do have regular visitors. Never met any of them or heard their names in the village, but I have seen riders and carriages come and go most weekends. At least over the last year or more."

"Does that include last autumn, particularly November?"

"I am sure it does." Sir George offered Lucien a cigar, which was declined, then lit one for himself. He took a puff before adding thoughtfully, "I recall a party on Bonfire Night, but I cannot say any other day in November with certainty. But around here not many weekends during the harvest go by without hunting or shooting on most estates."

"By regular visitors, do you mean repeat guests?"

"Yes, I believe so. Now that you asked, there is one carriage in particular with a pair of high-stepping spotted grays that comes frequently, at least twice a month."

Relatives? Friends? Associates of some kind? Lucien would need to know more about anyone that visited that often. He wondered if Miss Barnett had asked the servants about Harwick's visitors. If not, he might have to probe further or ask her to do so. The task might keep her and Lady Anne out of other mischief.

"I assume you had guests last November?"

"Most certainly. Every week, I dare say. My wife could tell you precisely." He straightened to give Lucien a hard look. "Are you suggesting one of our guests might have harmed the girl?"

"No, sir. But they may have seen a person or event having no importance at the time...a young woman carrying a bandbox, a rider near the pond, a cart crossing the marsh."

Sir George absently picked up his cigar box again, offered it to Lucien, then set it down when he realized he had a lit cigar smoldering in the flat silver cup used for collecting ash. He picked up the cigar and took a few puffs. "I suppose it is possible, but I would not like to see our friends drawn into something this ugly."

"I realize it is distasteful, sir. If it becomes necessary to talk with them, I promise to be discreet." Despite Sir George's concerns, Lucien intended to ask Lady Barnett for a list of their guests staying at the manor on November eighteenth. At this early stage in the inquiry, anything might later prove important.

The two men chatted a while longer, revisiting the subject of the Harwick household, but when Lucien was certain his host had nothing new to add, he thanked him and rose to leave. He paused at the door. "By the by, who would the constable ask to examine the remains?"

"Doctor Morehouse, the local surgeon. He is our only medical man."

"Is he likely to talk to me? Jones will never share the medical report."

Sir George humphed and pursed his lips. "I think Doc will see the need. Give him my name. It might help."

"Thank you. I will." After obtaining the doctor's direction, Lucien left Sir George to ponder the estate books, sent for his curricle to be brought round, and stopped in the small parlor to ask Lady Barnett for the November guest list. He waited while she finished going over tomorrow's menu with her cook and made his request as soon as the servant left.

"Oh, my, yes. That poor girl," Lady Barnett said softly. "Of course, I will copy the list. Anything to help. I keep all the names and directions from each party. It makes invitations so easy the next time." She stood and crossed the room to a dainty Queen Anne desk. "I shall have it for you this evening. Good success, Lord Ware. For her mother's sake, if nothing else. I would need to know what happened to my child."

"Thank you. My thoughts as well, my lady."

• • •

Lucien intercepted Doc Morehouse as he was returning to his thatch-roofed cottage with its cheerful blue door in Blinker's Marsh.

"Viscount Ware, is it not?" Morehouse said, offering his hand. "I have been looking forward to your visit."

Lucien gripped his hand. "Yes, I am Ware, but how did you know I would be calling?"

Morehouse's eyes twinkled. "I had an earful from Constable Jones. He warned me against talking to a nosy London lord asking way too many questions."

"Guilty, I'm afraid. The constable and I did not exactly start on a good foot."

"Knowing Jones for a number of years, I'm not surprised. Please, come inside. Would you like tea? Or something stronger?" the doctor added, rather wistfully, Lucien thought.

"Whatever you are having." Although it was barely two o'clock, it was never too early for brandy. Lucien soon found he had not been mistaken in the doctor's preference, although Morehouse salved his conscience by pouring a scant finger's breadth in his own glass. No doubt he still had patients to see.

They settled comfortably with their drinks in a small room the surgeon used as a study and library. Shelves stuffed with medical books, a dozen jars of unknown powders, and small paraphernalia of the medical trade lined three walls, surrounding a large desk cluttered with paper and two well-worn but sturdy chairs.

Morehouse gave Lucien a questioning look.

"I shall not pretend otherwise, "Lucien said. "I want your opinion on the skeletal remains form the pond."

"Jones wouldn't tell you anything, I suppose?"

"I didn't ask. Given his attitude so far, I felt it wasn't worth the effort…and would only rile him."

Morehouse chuckled and swirled his drink before taking a sip. "Yes, I see your point. What is your interest, if I may ask?"

"A family needing answers." Lucien explained what had brought him to the village, beginning with his grandmother's request. "There is a good chance the bones are those of Lucy Drayton."

Morehouse nodded. "I cannot dispute it. The victim was a young woman, but—not to be indelicate—there is nothing the Harwicks or her relatives, Heaven forbid, could identify by viewing the corpse." He opened a drawer on his desk, picked up a cameo necklace, and handed it to Lucien. "They found this in the mud beneath the bones. I've sent a description of it to Lucy Drayton's family, but I don't expect a reply for several days. If they confirm it belonged to her, I will feel confident in certifying the identity."

Lucien studied the cameo carefully, wishing for a moment that Lady Anne was present with her extraordinary memory for detail. The small, shell cameo of a Greek goddess was framed in gold and hung on a delicate gold chain. A family keepsake perhaps, passed down from a grandmother or great-grandmother. It saddened him to know Lucy would never pass it on to a child of her own. He returned the necklace to the doctor. "Once her identity is established, I am sure her mother would appreciate its return."

"Of course. There is little else I can offer them. It will be left to you or others to tell her family why this happened and by whose hand."

Lucien leaned forward. "What was the manner of her death?"

"The back of the skull was shattered. Several savage blows, I would say. No simple fall could do that. If she was stabbed or shot or even poisoned, there is no evidence left of it, but I can tell you the head injuries alone were severe enough to end her life. I have no doubts that she was murdered, but Constable Jones does not agree. He insists it was an accident."

Lucien sighed and leaned back. "Neither your conclusion nor his failure to accept it surprise me. Any possibility she was with child?"

Morehouse lifted a brow. "I found nothing to suggest it. No fetal bones were found, but with the condition of the body..." He shrugged, shaking his head. "I cannot say with certainty. For her family's sake, my official answer is no." Morehouse gave a soft snort and stood. "I hope you catch the scoundrel."

Lucien rose and retrieved his hat from the table. "Any thoughts who might have done this?"

"I'm sorry, I don't. It was a brutal attack. A man, I'd say. And I hope to God it was a stranger. Hard to believe anyone in our village would do this. When I have a response on the cameo, I shall send word to Barnett Park. Unless there is something else, my lord, I do not mean to rush you, but I have patients awaiting my attention."

"Of course. I won't delay you further. Thank you for your time and your candor. One day I hope to tell you the name of Lucy's killer."

After departing from the doctor's cottage, Lucien left Finn with the horses outside the local pub and wandered around the village another two hours. He had a drink in the tavern and then visited the trade establishments, a small apothecary shop, and a stand of fresh farm goods. At every opportunity, he attempted to strike up a conversation. Not all of the villagers would talk with him—maybe that was Constable Jones' doing or a natural suspicion of strangers—but when they did, he eventually asked about the skeleton at the pond. Often they brought it up themselves.

What he learned was Blinker's Marsh was rife with speculation. Most had already accepted as fact that the remains were those of Harwick House's missing governess, but why and how she died was answered by a myriad of theories, varying from an attack by a mysterious marsh creature—already mentioned by the footman—to more common suggestions of a random lunatic, an argument with *someone* unknown that turned violent, and even one unsubstantiated idea offered out of spite.

"I daresay she was no better than she should be. Been layin' with the master, I'd wager. Kilt herself, maybe, after finding she was…well, you know. These young girls think they be somethin' 'til they find there be consequences." This harsh opinion came from the pinch-faced woman at the produce shop.

Despite Constable Jones' well-known theory of accidental death, the majority of villagers accepted Lucy's death as a murder, however, and clung to the belief that such violence could only have come from one or more strangers who were now long since gone. Lucien presumed the tale helped them sleep at night.

On his way back to the pub to retrieve Finn and the curricle, he stopped at the blacksmith's shed where the smithy introduced himself as Joe Bates. The large, muscular man was working on the broken wheel of a farm cart.

Lucien's initial questions elicited the same responses he'd heard all day.

"Don't get many strangers, not unless they're visitin' one of the big houses," Bates said. "Never met the governess, current or past. Folks from Harwick House keep to themselves."

"So I've heard. Any trouble from the household or their visitors?"

"Nothin' I heard." The smithy picked up his mallet, glancing toward the cart.

Lucien took the hint. "Well, thank you. Have a good day."

Bates nodded and returned to hammering the metal bar into a new wheel brace. Lucien had nearly reached the roadway when the pounding stopped and Bates' voice brought him to a halt.

"There is somethin' curious though."

Lucien turned and took a step back. "Yes?"

The blacksmith frowned. "Might mean nothing. Probably don't. But two years ago about this time—yes, it was summer 'cause her papa died the winter before—a village girl went missin'. They said she done run away, but aint that what they said about this Drayton girl too?"

Chapter Six

Anne and Margret's afternoon walk started with an innocent stroll through the gardens, but it wasn't long before their conversation turned to Lucy Drayton, and they found themselves crossing the field toward the pond. Of course, they were curious. And they were not the only ones. Anne had watched from the window as several others from the manor and the local village make the trip earlier that day.

"I am surprised the captain and Lord Ware have not returned by now," Margret said, sounding a bit annoyed. "I wonder where they went? I supposed they're investigating without us...once again."

Anne frowned. "I don't think they are together. Lord Ware drove away in his curricle some hours ago, and Captain Wycliff was not with him. Perhaps the captain is riding with the other guests. Personally, I thought it was too hot, and a leisurely walk in the garden sounded much cooler." She flashed a grin at Margret and fanned her heated face with her hands. "I failed to anticipate a lengthy tromp across the fields without any shade."

"Only a little farther. You want to see where the bones were found, don't you?"

Anne wasn't sure why, but, yes, she did. It was an uncomfortable admission. Making a spectacle out of a young woman's tragedy was not quite the thing, and they could hardly justify it by claiming to help Lord Ware. He had already viewed the scene...and he had excluded them from further investigative activities, not that he was wrong. Her one terrible experience with cutthroats and murderers a few months ago should have been enough to keep her home with her stitching.

Yet here she was. Conscious of the extra weight of the small derringer she now carried in her reticule whenever she left the house, Anne expelled a sharp breath. At least she was prepared for trouble this time.

"Over here. Oh, Annie, I see broken reeds," Margret whispered. She shivered and hugged herself. "Maybe this wasn't such a good idea."

"Don't get miss-ish on me," Anne said. "We are here now." She picked her way across the squishy ground until she could see the piles of overturned mud and trampled marsh grass the constables had left behind—and all the footprints of those who had come to stare. An unsettling sight, Anne thought, knowing Lucy's bones had lain there, and she looked away.

She studied the rest of the scene, the fields and woods surrounding the pond. Was it mere luck that no one had observed the burial? With the openness of the fields and the trees shedding their leaves last November, the spot should have been at least partially visible from Barnett Park. She turned to look in the opposite direction and could see the back of Harwick House. In the dark, Lucy might have walked unseen or been carried down the narrow path through the trees, but she had been buried out in the open. Why? Was that not terribly risky?

Anne pressed the toe of her boot into the squishy ground. Of course it would have been easier and quicker to dig a grave in the wet earth. Perhaps the night had also been cloudy or moonless, lessening the danger of exposure.

"Shall we go now?" Margret's voice was barely above a whisper. "The place feels...I am not sure...just amiss. As though someone is watching us."

Anne's pulse jumped, and she looked furtively around, searching for a glimpse of someone or a movement among the trees. She found nothing to explain Margret's unease. "I do not see anyone. Your imagination, maybe. It is rather gruesome here."

"I wish we had not come," Margret said, still whispering. "I shall doubtless see her muddy grave in my nightmares for weeks, perhaps years. Are you not ready to go?" She gripped Anne's hand and tugged her back toward the manor. Glancing down at the wet hem of her gown, she pouted her lips in dismay. "Oh, my, look at that. It will soon be time for tea, and we shall need to freshen up before we are presentable."

"Oh, me too," Anne added, looking at her own muddy skirt.

On the walk back, Margaret was silent, and Anne soon became lost in thoughts of Lucy. At the house, they sought their separate rooms, and Anne found Jenny waiting for her with a gown already laid out.

"I saw you in the field returning from the marsh," the maid said. "Everyone but me has been there today, I think, but what were you looking at? Isn't the body gone?"

"Yes, the police took it away," Anne said, as she slipped out of her dirty boots. "I would not have wanted to see it."

"Then why go?" She helped Anne out of her gown and waited while her mistress washed her face and hands.

Anne shrugged. "Curiosity, I suppose." But it was more than that. Perhaps a need to understand the unimaginable. It made Lucy's death real somehow. "All we saw was mud and lots of footprints. Oh, I love this dress," she said as Jenny dropped the white tea gown with blue ribbons over her head. "It is one of my favorites and always makes me feel cool even in the heat."

They spoke no more about the pond, but the scene was burned into Anne's memory. The sludge, the smell of stagnant water. The discarded piles of muddy earth that seemed to haunt the spot, as though having given up their secret, they too waited for answers. Anne shook her curls. Now who was being fanciful? All the same, she felt a deep desire to see justice for Lucy. She would not rest easy until the killer had been caught and punished.

On her way downstairs, Anne realized she had not asked Margret if she was at home last November eighteen, and what about current guests? Had any of them been there? Shouldn't they be asked if they had seen anything? Anne tapped her chin in thought. Surely Lord Ware could not object if she made a few inquiries from the safety of the manor house.

With that thought in mind, Anne abandoned her pensive mood, put a smile on her face, and joined the other guests in the drawing room. Due to the heat and little afternoon shade in the garden, tea was served inside today. Anne took her lemonade to a seat near an open window in hopes of finding a hint of breeze. She was talking with the newly engaged couple, Miss Grant and Viscount Pemberton, when Margret waltzed into the room in a light and airy gown of pale-yellow muslin. Bubbling laughter indicated her good humor had been restored. Tea was almost over before the two women found themselves together.

"I saw you with Pemberton and Miss Grant. Could they talk about anything besides each other?" Margret grinned. "I would tease him about it, but I don't know her very well. I would not wish to embarrass her. She seems a lovely person."

"I thought so. We had a pleasant chat. How do you know him?"

"Our fathers were in school together. Even as a boy, Hugh came with his parents for the autumn hunting parties."

"Were they by chance here when Lucy disappeared?"

Margret's face registered surprise. "I cannot say for certain, but I think so. We had several parties around that time. Hunting season, you know." She raised a hand to cover her mouth. "Oh, Anne, I must have been here too. To think I might have seen her... or the murderer." She ended on a faint note. "If only I had looked outside or gone for a stroll that night."

"Don't trouble yourself about it now. Who else was visiting then? Anyone else who is here now?"

"The Halstons, I suppose. Oh, it's so hard to remember. Maybe Hugh will know. I could ask mama—she always keeps a guest list— but she would ask why I wanted to know." Margret shook her head emphatically. "We do not want to get her started on proper ladylike behavior."

Anne and Margret approached the newly engaged couple together. Hugh Pemberton showed little reaction to Margret's inapt 'questions, apparently used to his outspoken friend, and he responded quite amiably. "Yes, I believe we were here in November, but the hunt never went near the pond. The ground is soft and treacherous on horseback. I don't recall anything unusual happening, but that was months ago. I suppose I should have known you couldn't resist a mystery. Is that the date the governess died?"

"It's when she disappeared."

Anne enjoyed watching the easy exchange between her friend and Pemberton as Margret told him about Lord Ware's inquiry and even described their visit to the pond. His fiancée, Miss Grant, was not enjoying the story, however, fidgeting and frequently looking away from their blunt conversation.

Hugh finally noticed Miss Grant's discomfort and took her hand. "I apologize, my dear. We shall stop now. Margret and I have become quite use to talking about all manner of things we should not."

"You need not explain. It's just…that poor girl. So horridly sad. But if discussing it might help to find who did this, I do not mind."

But clearly she did. Margret appeared to perceive this, and after one final question—could he name any of the guests from last year's hunt, which he could not—they moved on to lighter topics of conversation.

That evening, when everyone gathered for pre-dinner drinks, Anne and Margret found an opportunity to speak privately with Sir Halston and his wife. The middle-aged couple lived six miles away and were frequent visitors. Anne smiled politely during the discussion of local events and people she had never heard of, only paying close attention when Margret brought up the discovery at the pond.

"Your father said it may be the governess who went missing from Harwick House," Halston said.

"Yes, Lucy Drayton. You visited last November, I'm sure, do you recall who else was here around the eighteenth?" Margret asked.

He shook his head. "In truth, I do not. The usual sporting crowd, I suppose. Why do you ask?"

"That's when Miss Drayton disappeared. I wondered if anyone had seen anything unusual that might assist authorities—such as unusual activity near the marsh."

"Oh, dear," Lady Halston interrupted. "I cannot bear talking about this dreadful affair again. There was too much talk at breakfast as it was. Since I wish to speak with Judith Rattrey before she leaves tomorrow, this would appear to be the perfect time. Please excuse me, my dears." She turned and smiled at her husband. "When you are finished, come find me."

"I am sorry we upset her," Margret said as Lady Halston walked away.

"She will be fine. Always been a tad squeamish." Halston eyed Margret. "You seem very absorbed by the matter. I saw you at the pond."

"I would not say absorbed, but interested. We had been helping Lord Ware to make inquiries on behalf of the Drayton family. Although no one expected this turn of events," she added.

"Rather unusual doings for young ladies…at least in my day. I hope Lord Ware is not allowing you to put yourselves in danger."

"Oh, no. He has been very strict," Anne said, feeling guilty that Lord Ware was taking the blame when he had definitely not approved of their current activity.

"We mostly talk to people we know and pass on anything that sounds important," Margret added.

Halston looked doubtful, but only said, "Be careful. Both of you."

"Of course we will," Margret assured him. "So did you see anything?"

"Can't say I did." Halston rubbed his chin. "One odd thing happened that I guess makes sense now."

"What do you mean?" Anne asked.

"It was the hounds. On the morning after…whatever occurred to Miss Drayton. We'd had perfect fox hunting weather, and I extended my stay for one last hunt on Monday. The hounds were excited, eager to leave. Suddenly two of them broke off baying toward the marsh, and of course the others followed. We had a difficult time recalling them."

"Oh, good heavens," Margret said softly. "They knew she'd been buried there."

"It may be so," he said gently. "If we had found her that day... but we did not. Hardly important now."

"I wouldn't say that. It makes it even more likely it is Lucy they found and that she died the night she disappeared," Anne said. "Thank you for talking with us."

"A sad business. Now, I must find my wife and a drink, perhaps not in that order."

Anne watched Halston walk away. If the hunters had discovered the body, they might have spared the family long months of waiting and wondering, but they could not have saved Lucy or spared the family's grief. It was too late.

She gazed around the room once more. What was keeping Lord Ware? Captain Wycliff had come down fifteen minutes ago and seemed to be gradually working his way toward Anne and Margret but still no sign of his lordship. She was eager to share the meager pieces of information she and Margret had gathered and was more than interested in what he'd been doing. Hopefully his late return was good news, rather than bad.

Chapter Seven

"What village girl?" Lucien stared at the blacksmith. Why had no one else mentioned another local disappearance? He walked back toward the forge. "Tell me about it."

"Not much to say. Twas Pete Mawbry's girl Jane. One day she was there, then poof. Just gone. Her mum says she run off with young Brodie Watts, but I happen to know he went to fight the Frenchies. He wouldn't be draggin' Jane along."

Lucien asked several more questions; the smithy mostly shrugged. Lucien knew from trips to Wellington's camps that some women followed their men to the battle fronts, but wouldn't she or the boy have told someone?

"What does his family say?"

"That she aint with Brodie. Just like I said."

Which made her disappearance suspicious and might even put the skeleton's identity in question.

After learning Jane had lived with her widowed mother, Lucien headed in that direction. He was deep in thought about this new information and swung around rather aggressively when he was hailed by a loud and quarrelsome voice.

"Viscount Ware. I would have a word with you." Constable Jones trotted toward him, his belly jiggling under the unaccustomed activity. "What do you think you're doing? Asking questions all about town? Did I not make it plain your interference was not needed or welcome?"

"Ah, Constable Jones." Lucien relaxed with a stifled sigh and produced a smile. "Good day. I admit I have been satisfying my curiosity. It is such an interesting affair. But I'm told you are doing a splendid job."

Jones hesitated, caught off guard by Lucien's amiable tone. He hooked his thumbs in his pants. "Yes, well, we are getting along. I suppose it is interesting to those not familiar with this sort of thing. I have seen all kinds of lawbreaking, and this is just another incident to me."

Lucien struggled not to laugh at this disingenuous speech. "I suppose that is true, you being a trained professional and all. But murder, missing girls? Surely your small village has not seen many of those."

"Well, uh—why, actually, we had another missin' girl a few years ago. Yes, sir, but it wasn't like this. Janie Mawbry run off." He narrowed his eyes. "You already heard, didn't you? Aint thinking of bothering Widow Mawbry, I hope?"

"Only to offer my sympathies."

"Why? Do you know her?" He bristled with suspicion again.

"I do not, but I had a cousin who disappeared," Lucien said, inventing as he went along and gauging Jones' response. "My aunt was devastated that she never heard where her daughter went or what happened to her. Aunt Vi found comfort in the church. I thought I'd share their story with Jane's mother in hopes it would help."

Jones eased off his belligerent stance. "She'll not listen to you. Not churchy, that one. I s'pose there's no harm in trying, but you gotta stop asking questions, stirring people up to believe there's a lunatic or some other wrong 'un on the loose. An unfortunate girl— likely the Drayton lass from up at Harwick House—wandered into the marsh at night and died in a sad mishap. No mystery about it."

"Maybe so," Lucien agreed.

"Mark my words, that's the long and short of it. Have a good day, sir. And remember what I said…no more questions."

Lucien gave a silent huff of resignation. Mishap? Not bloody likely, but Jones was not open to reason. Lucien waited until the constable was well down the street before continuing to the Mawbry house.

Jane's mother lived alone in a one room cottage. According to the smithy, an older daughter had married, moved away, and not been back. When Widow Mawbry answered his knock and reluctantly invited him in, he stepped over two nondescript dogs and pieces of scattered firewood. The floor hadn't been swept in recent memory, and unwashed clothes—evidenced by the strong oder of stale sweat—were strewn about. The widow exhibited the same lack of care in her person, dressed in shabby clothes, wrinkled and dirty, her stringy hair hanging about her face. He saw the avaricious glint in her eyes the moment he introduced himself. She was wondering if a visit from the Quality could be used to her advantage.

Since the only available chair was occupied by a fat, orange cat, Lucien chose to stand. She stared at him expectantly, and he came to the point. "I wanted to talk about your daughter Jane. I understand she left home two years ago. Have you heard from her?"

"Don't see it's yor bus'ness, but no. She dun run off."

"With Brodie Watts? I understand they were friends."

"Naw. Not him. I wondered at first, but his paw said Bro went to the war. Someone else, I s'pose."

"Another beau, you mean? Can you tell me who that would be?"

The woman cackled. "Beau? Now aint t'at fancy." She slapped her leg with one hand and laughed again. "Secretive, Jane was, but I daresay there was someone. Why you askin'?"

"You must have heard about the bones in the pond—"

"You thinkin' it be Janie?" She shook her head. "I heard 'bout it, a'right, but my Janie dint take no trunk like they found. Naw, she took nothin' and run off, with some man, I tell ya."

"You seem remarkably certain. I wonder if you know more than you say."

"You think I'd lie 'bout it?" she spat. Her indignant protest did not quite ring true. She sounded genuine, but her gaze kept slipping away.

"Not lie, exactly, but keeping something to yourself. Perhaps you have an idea where she went or why."

"Yer dead wrong. If I were to guess, I'd say London, but who knows? Demmed silly girl. Good riddance, I say."

Lucien bit back a sharp retort. Even though he had already taken a measure of the widow's character, her dismissal of Jane's fate caught him by surprise. If her daughter had run away, it was no wonder, but London would have been a terrible choice. Jobs were scarce, and its dark streets and alleys were not kind to country girls.

On the other hand, he had heard nothing that proved she had gotten as far as London. The bones they had found might not be hers, but were there other graves yet to be discovered? Did Blinker's Marsh indeed have a *wrong 'un* in their midst?

Upon leaving the Mawbry cottage, Lucien squinted at the sun sitting low on the horizon. He was at risk of settling for a cold collation for dinner if he did not return to Barnett Park soon. Finn would also be wondering how much longer he'd be, although Lucien doubted his groom was bored. The corner of his mouth quirked. Since Finn was waiting outside a tavern, he had likely charmed a pretty barmaid to bring him a pint or two.

Lucien started down the lane toward the main road when a man flagged him down. "Are you Viscount Ware?"

"I am." Lucien eyed the large man in the casual clothes of village life. "And you are?"

"Ellis, Dan Ellis." He pointed to the cottage behind him where a woman stood in the doorway. "My wife and I live here. Was that Janie in the pond?"

"No official identification yet. Do you have reason to think it was?"

"Just you being here."

Lucien should have known. In a village as small as Blinker's Marsh, it was impossible to go unnoticed or without everyone knowing your business. Maybe the town gossip would work in his favor this time. He shrugged. "Means nothing. I just heard of Jane's disappearance and thought it was odd. Two girls missing in such a small place, I mean. I take it you knew the Mawbry girl."

"My wife and I saw her every day. When she was little, she used to come to us when her ma was gone and there was no food. Then later, she'd stop just to talk a while." He nodded his chin toward the Mawbry cottage. "Did she tell you about that last day?"

"She said her daughter ran away without warning."

Ellis snorted. "Mattie said she wouldn't tell you, that's why my wife sent me out here. Well, the truth be, her mum threw her out. They had a big row. We could hear their voices from our back garden."

"What was the row about?"

"That I can't say. Couldn't make out the words, but it was worse than usual. Her mum was always getting after her, but that day the screeching frightened Mattie's hens. She wanted me to go over and put a stop to it, but then Janie came storming out the door, and her mum was throwing clothes at her. Told her to 'Get out and never come back.' Janie was crying and picking up things. Aye, and she was yelling back. Mattie and I came around the house and tried to talk to her, but she shook her head and took off running through the woods." Ellis looked down at his feet and shook his head sadly. "Thought she'd be back. Always was before. I wish now we'd done more—followed her maybe. 'Cause we never saw Janie again."

"Was there anyone else she might turn to for help?"

He shook his head and raised his hands in a bleak gesture. "I just wish we knew she was alive and well. I'm feared that aint the way of it."

Recognizing the man's genuine concern, Lucien offered him the best he could. "If I learn anything, whatever it is, I will send word."

"Thank you, my lord. My wife and I appreciate it."

With nothing more to say, Lucien continued down the lane. As he turned onto the main roadway, he glanced back. Ellis was still standing with his hands stuck in his pockets. If only Jane had confided in this couple who clearly were fond of her. Instead, Lucien was now inquiring into the welfare of two young women, and he had little hope of finding either in the circumstances he'd wish them to be.

Despite the lateness of the hour before dinner, Lucien took time to write a brief note to Rothe, asking him to locate Brodie Watts and confirm that Jane wasn't with him. Then he splashed water over his arms and face and slipped into fresh clothes. After dispatching the note by a passing footman, he joined the gathered guests downstairs. The butler announced dinner just as he spotted Lady Anne, Miss Barnett, and Captain Wycliff. The captain waved, and they waited for Lucien as everyone moved toward the dining room.

"We feared you had gotten lost," Wycliff said with a grin. "Have you been off investigating again?"

"A bit," Lucien confessed. "I learned something of interest, but there's no time to discuss it now. It will have to wait until after dinner."

While the captain escorted Miss Barnett to the table, Lucien offered his arm to Lady Anne. She tilted her head to search his face. "My, how mysterious you are. We have a little to tell you too, but from the sound of it, I'd say you discovered something more intriguing."

"Do you think so?" Lucien was amused by her angling for a hint. He leaned over as he held her chair and whispered in her ear. "You have to wait just like the others, Miss Curiosity."

She smothered a laugh, clearly unrepentant at being caught out.

Dinner and the music afterward dragged on so long that even Lucien was getting impatient. He did not want to risk being overheard linking the disappearances of the two women. Constable Jones was not wrong when he said the mere suggestion of a killer preying on young women would cause alarm, even hysteria, within the community. As a consequence, Lucien dodged his friends all evening and was the recipient of their increasingly annoyed glances.

As soon as the impromptu music stopped, he approached Lady Anne. "Can I interest you in a moonlight walk through the gardens?"

"I should tell you no after making us wait like this," she said giving him an arch look. "But you know very well I will not. Let us go before you think of some other reason to delay."

"No fear of that. I am nearly as eager as you are," he said taking her arm. He lifted a brow at the other couple. "Join us?"

Miss Barnett frowned at him. "As though we had not been waiting for hours."

"Lead on." Captain Wycliff chuckled. "You may count on us being directly behind you."

Once gathered in their favorite spot at the far end of the garden, they listened spellbound to everything Lucien had learned that day. He saved the Mawbry girl's disappearance until the end.

"Oh, no," Lady Anne gasped. "Not another."

"It's true. I had forgotten," Miss Barnett said in a hushed voice, darting a look at the growing shadows and shivered. "A madman must be on the loose."

Lady Anne turned to stare at Lucien, moonlight catching her concern. "Could that be? Is some maniac killing these women?"

"We should not assume the worst," Lucien said. "Jane Mawbry had plenty of reason to leave home after the row with her mother. She may be living somewhere else by choice. Two disappearances, however, is at least a suggestive twist of fate."

The captain frowned. "All the more reason for the ladies to stay out of your inquiry from here on."

"By all means," Lucien concurred.

"Surely you don't mean that," Miss Barnett protested. "We were very circumspect in our actions today." She told them about the visit to the pond and questioning the three guests about last November, including the odd behavior of the hounds. "So you see, we learned something without putting ourselves in any danger."

"This time. But merely asking questions can be dangerous," Wycliff warned.

Lucien nodded. "If I had known how serious this would be... Well, I did not. But we should all be more circumspect for our safety, for the reputations of others, and to avoid adding to the fear already spreading in the village." He turned to Anne. "Did you notice anything significant at the pond?"

She looked at him confused. "You have been there. There was not much to see, except mud."

"I did not know about Jane at that time. Did you see any *place* we should examine further?"

Her face cleared. "Oh. Oh, I see. You mean another burial spot."

Margret gasped. "Jane's?"

"We must consider the possibility," Lucien said.

"But how would Anne know? She doesn't even live around here." Miss Barnett stopped abruptly. "Oh, that memory thing." She looked at Anne then turned to the captain. "She has a really astonishing ability to recall everything she has seen. Rather handy, don't you think?"

"Indeed." But Wycliff looked bemused.

"I am sorry, but I did not see anything suspicious," Lady Anne said. "It has been two years since Jane vanished, and the ground is wet and muddy. What evidence would there be?"

Lucien shrugged. "Nothing, I suppose, but I had to ask. Your ability is too unique to ignore when it might make a difference."

"Oh, la, sir, any time," she said a bit too blithely to be believed. "I, of course, am ever at your whim."

Lucien lifted a brow. "Should I consider that a set down?"

"As you like." Then she relented. "I was only funning…mostly. You know I will help when I can. It is just that…well, I would rather my little oddity was not widely known."

"Total recall is scarcely 'a little oddity,'" Lucien said.

"Egad, yes, my lady. You are too modest." Captain Wycliff bestowed her with a look of admiration. "But I shan't repeat it. Your secret shall remain among the four of us."

Lady Anne still seemed uncomfortable, and Lucien turned their discussion to where Jane might be if she had left on her own. "If Jane ran away, she would have known the road to London and could easily have walked the two or three miles looking for shelter and work."

"Or she could be at the war front with Brodie Watts," Miss Barnett reminded him.

"I've already written making a formal inquiry about that," Lucien said. "But I think London is more likely. Perhaps I should seek assistance from Bow Street and London's constabulary."

"Yes, I think you should." Lady Anne nodded with an eager look. "Oh, I hope they find her." She sighed when the captain raised a brow. "Yes, Captain, I know her situation in town could be very poor, but we could help her, and regardless, is it not better than being dead?"

Chapter Eight

During the night, a cool wind swept through the area, and Sunday morning dawned clear and mild. All six of the younger set, four of the older gentlemen guests, and Sir George took advantage of the break in the heat by riding out for a last jaunt. The servants were busy packing bags and trunks so that guests were prepared to disperse to their own homes after breakfast or at the latest by early afternoon.

Lucien and his friends returned from the ride laughing over Miss Barnett's futile attempts to convince a cow to remove herself from the middle of the riding path. The solemnity overshadowing recent days had temporarily lifted, and they trooped into the house, looking forward to a hearty breakfast.

Lucien was met by a footman with a folded note. He read it, his smile fading.

"Not bad news, I hope," Lady Anne said.

"Nothing unexpected. It is from Dr. Morehouse."

"What's that?" Sir George asked, stepping toward them. "Has something happened?"

The hallway became quiet as the other riders strained to hear what was being said. Lucien saw no reason not to share what was bound to be all over the village by now.

"Yes, sir. Lucy Drayton's family identified a necklace found with the bones, and Dr. Morehouse has officially declared the remains to be hers."

A few sighs, but mostly the confirmation was received in silence. None of the guests had known the young woman nor were they in any way involved. Yet the report had a dampening effect on everyone's spirits.

Sir George heaved a sigh. "I am sorry for the family. I shall write to them. Does he state the cause of death?"

Loath to get into the gruesome details, Lucien said, "An inquest tomorrow at two will issue an official ruling."

Sir George's eyes flickered. "Yes, yes, of course." He knew Lucien had evaded his question. "I will make a point to attend. By the by, Ware, I would like to speak with you after breakfast regarding another matter." Sir George strode toward the family's private rooms, and the guests scattered to change before breakfast. The light-hearted laughter had died in the hallway.

• • •

Lucien changed quickly and settled for coffee and toast, finishing his morning repast before the others came downstairs. He had things to do prior to meeting with Sir George, and he hurried back to his room and wrote a second message to Rothe, this one more detailed regarding events in the Blinker's Marsh area. The anticipated coroner's verdict made determining the fate of Jane Mawbry even more urgent. If a murderer was preying on young women this close to London, authorities in town needed to take steps to protect their own citizens and to determine if he had already made forays into town.

Once the letter was written, Lucien slipped out to the stables, gave it to Finn to deliver to Whitehall, and tasked him with replenishing Lucien's wardrobe as he would be staying in the area several more days to continue his inquiries. Constable Jones was likely to let the matter of Lucy's death languish, as he had Jane's, and Lucien did not yet have the answers the Drayton family deserved and his grandmother would demand.

Finn grinned from ear to ear at the proposed trip. "Aye, m'lord. Y' can count on me. Be back 'fore you know it."

"No racing," Lucien cautioned, but his groom's enthusiasm amused him. Since Lucien preferred to drive himself, Finn rarely got a chance to try out the matched bays on the less congested roads outside London.

Returning to his room, Lucien eyed his travel bag. *Now or later?* Packing would only take a few minutes. He had sent much of his clothing to Hays Mews with Finn. With the houseparty ending, Lucien would be moving to an inn some three miles away. He shrugged and turned away. Sir George had waited long enough.

Lucien tapped on the open study door.

"Ah, come in, Ware." Sir George rose and waved him to a chair. "I apologize for this invitation being so tardy. I meant to speak with you earlier in the week, suggesting you extend your stay with us until your inquiries are complete."

"Most generous of you, sir, but I do not want to impose longer than I have already. I had thought to put up at the posting inn for a few days."

"Nonsense. No imposition at all. Our home is by far the most convenient spot for you." A twinkle entered his eyes. "I might add that Lady Anne will be with us for another week or more, and I intend to invite Captain Wycliff to extend his stay."

"A most convivial party. You tempt me, sir, and as long as it will not be an inconvenience, I am happy to accept. Thank you."

"Delighted, my boy. Of course, that is not all I wanted." Sir George's gaze was direct. "What did you not say about Morehouse's message?"

"Nothing critical. I was merely sparing the ladies the details. The good doctor will testify the governess died from repeated brutal blows to the head with a blunt object, that her death was caused by a person or persons unknown. The obvious verdict is murder."

"As we feared."

"Yes, rather predictable, considering the remains had been buried. Sir, I wonder that you had not mentioned this was the second missing girl from the neighborhood."

Sir George's eyebrows rose, he frowned in thought, and then Lucien saw comprehension cross his face. "The Mawbry girl. Yes, I had forgotten. He mother said she'd run off and that was rather the end of it. I suppose it does look suspicious now. Have you been making inquiries regarding her?"

"I have. And I must say, I don't believe her mother's story."

His host started to lean back in his chair, shaking his head, then jerked upright. "By Gawd, Ware, are our ladies in danger from some madman?"

"I cannot say, not for certain." Lucien repeated what he had learned in the village, including his conversation with Mrs. Mawbry's neighbor Daniel Ellis. "Jane was alive when her mother washed her hands of her. However, she was last seen running into the woods near the marsh rather than south toward London."

Sir George seemed to absorb that. "Ellis is a good man. Reliable. I shall speak with the ladies to have a care for their safety. What else can we do?"

"I have no clear path as yet," Lucien admitted. "I have sent two messages to London. With luck, those answers will suggest a direction for inquiry."

"Egad. The more I think about it, I am loath to allow Margret or Anne to set foot off the estate with a killer out there…somewhere."

• • •

Lucien scowled as Finn entered the stable yard with a flourish less than three hours later and drew the curricle to a halt. As expected, his groom had made good time, but he had not expected him to return with Lucien's valet and three large bags tied on the back.

"Talbot, I do not recall sending for you."

"Nor did you say I could not come, my lord." Talbot climbed down, straightened, and looked his master up and down. "A good thing I did." His eyes widened. "Good heavens, sir. What terrible misfortune has befallen your boots?"

Lucien looked down. Indeed, they had not quite recovered their high shine after the dunking in pond water and mud. He sighed. Talbot would never let him hear the end of it. "Well, since you are already here, I suppose they could use a little attention."

"Very good, sir." Talbot's tone indicated he had never doubted the outcome. "I understand we are moving to an inn today."

"Plans have changed. Sir George has invited me to extend my stay, and now I will have to beg him to accommodate my well-meaning but disobedient valet." Lucien turned away hiding a smile. If he did not sometimes get in the last word, Talbot would soon be running his life.

Arrangements were quickly made. With other guests leaving, Lucien was moved to a bedchamber with a manservant's room next door. Talbot came through the connecting door with the two largest bags, set them down, and opened one to pull out a pair of glossy boots.

"If you would change your boots now, my lord, I will see if I can save your Hessians, and I really should brush your jacket."

"Do not fuss, Talbot." But Lucien sat on the bed and pulled off his boots. "Any news from home?"

"Nothing to remark on. I brought the mail that might be of interest. The Dowager Countess has called twice, and young Sherbourne asked after you yesterday. The city is unbearably hot." Having dispensed with this summary, Talbot finished his unpacking, took a last longing look at Lucien's jacket as though he might seize the opportunity to start brushing, snatched the offending boots, and left.

Lucien thumbed through the mail, setting most of it aside. He opened a message from Rothe and grimaced. A new assignment, obviously sent before the marquess received Lucien's messages. That must be why his partner had called, and whatever it was, Sherry would doubtless take care of it. In any event, it would have to wait for Lucien's attention. He dropped the note on the table. He needed more time to pursue Lucy's killer and solve the mystery of Jane Mawbry's disappearance.

To avoid the bustle of pending departures and prolonged goodbyes, Lucien decided this was an opportune moment for a return visit to Harwick House. Sir George's comments about regular guests at the neighboring estate had kept running through his head. Such visitors were likely acquainted with Lucy Drayton, and Lucien had spotted two carriages and a couple of riders heading toward Harwicks' last night; time to make their acquaintance and to hear what the Harwicks had to say now that Lucy's body had been identified.

He chose to walk on such a pleasant day, quietly leaving by the manor's side door, cutting across the field, and skirting the marsh this time so Talbot would not complain of his boots again. He took the path through the woods, emerged at the Harwicks' stable yard, and was pleased to see the Harwicks and four guests drinking wine and lemonade in the garden. Mrs. Harwick and a female guest held dainty parasols to protect their fairer skin from the bright sun.

Harwick rose and came to meet him. "Lord Ware, I had not expected to see you again."

"Oh, why is that? I say, have I intruded?"

"Oh, no. Not at all. It just that I assumed you had returned to London by now."

Lucien accepted the lie. The whole village was aware of his presence. Surely the Harwicks were not *that* isolated.

"I am reluctant to leave without knowing exactly how Lucy Drayton died."

"Ah, yes, I see. A tragic accident to be sure." Harwick paused and finally cleared his throat as keeping Lucien standing at the edge of the woods grew awkward. "Pardon, my manners. Will you join us for a drink? A little port or champagne? Or lemonade if you prefer."

"My pleasure. Port would be excellent."

Lucien followed his host to the small gathering, and Harwick made introductions. No one appeared pleased about it. Lucien was intrigued by this reaction and studied the visitors. They were all somewhere in their thirties. The gentlemen wore typical country dress of knee breeches and boots. The lady sitting with Mrs. Harwick was introduced as Mrs. Cluett. She wore a pale green gown a few years out of date, and her reddish-brown curls were drawn up off her shoulders in deference to the heat. She appeared aloof and did not look at him directly, holding the parasol so it shaded her face most of the time. Mr. Cluett, dark-haired with indifferent brown eyes, stood behind her and returned Lucien's brief bow.

His wife spoke in a clipped voice. "A pleasure to meet you, viscount. How can you walk about on such a very warm day?"

"A short walk only. I am staying at Barnett Park." He gestured toward the mansion's roof that could be seen through the trees.

The other men—Mr. Faegan, also dark-haired, and Mr. Ramsey with flaxen curls swept back in the latest style—nodded at the introduction but did not come forward. Lucien felt he had interrupted something, and they were anxious for him to leave. No, more than that—he felt a distinct animosity toward him. His interest grew.

"I assume you will attend tomorrow's inquest," Lucien said conversationally, looking at Harwick.

The man frowned. "Why would I? The girl left without notice. I'm sorry for the accident that brings sorrow to her family of course, but this does not concern us."

This was the second time he'd called her death an accident, and Lucien could not resist correcting him. "But it was not an accident. Surely the constables told you they expect a coroner's verdict of murder."

"No, they did not. Constable Jones asked a few questions and said it was likely she had suffered a chance fall."

"The doctor does not agree."

"Does he not?" Harwick looked at a loss for words. "Well, I am persuaded they will sort it out without us."

"Perhaps your guests knew her?"

"A servant?" Mrs. Cluett said with disdain. "I hardly think so." She turned to look at Mrs. Harwick. "Was this woman not your governess?"

"She was, although only for a few weeks. I daresay you never saw her." She appealed to her other guests. "Charlie? Peter? Did either of you ever meet the Drayton woman?"

Harwick interrupted. "Of course they did not. You are ridiculous to ask, my love." His denial came as the two men, as though on cue, shook their heads, murmuring denials.

Lucien's jaw tightened. They were going to deny everything,

even meeting a woman who had been a member of the household, but some perverse streak made him keep trying. He turned his head toward Harwick. "Have you recalled anything further after our previous talk? Perhaps someone Lucy had befriended, a local beau? Unusual occurrences in the neighborhood or strangers hanging about?"

Harwick heaved a sigh as though he had concluded the fastest way to rid himself of Lucien was to answer his questions. "We don't encourage anyone to hang about our property, so no, no strangers. My wife and I tried to think if Lucy had befriended anyone, but other than our maid Bethy, there was no one. She was a timid, mousy girl, kept to herself, and then she was gone." He shrugged. "I am sorry, Lord Ware, but that is all we can tell you."

"It is unfortunate. Oh, I nearly forgot. Were you aware another girl, Jane Mawbry, disappeared from the village two years ago?"

Harwick stiffened. "No, why would we? We rarely go into Blinker's Marsh."

"Or indulge in village gossip," his wife added. "You must excuse us now, Lord Ware. Our friends are here only for a brief stay, and we have much catching up to do."

Lucien nodded and rose, accepting this blunt dismissal. As he returned through the woods to Barnett Park, a smile lurked at the corners of his mouth. They had done their best to be disobliging, and yet he found some satisfaction in the exchange. The eyes are always a giveaway, and little things stood out. The visitors were not as ignorant of Lucy as they pretended. How would Mrs. Cluett have known the girl was a governess unless the name had been discussed? And Jane Mawbry? Despite Harwick's insistence the girl was unknown to all of them, Lucien saw Faegan and Ramsey exchange a fleeting look. They knew something. And if all was as innocent as they claimed, why the simmering hostility?

A grim smile emerged. They were hiding secrets at Harwick House…thereby giving him four more suspects for his inquiries.

Chapter Nine

When Lucien strolled up to the Barnett mansion fifteen minutes later, tea was being served. The greatly reduced party—the older Barnetts, Miss Barnett, Lady Anne, and Captain Wycliff—had noted his absence.

"A hot time of day for a walk," Sir George said as Lucien approached. They were once again gathered under the garden's large shade tree.

"Yes, Mrs. Cluett thought so too."

"Who is Mrs. Cluett?" Margret asked.

"I gather he has been visiting at Harwick House. I noticed they have guests again." Her father looked up from a letter he had been reading. They were seated in chairs the servants had placed in a circle under the tree. A table in the middle held the tea tray and a large plate of small sandwiches, biscuits, and seedcakes.

"You have the right of it, sir. Although I must confess I was not a welcome visitor."

"Truly?" Miss Barnett's eyes lit with curiosity. "Were they uncivil?"

Lucien came to a halt beside Lady Anne's chair. "Not exactly, but they clearly did not want my company nor to talk about Lucy or Jane." He pulled up a chair, chose two finger sandwiches, and repeated the essence of his short visit. "They were not as unconcerned as they presented, although when I asked Harwick about the inquest, he as much as said he could not be bothered to attend."

"A rather callous attitude." Lady Barnett sounded both surprised and indignant. "Miss Drayton worked for them."

"Not long enough to matter nor for their friends to meet or even lay eyes on her."

"Is that what they said?" Lady Anne asked.

"'Fraid so."

"Fustian! She was a governess not a scullery maid," Miss Barnett said. "Of course they saw her with the children. Mama is right, they are cold and heartless. And deceitful. Someone in that house knows what happened to Lucy."

"Now Margret." Her parents spoke in unison, making Lucien smile as he wondered how often they had reprimanded their impetuous daughter over the years.

"You cannot toss about serious aspersions without proof," her father added.

While Margret was defending her accusation, Lucien spoke quietly to Lady Anne. "You are very reserved today."

"Nothing to say. It has all been said, rather well, I thought." She sighed. "I feel badly for both young women. They were not much younger than I, but they had so little. I feel almost... guilty."

"About the advantages of our birth?"

She nodded.

"Rank does not guarantee happiness, but I too have felt the weight at times. Particularly when I see soldiers living on the streets and in the rookeries. We were born to privilege, Lady Anne, and I believe it comes with a responsibility to make life better for others."

"Is that why you do these inquiries? To make things better?"

He gave a wry smile. "Perhaps. I enjoy the challenge, but I'd like to think a part of the reason is that noble."

"Why do you two look so serious?" Miss Barnett interrupted. "Are you telling her details we have not heard?"

"No. Not a word," Lucien said, holding his hands up in self-defense. "You've heard it all."

"I was remarking on the sad lives of these young women," Lady Anne said.

Miss Barnett's face fell. "Yes, it is dreadful."

"Goodness. All this gloom. Let us talk about something more

cheerful," her mother said. "Have you seen the pups that were born last night?"

"A sturdy litter of five," Sir George added. "Excellent future hunters, for sure."

With Miss Barnett and Lady Anne exclaiming over this happy event, and Lucien and Wycliff serving as escorts, they did as Lady Barnett had bade them and trooped off to the stables.

• • •

"Is that someone at the door? Who would be arriving at this time of day?" Lady Barnett set down her table fork and looked expectantly toward the dining room archway. The sound of voices from the manor's front entrance had drawn everyone's attention, and a moment later the butler appeared.

"Yes?" Sir George prompted.

"A gentleman to see Lord Ware, sir. An Andrew Sherbourne."

"Sherry? This is a pleasant surprise." Lucien rose and gave a nod to Sir George. "Pardon me, sir. He is an old friend." He started for the door, frowning with a mixture of concern and impatience at the unexpected interruption. What would bring Sherry here? Had Prinny or his friends gotten into serious trouble again; or provoked a war with yet another country?

"Invite him to join us, Ware. When your business is concluded, of course."

"Thank you, sir. I shall ask."

Entering the front hall at a brisk stride, Lucien relaxed when Sherry turned and gave him an apologetic grin. Not a national crisis then.

"Sorry to interrupt your holiday. Don't rebuke me too harshly."

"Not at all," Lucien said, clapping him on the shoulder. "I am always glad to see you but curious on this particular occasion as to why. Rothe, I assume. Has this latest assignment gone awry?"

"Not exactly, but it has gotten complicated. Can we speak privately?"

"Of course. How urgent is it? We were just sitting down to dinner, and Sir George invited you to join us."

Sherry's grin broadened. "Most anything can wait that long, but I am not exactly dressed for dinner."

"No one will mind. They know you just arrived."

"In that case, lead the way."

Lucien introduced him to the rest of his dinner companions, making no further explanation of their relationship than he had already given. Of course Lady Anne knew he was also Lucien's fellow agent and partner, but he was confident she would not mention it.

Sherry made a cheerful addition to the dinner table, and he quickly discovered Sir George and his father, Baron Sherbourne, had been at Eaton together.

"I fear we were a couple of young scamps. In fact there were five of us who managed to get into more than our share of mischief," Sir George admitted. Chuckling, he refused to recount any specific adventures. "I will not tittle-tattle upon your father...or myself."

Dinner conversation remained casual, and no one brought up the local murder or surrounding events. It was not until the gentlemen retired for cigars and brandy, that Sherry said to Lucien in an undertone, "I assume Sir George knows why you are here?"

"He does." Lucien turned and included the others. "Sir George, Captain Wycliff, and I have openly discussed matters regarding Lucy Drayton and Jane Mawbry. Have you brought information on either inquiry?"

"Not happy news. They located Brodie Watts. Jane Mawbry is not with him. The city's constables and Bow Street have the description of her that you provided, but so far nothing has been reported."

"I feared as much." Lucien drained his glass of brandy. The news, though anticipated, made her prolonged absence more alarming.

"Most unfortunate." Sir George blew a ring of smoke from his cigar. "I had held out for a different outcome. Now I wonder if she too is dead."

Sherry's gaze darted to Lucien's face. "Lucy Drayton is dead?"

"Yes. A skeleton was found in the marsh, and her relatives confirmed the trinket found with it was hers."

"I see. Anyone under suspicion?"

Lucien hesitated. He was reluctant to publicly name the Harwicks and their guests. If he was wrong, he might unduly prejudice Sir George against his neighbors. After all, he had no proof, just some small inconsistencies and niggling worries. "Nobody definite. The household where Lucy Drayton worked has to be considered, and the local constabulary barely spoke with them."

Sir George snorted. "I predicted that. Constable Jones is a nice enough fellow when there is nothing to be done, but he is lazy and not likely to take any action that might disturb his comfort. Nor does he welcome advice from anyone."

"Do tell." Sherry's muttered remark drew little more than a shrug from Lucien. Local constabularies tended to either be friendly and welcome assistance, or they were territorial, refusing cooperation.

"Then he shan't be happy about this." Sherry took a folded paper from an inside coat pocket and handed it to Lucien. "The Prince Regent authorized this order that was sent to Constable Jones just before I left London. The Crown has officially placed you in charge of both inquiries, my friend. Jones has been ordered to turn over all reports and render any assistance you require. From what you have said, I predict he will either hide out to avoid you or be on your doorstep by morning."

"He'll be here," Sir George said with certainty. "Mad as a wounded buck. I shall warn our butler to expect him and have the footmen standing by."

"Well, that sounds like fun." Lucien gave Sherry a sharp look. "What's going on? The palace rarely interferes in local matters, and Prinny is in Bath. This took some effort to achieve."

Sherry returned his gaze and held it. "I just take orders."

Lucien got the point that Sherbourne couldn't relate anything further in public and shrugged as though it was unimportant. Rothe was obviously behind this, but why? What possible interest could Whitehall have in these young women?

"Yes, well," Sir George stood, bringing the other men to their feet. He gave Sherbourne and Lucien an appraising glance. "I believe the captain and I should rejoin the ladies in the drawing room while you continue your conversation. Sherbourne, I hope you will at least stay the night."

"I would be grateful, sir," Sherry said. "I was not looking forward to a long ride in the dark."

When the door closed, Sherry sat again. "I like them, Sir George and the captain. You appear to trust them, but I wasn't sure how far."

"They're good men." Lucien poured another brandy for himself and Sherbourne before resuming his own seat. "But they do not need to know everything. So what trouble has Whitehall uncovered now?" he asked, casually rolling the glass between his fingers.

"Treasonous activities." When Lucien scowled, Sherry said, "Yes, I know, we said no English dissidents, but this time, I allowed Rothe to talk me into it. There was a whiff of something out of the ordinary, something truly dangerous. When I first started poking around, it appeared I was wrong—just more revolutionary talk from locals angry over poverty, the laws, the wars, you name it." Sherry leaned forward. "But recently, I became certain outsiders are stirring the resentment. In fact, I'd wager good blunt it is French agents."

"Why? Someone is always feeding the flames. Even our own politicians when it suits them. The last time I saw Salcott, he mentioned several Whigs—Toomey, Southway, and Martin leading the charge— making very outrageous speeches in the House of Lords."

"This is different. French-speaking strangers are meeting in secret with rebel bands."

Lucien steepled his fingers. "Even so, how did that translate into Prinny's order regarding these two local women?"

"The Harwicks, in short. They are rumored to be part of a rebel group...and may even be harboring the French agents."

Lucien sat forward, exhaling a quick breath. "I believe I've met them."

"Are you serious? I thought the gossip of gentry being involved might be just another of numerous bad tips."

"Not this time, I'd say. Two men and a married couple are presently visiting Harwick House, going by the names of Mr. Faegan and Mr. Ramsey—Charlie and Peter, although I do not know which given name is which—and Mr. and Mrs. Cluett. They are passing themselves off as Quality." He went over the particulars of his visit to Harwick House, describing the aloof Cluett woman, the two dark-haired men who never spoke above a murmur, their stylish, light-haired friend Ramsey—and the underlying enmity he'd experienced. "Now that you have raised the possibility some of them are French agents, their hostility toward me may mean they know or suspect who I am from our work inside France."

Sherry whistled under his breath. "Bloody hell. A sorry turn of events that would be."

Lucien and Sherry had spent four years spying for the Crown in the courts and among the social elite on the Continent. When their commitment to the War Office was completed, and while extracting themselves to return to England, their spy activities had been publicly exposed through a personal betrayal. Neither man would be safe on the Continent for years to come, but until now, they thought they had gotten away without leaving a trail. Lucien sighed. Peril may have followed them home...or even stumbled upon them by a chance of fate.

"You should pull back from this assignment," Sherry insisted.

"Not bloody likely. But you should consider it. There is a reward for both our deaths, and if I have been compromised, so have you or soon will be by association. I'm already deeply involved here. It makes sense for me to carry it through. I will not back away. I may not be sure who did what, but there is at least one murderer at Harwick House. And now you tell me they are suspected traitors and spies." He clenched his jaw. "In truth, Sherry, Rothe no longer holds my reins in this matter."

Sherry looked hard at him for several moments. "You haven't been caught up like this in an investigation for a long time. It appears personal, more so than just a request by the dowager."

Lucien slumped back in his chair and shrugged. "Perhaps. An innocent young woman—maybe two—has been murdered. The families deserve to know what happened and why." And maybe he resented the fear and disruption inflicted on a peaceful village—or the mournful empty eye sockets of Lucy's skull. He knew he felt compassion for Lucy's family and for the couple who wanted so badly to help Jane. The spectre of treason within Harwick House was the final insult. "It would give me great satisfaction to uncover the truth…and to know the guilty would hang."

"I'm with you, of course. How much should I tell Rothe?"

Lucien shrugged. "Whatever you have to. Do not lie to him for my sake."

"Our sake," Sherry corrected. "Maybe I shall leave a message with his secretary that I delivered the information to you…and forget you mentioned what is, after all, just a suspicion on your part."

Lucien gave him a lazy smile. "That would be one solution." He stood. "We should join the others. They must be wondering what is taking so long. In the morning, if the weather holds, we might ride, or better yet, walk through the woods and take a good, long look at Harwick House and its visitors."

• • •

"What a surprise," Miss Barnett said when Lucien and Sherry entered the drawing room a few minutes later. "We thought you had forgotten us and retired for the night."

"Did you now?" Lucien said with a teasing smile. "And here I was telling Sherbourne we had to hurry back or you would fret that something was happening without you."

Sir George laughed. "I think you have figured out my daughter, my lord."

"So what is going on?" she demanded, looking at Lucien and Sherry.

When they hesitated, Lady Anne intervened by laying a hand on her friend's arm. "Margret, you know there are private matters that one cannot share with others." She shot a glance at Lucien. "I believe this is one of them."

"Oh, um, I guess I had not thought... I did not mean to... I beg your pardon." Miss Barnett looked flustered and the captain rescued her.

"We were just preparing to play cards," Wycliff said, getting up and extending his hand to Miss Barnett. "Let us not plague the viscount with our curiosity. What can be played by seven?"

"Oh, not me," Lady Barnett protested. "I have embroidery to finish."

"I would rather watch," Lady Anne said.

"As would I," Lucien agreed.

"All the better. Two against two." Sherry turned to his host. "Sir George, shall we show your daughter and the captain how Whist should be played?"

"Splendid idea."

"You shall not think so when you go down to defeat," Miss Barnett shot back, having recovered her composure. Laughing, they took their seats and shuffled the cards.

Lucien led Lady Anne to seats near the open windows. They could still see the card game yet be private and pick up the light breeze that had sprung up at twilight.

"Can you not tell us why Sherbourne is here?" she asked, keeping her voice down.

"Not so accepting of private matters after all, eh? You already heard his report on Jane Mawbry."

Lady Anne let out a sigh. "Are you persuaded she was killed too?"

"Not yet. We have no real evidence of it. I intend to make inquiries throughout the countryside again, particularly farms and cottages between here and London. We were only asking about Lucy before. Someone may know where Jane Mawbry went."

"Hmm, yes. that is true." Lady Anne pursed her lips. "Sherbourne could have sent you a note about Jane. Instead, he came to see you. I cannot help but wonder why."

"You are much too curious. He wanted to warn me of the Prince Regent's order, and he is working on another matter he wished to discuss. As you say, a private matter."

"Ah, yes, the order. Sir George told us about it. Since Rothe must have arranged it, I think this isn't just about two young women. Why would the war office become involved in such local issues? Unless there is something else going on." She tilted her head, a faint frown crossing her brow. "Has some trouble occurred in the government? Or is it French spies again? Does it involve Harwick House?"

Lucien stifled his surprise and laughed. "Why would you ask that? You cannot expect such excitement every time we meet." Lady Anne was observant and perceptive—and she had been privy to his secret life last winter—but he hadn't expected her to arrive at such an accurate conclusion. Had he or Sherry said something to give it away? Or was Lady Anne just that good at putting the facts together? If so, Lord Rothe had lost more than he thought when she'd refused to join Prinny's spy unit. "Never mind," he said, fearing someone might overhear them if this continued. "We should talk of something else."

"Which is an answer in itself. Why can you not tell me? You did last winter."

"Not by choice. You were already in the middle of it and at great risk. I could not leave you unprotected or unaware of the danger."

"Did I not assist you in the end?" she asked archly.

"Of course, you did. I have not forgotten, but you also suffered harm, and it could have been serious. I would not have that happen again."

"Very gallant of you, my lord. But am I not presently at risk with a killer—and French spies—in the neighborhood?"

He raised a brow in reproach. "No one is talking about French spies, except you. As for Lucy's killer…yes, he could still be in the neighborhood. Exactly why you must be careful and follow Sir George's advice. As long as you and Miss Barnett quit nosing around and do not to go anywhere unescorted, you should be safe enough."

She gave a soft huff. "Oh, fine, I suppose. I shall say no more about it. For now." She turned her back to him and began watching the card players. "Oh, good game. The score is almost even."

Both in the card game and our conversation, Lucien thought. She may have put her curiosity on hold for tonight, but it would not last. She was so close to the truth that from now on, he and Sherry would have to be circumspect of everything they said and did. Past experience persuaded him that Lady Anne was quite capable of plunging headlong into trouble without the least intention of doing so.

Chapter Ten

At breakfast the next morning, Lady Anne and Miss Barnett attempted to arrange a riding party that would meet Sir George's restrictions. They appealed to Lucien, but he declined on the grounds that Sherbourne would be leaving that morning, and he wanted to see him off. Lady Anne gave him a speculative glance, but he kept his expression bland until she was distracted by Captain Wycliff's offer to accompany them. The three of them set off with two footmen around ten o'clock.

As soon as the riders were out of sight, Lucien and Sherry took off on foot toward the path in the woods, arriving in a copse of trees behind Harwick House within minutes. Taking care to stay out of sight, they changed position several times so that Sherbourne got a good look at the entire house and grounds. Oddly enough, they failed to spot the residents or their guests.

After mapping the layout by memory and knowing they could not linger for fear of being caught in a lie by the ladies, they swiftly returned to Barnett Park. It was close. Andrew had just brought his saddled horse from the stable when the riders returned.

"I thought you'd be gone by now," Lady Anne said as she dismounted beside them. "You could have come riding after all."

"One thing and another delayed me." Sherry waved a vague hand. "I'm delighted for another opportunity to say good-bye."

"Did you have a pleasant ride?" Lucien asked.

"Lovely. You should have come with us," Miss Barnett said archly. "We met up with the Harwicks and their guests out riding. The men are quite handsome."

Worst luck. They'd missed the very people they'd hoped to see. At least the mysterious guests were still around. "Did you stop to chat?"

"Certainly. They were very polite to us."

Lucien lifted a brow at Lady Anne. "What did *you* think of them?"

"Well-enough looking. Reticent more than polite, I'd say. Mr. Harwick and Mrs. Cluett did all the talking. I don't think the names of the two gentlemen who kept to the back were ever mentioned."

And she *would* remember, Lucien thought.

Miss Barnett nodded. "Mrs. Cluett was rather overbearing. She talked so much Mr. Harwick forgot to introduce the other two gentlemen. Although one of them did smile at me rather impertinently," she added with a saucy look at Wycliff.

"Should I be worried about competition?" he asked with a grin.

"Always, sir," was her nippy reply.

While Miss Barnett continued to flirt with Wycliff, the riders handed over their horses to stable boys and began to move toward the house. Lucien turned the opposite direction and walked Sherbourne and his gelding toward the road.

"I should return within a day or two," Sherry said, swinging into the saddle. "Rothe will want an updated report on the activities at Harwick House. Watch your back, my friend. I am loath to train a new partner. If you have indeed been identified as Mr. Simon Grey from Paris, you may well be in danger."

"See you soon." Lucien watched until horse and rider broke into a gallop at the end of the Barnetts' circular drive. He turned toward the manor to join the riding party, but they had already entered the house. Wishing to question Lady Anne and Miss Barnett further about their brief meeting with the Harwick party, he lengthened his stride and crossed the empty cobblestone stable yard thinking of other ways he might obtain information on Harwick's guests.

The loud report of a long rifle jerked him from his reverie. Instinctively turning toward the sound, he was staggered by a sudden sharp blow and pain in his left upper arm that sent him reeling. He sucked in a quick breath with a muttered oath as he hit the ground, and he scrambled into a crouch. Observing movement under the trees near the pond, he straightened and raced in pursuit. Lucien knew he'd been hit, but so far it was not a bother. He was nearly half-way across the field when pounding hoof beats sounded behind him.

"Where is the shooter?" Sherbourne shouted.

"The woods. By the tall birch." Lucien kept running, but Sherry's horse galloped past, easily leaving him behind.

By the time Lucien reached the edge of the woods, Sherry had leapt from his horse and disappeared among the trees and dense foliage. Lucien peered into the brush deciding which way to go and finally realized how profusely his arm was bleeding. He ripped off his cravat, wrapped it around the wound, and, ignoring the increasing pain, he plunged into the brush, following the sounds of a rapid pursuit. The snapping of branches suddenly stopped, and Lucien halted, listening.

When someone came toward him at a cautious pace, Lucien backed away and stepped behind a tree. If this was the shooter doubling back, he could be in trouble with one arm relatively useless. He reached for the knife in his boot.

Sherry broke out of the underbrush. Lucien relaxed, took his hand off the knife, and stepped into sight.

"Lost him, devil it. Actually, I never had him in sight." Sherry grimaced as he spotted the bloody cravat. "How badly are you hurt?"

"A scratch. Where did you lose him?"

Sherry shrugged. "He must have found a hidey hole in the woods. I went all the way to the manor but saw nothing amiss. Did you get a good look at him?"

"None at all. I wasn't aware of trouble until I heard the rifle report and was hit. I saw a glint of metal and something moved under the birch tree. Nothing else."

They turned toward the sound of running footsteps coming across the field. "Good lord, Ware," Captain Wycliff called, "what the devil happened? Were you shot?"

"Just nicked my arm."

When the captain reached them, Lucien repeated what he knew, while Sherry waved off Sir George, Finn, and a few servants who were streaming across the field with guns in hand. "Go back," he yelled. "The shooter's gone. We'll be right with you."

Sir George nodded and turned back, herding everyone before him. They stopped at the stable yard to wait.

Sherry tried to get Lucien to take his horse, but he declined. In fact, Lucien doubted his ability to get on the horse. He felt a bit woozy, and his arm ached, but he had suffered worse injuries during the war. He clutched his arm against his chest. Despite the cravat, blood still seeped through to drip from his elbow. Gritting his teeth, he walked between Sherry and Wycliff, hoping he would not disgrace himself by passing out before they made it back. He avoided Sherry's worried look.

To distract himself and Sherbourne, Lucien asked Wycliff about the Harwick riding party. "When you saw them this morning, was anyone carrying a long rifle?"

The captain's brows shot up. "You think one of them did this? By Jove, that would fit with your suspicions. Let me think…yes, I recall wondering if they had been shooting rabbits. One of them had a rifle in a saddle bucket, but I cannot be certain who it was." He gave Lucien a sideways glance. "The shot came from somewhere near Harwick House?"

"The woods below…from among the trees."

Wycliff glanced over his shoulder. "It would take a marksman from that distance."

A wave of dizziness caused Lucien to stumble on the cobblestones as they reached the stable yard, and he went down on one knee. Sherbourne and Wycliff pulled him to his feet, holding him steady, but those waiting near the manor doors had already run forward to help.

"Oh, my lord. You *have* been shot." Lady Anne's face swarm before his vision, but Lucien tried to reassure her.

"I'm all right. Truly, I am. Just a misstep." But his words came out raspy, causing more alarm to flash across her face than if he had said nothing.

Sir George sent for the doctor, and Lucien was half carried to his bedchamber. Talbot fussed like a mare with a new foal as he removed Lucien's coat and shirt and pulled off his boots. Having disposed of the bloody cravat, he washed away the blood, rewrapped his master's arm in a clean cloth, and insisted he lie on the bed. Lucien gave in but sat propped up by pillows. With nothing more to do, Talbot fretted helplessly while they waited for the doctor.

Sir George disposed of the ladies hovering in the hallway by shutting the bedchamber door after promising he would send word once the doctor had examined Lucien. Having accomplished his goal, he turned toward the bed, his brows lowered in a bushy scowl. "What the bloody hell happened out there, gentlemen?"

"It was a rifle shot, but I saw no one," Lucien admitted. With Sherry's help he recounted what he could of the incident and the pursuit of an unknown shooter. The tale was told quickly because there was so little to tell.

"Not much to go on," Sir George growled. "Can't go around accusing people without some evidence."

"I agree," Lucien said. He turned his head to Sherry. "What brought you back? I thought you were on your way to London."

"The rifle shot. Didn't seem right. I came back to take a look, saw you running toward the woods, and realized what must have happened. Although I didn't realize you'd been hit. Why the devil were you chasing him? You weren't even armed, were you?"

"Sherry, does it matter now?" Lucien said wearily.

"Why would anyone do this?" Sir George asked. "Because of your inquiry?"

Lucien hesitated to answer. He just wanted everyone to go away until he could think clearly. He tried to deflect Sir George. "It could have been an accident. A poacher, maybe."

"Bollocks. I am not a green boy, my lads." Sir George looked at Lucien sternly, then at Sherry. "What have you kept from me? In light of this shooting, I think it's high time we heard it all." He waited, making it plain he was not leaving without an explanation that satisfied him.

Sherbourne looked toward the bed. "He is right. We have to tell him."

Lucien heaved a sigh, letting his head sink into the pillows. "Then you do it."

"Would you prefer I left?" the captain asked, looking uncomfortable. "If this is something private…"

"No, you should stay. It affects everyone." Lucien closed his eyes. He really was very tired.

"Lucien?"

He heard the worry in Sherry's voice but could not bring himself to open his eyes. "Tell them. I just need a moment."

Talbot was by his side, easing him further into the pillows and propping his arm.

"Rest easy, my friend. I can take it from here." Sherry paused as though collecting his thoughts. "We—Lucien and I—were covert agents for the Crown for four years. Mostly in Paris. Since our return to England we have done some work for the War Office from time to time."

"Is that why Ware came to Blinker's Marsh?" Sir George asked.

"No," Lucien muttered. "It was Grandmama."

"The Dowager Salcott," Sherry clarified. "Quite a formidable lady to whom you'd never want to say no. But his private inquiry changed yesterday with the intervention from Whitehall, and now this shooting…it may mean our past has caught up with us."

"I don't understand. In what way?" Sir George asked.

"Lucien's inquiry and the Crown's concerns regarding recent rebel activities have crossed paths. And Lucien may have been recognized by someone in the Harwick party as a former agent for Wellington."

When Sherry stopped there, Lucien murmured, "Go on. Tell it all. They have to know enough to protect themselves, and we may need their help before this is finished."

"I think Rothe would agree with that," Sherry said. He related Whitehall's concerns that French agents had infiltrated local revolutionary bands and that the Harwicks were French sympathizers. "Since Lucien was already involved with Harwick House, Whitehall—and the Prince Regent— put him in charge of the local inquires with a mind to legitimize his ongoing presence."

Sir George was silent for so long that Lucien forced his eyes open. His host looked stern, even angry.

The older man finally said, "There's only one way they'd know about Ware's past."

"Fraid so," Sherry said. "They're privy to French intelligence, and someone in that household it likely a French agent."

"Not conclusively," Lucien objected. "The shot at me could have nothing to do with France and everything to do with Lucy's killer thinking I'm closer to unmasking him than I am." He struggled to sit, but the room seemed to move in waves, and he lay back again.

"Well, which is it? Are they spies or killers?" Sir George asked, his frustration coming through.

"Both," Sherry said.

"Or neither," Lucien muttered.

"Bollocks." Sir George appeared taken aback. "Surely you are not serious, Ware," he said frowning at Lucien. "Under the circumstances, it is quite apparent they are guilty of something."

Sherry snorted. "Lucien's injury has put him out of sorts, sir. Harwick House is clearly at the center of trouble in the neighborhood."

Lucien struggled to sit up. "Help me up, Sherry. I may be out of sorts, but one thing is clear, I must leave Barnett Park before others are harmed."

"What? I'll not hear of it," Sir George said.

"The ladies, sir," Lucien urged.

"Nonsense. You think I cannot protect my own? If these ruffians are after you, you are safer surrounded by friends."

A rap on the door interrupted further discussion. Lucien was relieved by the sight of Doc Morehouse. He didn't feel up to snuff. Perhaps chasing the shooter had not been such a wise idea.

The doctor took one look at Lucien's face and ordered everyone else from the room. Considering Morehouse's rather harsh tone, Lucien wasn't surprised that no one protested. The moment the door closed, the doctor's voice softened.

"Now, lad, what kind of trouble have you gotten into?"

The doctor took one look at Lucien's face and ordered everyone else from the room. Considering Morehouse's rather harsh tone, Lucien wasn't surprised that no one protested. The moment the door closed, the doc...

Now lad, what kind of trouble have you gotten into?"

Chapter Eleven

"Anne, did you hear me?"

Lady Anne looked up at the sharpness in Margret's voice. She had been waiting in the small parlor with Miss Barnettt and Lady Barnett for the doctor's report, and she was trying hard to stay composed. She sipped her tea and spoke when spoken to— or thought she had—but she kept listening for someone to come down the stairs.

"I apologize, Margret. Did you say something?"

"Only three times now. You must not fret so. Surely Lord Ware's injury is not serious. After all, he chased that horrible person who shot him and walked nearly all the way back."

"Morehouse is an excellent doctor," Lady Barnett added, reassuringly.

"I'm sure you are correct—he will soon recover." But Anne wasn't sure at all. She had been shocked by his near collapse...and the sight of so much blood. Stories kept flitting through her mind of soldiers who had ridden miles or kept fighting long after they had been mortally wounded. She took a steadying breath and set her jaw. She must not think such thoughts.

Oh, why did someone not come? Taking another sip of tea, she told herself once again that her anxiety for Lord Ware was nothing out of the ordinary. Margret was worried too, was she not? They all were.

After what felt like hours, the doctor arrived, hurried up the stairs, and Lord Sherbourne and Sir George came downstairs to join them. One look at Sherbourne's drawn face made her swallow hard. She gave him a look of entreaty, and he came to sit by her side.

"Do not worry, my lady. His arm will mend."

"He is young and healthy," Sir George added to the room at large. "He was conscious and talking when we left. He should have sought care rather than chasing after the fellow, but Morehouse will fix him up. I dare say he will need extra care for a day or two. Perhaps I should hire a woman from the village to help."

"He has Talbot," Sherbourne said, "who is well up to the task. This is not Ware's first injury."

"I can sit with him when his valet needs rest or just a break," Anne said. "My mother has been ill for many years, so I am familiar with the routine of a sickroom. My maid will be nearby to assist if necessary."

"Very kind of you to offer," Sherbourne said. "Once he is settled, I must ride to London to report this latest development. I shall return by nightfall…if I may impose on your hospitality again?" he asked, turning to his hosts.

"Of course, you are welcome," Lady Barnett said, warmly. "You need not ask."

"As long as you like," Sir George added. "I've been thinking over the situation. If you believe it's likely someone will make another attempt on his life…well, I wonder if we should send the women to stay with friends—or," he hastily amended at his wife's astonished look, "at least Lady Anne and Margret."

"We are not to be fobbed off like that," Margret said, getting in before Anne's protest. "I too may be needed to sit with his lordship. Surely Father and Captain Wycliff can keep us safe."

Sir George turned to the captain. "Do you have a firearm?"

"Not with me. If you wish me to stay, perhaps Sherbourne could stop by my lodgings while he is in town. I would be honored to assist in safeguarding the ladies."

"Then by all means, we shall do it." Sir George eyed his daughter with a look that was beyond speculative. "Whatever makes my daughter feel secure."

Sherbourne nodded. "I shall bring my pistol too. I wager Lucien has his in his bags, but I will verify that with Talbot."

"Very good," Sir George said. "Our servants will need to be told something. If I recall correctly, our footmen are decent shots. I will see the staff is prepared for whatever comes."

A short time after this discussion, half the household was scurrying around in the back rooms, polishing firearms and gathering munitions, but when Doc Morehouse descended to the drawing room, the family, Lady Anne, Sherbourne, and Wycliff were still gathered to hear his report.

"The viscount is resting comfortably," he assured them, setting his bag down and accepting the half-finger of brandy Sir George handed him. "I have bound his arm, and over his strenuous objection, his valet and I managed to dose him with laudanum." Morehouse smiled. "He won't be an easy patient, I predict, but I am hopeful he will remain quiet for at least a couple of days. I'm concerned about the great amount of blood loss, but the bone in his arm was nicked rather than shattered. He should heal rather well, if there are no complications. Did any of you see what happened?"

So once again the story was related: the shot, the unsuccessful chase, and Lord Ware's near collapse upon his return to the manor.

"Ah, that explains the excessive blood loss." Morehouse shook his head. "The young can be rather foolish. Give him plenty of tea, as much as he will drink, and I'll see him tomorrow."

"I assume we must watch for signs of a fever," Anne said.

"Yes, that is the greatest risk. Someone should stay with him through the night."

"We shall be diligent," Lady Barnett said. "Thank you, Mr. Morehouse."

Similar sentiments were expressed by the others. Morehouse set down his glass and picked up his bag. "I must be off."

Anne stopped him with a question. "One last thing before you go, can you tell us what happened at the inquest?" She saw his look of surprise. Ladies didn't usually concern themselves with such matters, but he recovered quickly.

"Nothing unexpected, my lady. Half the village pushed inside the tavern to gape, and the heat was stifling. Be that as it may, the coroner reached the only sensible conclusion—unlawful murder by persons unknown. A sad affair."

"What happens next?"

"I hear that is up to Lord Ware. Constable Jones says he's washed his hands of the matter."

"Not exactly what happened," Sir George said and went on to explain the Crown's order.

"Ah, I thought Jones was more prickly than usual. I guess I better get my patient back on his feet if we're to get this murder solved."

After the doctor left and Sherbourne departed for Whitehall, Anne and Margret went up to see the patient for themselves and to offer their services to Talbot.

"Very kind of you, my ladies." Talbot glanced toward the bed with a satisfied smile. "As you can see, he is sleeping now, and there is nothing to do. However, he must be watched constantly the next couple of days. I can manage his care, of course, but if Lord Sherbourne isn't on hand, it might be nice to have someone step in for brief periods."

"I shall be available at any hour," Anne promised. "You must stretch your legs and sleep at some point."

As Anne and Margret descended the stairs, Margret asked, "So what are we supposed to do about solving the murder or about Jane? Sit around until someone else gets shot?"

"I hardly think that will happen," Anne said. "It is Lord Ware they are after, and he is safe enough inside the manor. But I know what you mean. I feel as though I should be doing *something.*"

"Hmm, yes." Margret stopped to face her friend at the bottom of the staircase. "Why was Lord Ware so curious about the Harwicks' guests? Does he think they harmed Lucy or Jane?"

"I'm not certain," Anne hedged. "But he and Lord Sherbourne were both asking about them—not just their names, but where they are from, that sort of thing—how they know the Harwicks, and why they are in Blinker's Marsh. I suspect something else is happening, not just the missing girls."

"I think so too. But what? You know something you're not telling me, Anne. Exactly what do Lord Ware and Lord Sherbourne do for Whitehall? I've heard Lord Rothe mentioned…"

"Please don't ask me," Anne said. "It would be good if you kept your speculation to yourself."

"But—"

"No, please, Margret, I am serious."

Margret eyed her a long moment. "Oh, very well. But I know I'm right." She shrugged when Anne failed to respond. "Maybe we could help them—whatever they are doing—by getting the information they wanted."

"How?" Anne asked cautiously.

"Since we were introduced on our morning ride, would it not offend propriety if we failed to make a house call?" Her eyes gleamed with mischief.

Anne returned a conspiratorial smile. "Oh, most improper. We must remedy that immediately. but what about your mother? Will she agree to go?"

"It's not her but father who worries me. Apparently she was quite adventurous when young. Although she refuses to talk about it, Father blames her for my high spirits whenever I do something he disapproves."

"Then by all means, let us recruit her assistance. And Captain Wycliff?"

Margret cocked her head. "I believe I can talk him around. He might even go with us."

As it happened, the gentlemen removed themselves as potential obstacles to Anne and Margret's plans. Sir George felt it was his duty to report Ware's shooting to the local constabulary. "I shan't tell them anything they should not know," he said. "But they have a duty to protect Blinker's Marsh, and they cannot do that if they are not made aware of what has occurred. I also intend to speak with a few neighbors. Captain Wycliff, would you care to go? I would enjoy the company, and having a military man at my side might impress Constable Jones."

"Gladly, sir. I am at your pleasure."

They had barely ridden out of the stable yard before Anne and Margret presented their plan to Lady Barnett.

"Heavens, girls, your father would never approve."

"That is probably true," Margret conceded. "But he is not here. What could happen on a simple house call? We will have a footman and coachman to guard us, but I cannot imagine they would be required to do so." Her smile turned eager. "Are you not dying to know more about their mysterious guests and why they're here? And if one of them acts guilty for shooting Lord Ware?"

"My goodness, Margret. I hope you're not planning to accuse them?"

Margret laughed. "I promise not to do so. Please, let us go."

"We could learn other things just by listening," Anne said. "They might let something slip. Lord Ware questioned whether they are who they say they are, and I found it odd two of the men didn't speak. Was that because they are foreigners? From where? One of them looks very French."

"If nothing is wrong, mama, well, then we will have done our duty in making a neighborly call," Margret coaxed.

Her mother pursed her lips. "I am sure we should not, but it is hard to always be excluded, and I too am curious. Where is my blue hat?" She laid her knitting aside and rose. "It goes so well with my best afternoon tea gown."

• • •

Anne shot Margret a rather desperate look. They had been at Harwick House almost fifteen minutes and learned nothing. Since a visit beyond half an hour would be deemed improper by high sticklers, they were running out of time.

Margret suddenly said, "What a lovely house this is. I have ever wondered about the grand ballroom. May I see it?" She stood and gave the handsome, fair-haired Mr. Ramsey an expectant, coquettish look. "Perhaps you could show me around?"

Anne nearly choked at Lady Barnett's appalled look. Margret's mother might have been spirited in her youth and still willing to bend the rules upon occasion, but her daughter's lapse in polite etiquette had left her momentarily speechless.

"Miss Barnett, you are so taken by old houses…" Anne began with a polite laugh, hoping to make an excuse for her friend's impulsive behavior and forestall Lady Barnett's protest, "I am afraid you have allowed it to override your good manners. What must the Harwicks think?"

"Oh, goodness, I *am* sorry," Margret said, feigning remorse. "I hope my enthusiasm did not offend."

"Not at all. It is quite all right," Mrs. Harwick said stiffly, making a half-hearted effort to hide her disapproval. "We would be delighted to have your opinion on a room that is one of my personal favorites." She turned her head and gave Ramsey what Anne thought was a warning look. "Mr. Ramsey, would you do the honors?"

"Absolutely, my pleasure." He strolled forward and offered his arm to Margret with a flirtatious smile. "Shall we, Miss Barnett?"

Anne felt a moment of unease. Ramsey clearly thought Margret wished to be alone with him. Well, Margret could take care of herself. And her friend's boldness had given them an answer to one question. While Ramsey looked English, he had a definite accent. Not French, but Italian, maybe. Now, if she could get Mr. Faegan to speak up…

She turned her head to smile at the dark stranger. "Mr. Faegan, I do not recall where you said you were from."

"I don't believe he said," Mrs. Cluett interjected. "Charles does not understand English, Lady Anne. His home was in the Flemish town of Ghent. His family fled the occupation by Napoleon, and out of necessity they changed their family name." She turned to him and asked in French, "What was your original surname, Charles?"

He hesitated, his eyes flitting to Mrs. Cluett, then he bowed his head toward Lady Anne. "Lacroix, mam'selle."

His accent was thick. French was clearly his native tongue, and although it was frequently found in Flanders, it was not the dominant language. Mrs. Cluett had certainly been ready with a story to explain his accent—maybe too ready. And, for a man who could not understand English, Faegan's eyes and expression had appeared to follow the conversation among the women quite well.

"It must be difficult to get around England without understanding the language," Anne said, giving him an encouraging smile. "I admire you for choosing to come here."

Again, it was Mrs. Cluett who answered, sharply this time. "They had no choice. They would have faced the guillotine if they remained in Ghent."

"How dreadful," Anne answered, unruffled. Even if true, there were many countries where his family might have found sanctuary. Why England, where French was certainly not in vogue? Faegan or Lacroix, if either was his true name, might be a French connection that would interest Lord Ware. And then there was Mrs. Cluett, there was something about her that Anne did not trust.

Lady Barnett had been watching the hall door and finally said, "I wonder what is keeping my daughter and Mr. Ramsey? We really should be going."

"Lost track of time, I'm sure." Mrs. Harwick looked at Faegan. "Would you look for them?"

"Qui, mam'selle." He turned and left the room.

"He appears to be learning English quite rapidly," Anne murmured.

"Uh, yes, well, he is can often infer much from the situation," Mrs. Harwick said before lapsing into uncomfortable silence.

No one else remarked on the exchange, but Mrs. Cluett's lips pressed in a tight line.

The awkwardness was broken by Faegan returning, followed by Margret laughing at something Mr. Ramsey said. She was hanging on her escort's arm. "It is a fantastic ballroom," she said turning to her mother and Anne. "I can just imagine the grand affairs that were held there a century ago. Oh, are we leaving so soon?" she asked as her mother swept to her feet.

"Yes, dear. We must not overstay our welcome." Lady Barnett nodded to the guests, expressing her pleasure at meeting them, before turning to Mrs. Harwick. "I look forward to entertaining you at Barnett Park. Thank you for your gracious hospitality."

Anne drew her handkerchief up to cover an irrepressible smile. Gracious hospitality? What a plumper! Their visit had not been well received, not for a moment.

• • •

"Oh, Margret, you will be the death of me," her mother lamented as they settled inside the carriage for the short trip home. "To be so bold."

"But it worked, Mama. Just wait until you hear everything the amorous Mr. Ramsey told me."

"The what? Amorous! My heavens," Lady Barnett cried, regret and consternation flooding her face. "Was he ungentlemanly? Oh, what will your father say? I blame myself for allowing you to talk me into this visit."

"Please do not fuss, mama." Margret laid a gloved hand on her mother's arm. "I did not let him get seriously out of line. He merely tried to kiss me."

"As if that was not a bad thing," Lady Barnett said in fatalistic tones. She rallied immediately and turned to her daughter with a stern expression. "Do *not* tell your father. He might feel duty bound to call Ramsey out, and then…my goodness, where would we be? You mustn't tell anyone."

"I shall not. I promise. It was nothing. Do you not want to hear what he said?"

"I do," Anne said, breaking into the mother-daughter exchange, hoping to redirect Lady Barnett's thoughts. "I am most eager."

"Hush now, both of you. We are home now, and it will have to wait," the older woman warned as the coach came to a halt. "Come to my room where we may talk privately. And someone bring the sherry. I could use something stronger than tea after that most disagreeable visit."

By the time they were gathered in her bedchamber, Lady Barnett had a firm hold on her self-control. The sweet sherry helped them all, and the younger women soon were laughing over the awkward adventure. Even Lady Barnett admitted parts of it were humorous in retrospect.

"And it wasn't for nothing," Anne said. "We learned Mr. Faegan is really Charles Lacroix from Ghent, or at least claims to be. Nor is Mr. Ramsey an Englishman with that accent. He sounded like the neighbor's cook back home, and her family came from Italy."

"Very clever of you, Anne. He is from the island of Sicily." Margret smiled. "And very talkative when his mind is on seduction. All I had to do was pretend to admire him, and he talked on and on."

"Oh, Margret." Her mother sighed. "I hope you did not do anything a lady should not."

"Well, maybe a little," Margret said, then relented with a giggle. "No, mama. I did not. But I allowed him to think I might."

"Dear me," Lady Barnett said faintly and took another sip of sherry.

"So what else did he say?" Anne urged.

"They have all been friends or acquaintances—he does not like Mrs. Cluett very much—some five years. They didn't meet in England, but I could not get him to say where. He and Mr. Faegan travel together—often, I take it—but once again, he was vague about where, except they visit Harwick House two or three times a month. He told me that because he asked to see me again." She laughed. "As though I would agree."

"I wonder why he dislikes Mrs. Cluett." Anne mused. "Did he say?"

"Not really. He didn't actually say he disliked her—it was the way his mouth twitched and his tone hardened, as though he resented her but had to hide his animosity." Margret shrugged. "Another very strange thing...he went silent and stiffened when I mentioned

Viscount Ware. In fact, I had to coax him after that to get him talking about anything other than the architecture of that dratted ballroom. It was quite undistinguished, by the by. I was hard pressed to find things to admire so as to extend our conversation."

Anne gave a laugh. "I am sure you were masterly. His reaction to the viscount *is* odd as though Ramsey might have known him before."

Margret frowned in thought. "He might have. Yes, Anne, Ramsey started to say something about seeing someone in Paris and then stopped. He said it was unimportant, but I am certain he was lying."

Anne drew in a quick breath. Paris. Did he know Lord Ware from the war? Had he shot him because of his spy years in France? Thank goodness they were safely away from Harwick House. If Ware and Sherbourne's present activities involved the war, the situation could indeed be dangerous for everyone.

"Has Lord Ware said he knew him?" Margret asked, studying her friend.

"No. He has not." Nor did she intend to speculate with Margret. If she did, she would be tempted to reveal everything she knew or had guessed about his history with the War Office. She could not do that. The viscount's activities were not her secret to tell.

"It is strange, is it not?" Margret said thoughtfully. "I wonder if any of this information will help Lords Ware and Sherbourne."

"How can it not?" Anne dropped her eyes to study her hands. "But who among us is brave enough to tell them how we got it?"

There was a moment of weighty silence.

"*I* shall tell Sir George we felt compelled by civility to make a house call after meeting them this morning, that it would be very odd and impolite if we did not," Lady Barnett said. She eyed both young ladies. "He need know nothing more. Anne, you are the obvious choice to talk with Viscount Ware and Sherbourne about anything else. You have a longer acquaintance. If you feel compelled to tell them *everything*, please caution them not to share certain matters with my husband."

Margret gave Anne a sympathetic look. "I fear she speaks the truth. It is up to you to talk with them. Do you think they will be very angry?"

"No more so than the captain," Anne said, raising a brow. "And you shall have to deal with him."

• • •

When Sir George and Captain Wycliff returned to the manor an hour later, Lady Barnett followed her husband into his study. The captain waved but didn't stop to talk. He went upstairs to change, thus allowing Margret a reprieve from her own confession. Anne and Margret waited on pins and needles for her mother to return, but long minutes passed and still no word from the study.

Capt. Wycliff arrived in due course, but he didn't appear to notice the ladies' preoccupation and launched into a description of his afternoon talking with neighbors and the village constables. "Constable Jones was his usual blustery self, ragging on about his theories of insane strangers in the neighborhood and careless poachers. I wasn't sure whether he meant the shooter was an insane stranger or he was referring to us. When we left, he was set on searching the village for I am not sure what—strangers, maybe, or rifles or evidence of poaching."

"At least he is doing something," Anne said. "That should warn the villagers of potential danger in the neighborhood."

"Sir George told the local gentry a bit more and hinted at our suspicions of Harwick House and their guests."

Conversation was interrupted as Margret's mother walked briskly through the drawing room to the outside French doors. She'd been closeted with Mr. Barnett more than a half hour, and her mouth was firmly set. Her direct gaze appeared to carry a warning. "If any of you need me, I shall be in the garden. My roses need pruning." She closed the door behind her with a loud click.

Working in the garden in this stifling heat? Anne wondered. Lady Barnett must feel a strong need to get out of the house for a while…and away from Sir George, perhaps. Before Anne could even think about how he must have taken the news of their visit to the Harwicks, he appeared in the archway and surveyed both young women with a jaundiced eye.

"I promised Lady Barnett I would not rebuke you, but I am compelled to say I do not approve. You behaved recklessly." His gaze turned to Margret. "I am disappointed but will say no more." With that, he left, and Anne heard his study door close with more than necessary force. The doors in this house were being sorely used today.

"To what was he referring?" Captain Wycliff asked, his eyes narrowing on Margret's face before looking at Anne. "What have the two of you done?"

"If you are going to be a bear about it, we shall not trouble Anne with our quarrel." Margret stood. "We shall talk in the library."

No more than ten minutes later, Margret was back. "I told him we went because it was the proper thing to do. He has gone off in a huff. To the stables, I think. I suspect it was to avoid saying something I would not forgive." She glowered at the windows that opened on the stable yard.

"Do you think Sir George and the captain will remain angry for long?"

Margret sighed. "Father won't. I daresay he will be aloof at dinner, but over it by morning. As for the captain, I do not know. He says we were reckless with our safety, but you know we were not." She stood, lifted her chin, and went to gaze out the window. "He needs to understand he cannot run my life. We are not married or even betrothed." She turned and gave Anne a determined look. "Even if we were, I will not be ordered about."

Her independent spirit was one of the traits that made Margret and Anne such close friends, but Anne would not be lured into making disparaging remarks about the captain. Friendships have limits, and chances were good Margret and Wycliff would get beyond this rift. The less Anne said about it, the better. Instead, she suggested they play cards and stay out of everyone's way for a while, and Margret agreed.

Captain Wycliff's response had given Anne pause. Unless their visit to Harwick House was to be useless, she had to speak with Lord Ware or Lord Sherbourne, and her mind was only half on the card game as she wondered how they would react. Which of them should she approach? She was better acquainted with the viscount and telling him should be the obvious choice, except Anne suspected his reaction would mirror the captain's—or worse. Talking to Sherbourne would be the coward's way, yet she could not put off the telling either. Her final decision would have to guided by the viscount's condition.

Sherbourne returned to the manor less than an hour later. Anne hurried to the drawing room door, just in time to see him give his traveling bag to a footman and go straight up the stairs to Lord Ware's room.

"Was that Sherbourne?" Captain Wycliff asked walking into the drawing room as Anne returned to the game table and picked up her cards. "Did he bring any news?"

Wycliff acted as though the row had never happened, and Anne followed his lead. ""He did not stop to talk. I'm sure he will be down as soon as he has seen the viscount."

"No doubt." Wycliff came to stand beside the card table. "May I observe?"

"You are welcome to play," Margret said, looking up at him with a tentative smile. "It is just a friendly game of Vingt-et-un."

They had just started a new game of twenty-one to include the captain when they heard footsteps on the stairs and Sherbourne joined them.

"Talbot says Lucien has been sleeping fitfully," he said in response to their anxious looks, "and I did not want to disturb him. Have you heard anything while I was gone?" It was a perfunctory question, and his brows lifted in surprise at the sudden silence.

Anne put down her cards and stood. Choice made. "I think we should take a stroll in the garden, my lord. I have a bit of information to report."

Chapter Twelve

Margret was hovering near the hallway and pounced on Anne, dragging her into the front parlor the moment Sherbourne went up the stairs. "What did he say?"

"Not terribly much," Anne admitted. "He was surprised, I could tell, and he frowned a couple of times, but mostly he just listened." She grimaced and shook her head. "Afterward, he said Lord Ware might not take it as well as he had. I felt he was warning me, but I could be wrong." She shrugged. "His lordship has no right to take me to task. He is merely a friend."

"Oh, come now, Anne. You are talking to me. I have seen how you look at the viscount and how worried you have been. And he is surely interested in you, or he would not keep coming around."

"I have seen little of him the last couple of months. Regardless of all that, what can he do about our call on the Harwicks? It is done. I am hopeful he will admit we were of some assistance."

"I thought we did quite well, and so I told the captain."

Anne wasn't positive any of it had been of value. While Sherbourne had listened attentively, he had not said if the information was useful or not.

"We did what we could," Anne agreed. "I am not sorry, not even a bit."

"Nor am I."

On that note of agreement, they parted to change for dinner. As Anne reached the guest floor, she peeked down the men's wing. Lord Ware's door was partly open. If Sherbourne was telling Ware of their visit, she did not hear any yelling or ranting. Perhaps he was taking it better than predicted. She would stop to visit him immediately after dinner—when Sherbourne should

112

still be with the other men—and get any unpleasantness over and
behind them.

Her plan was thwarted when Sherbourne did not come down
to the table. Instead, trays were requested, and Anne grew uneasy.
Why did it take both Sherbourne and Talbot to care for him? Had
the doctor not said he would be sleeping most of the day?

Dinner was nearly over when Anne heard voices at the front
entrance and then footsteps going up the stairs. Her concern grew.
"What is happening, Sir George? Was that the doctor?"

"I assume so. His lordship has been more restless than
anticipated, and Sherbourne wanted Morehouse to take a look at
him. A mere precaution."

Anne doubted it. Sherbourne had seen many men injured
during the war. He wouldn't send for the doctor unless it was
necessary. She set down her wine glass. Restless could mean Lord
Ware had a fever or was developing one. That would be serious,
indeed. She pushed back her chair. "If you will excuse me, I am
going up. I may be able to help." Not waiting for a response, she
hurried to the door.

"I am sure that is not necessary," Sir George called to her, but
Anne did not turn back.

Margret caught up with her on the stairs. "They will not let us
in, you know."

"Maybe not, but I shall insist they talk to me." She marched up
the stairs and knocked on the door.

"Who is it?" She recognized Sherbourne's voice.

"Lady Anne."

"And Miss Barnett."

Sherbourne opened the door a few inches but barred the way
with his body. "This is not a good time, ladies. The doctor is here."

"We know that. What is wrong? Has he taken a fever?" Lady
Anne firmed her jaw. "You might as well tell me for I am staying
here unless you do."

Sherbourne shook his head but spoke to someone behind him
and received a muffled response.

"Well?" she prodded.

"Doc Morehouse says he will talk with you soon, if you will go back downstairs and wait until he is finished. Be patient, Lady Anne, until we can sort this out." Sherbourne's face was clouded with worry. "I promise we will not keep anything from you."

"Very well, I shall go and wait for his report. I...We just want to help."

"I know. Try not to worry."

• • •

"No, he doesn't have a fever," Morehouse said, sitting down in the drawing room and accepting the cup of tea that Lady Barnett offered. "The laudanum is keeping him asleep, but he is moving around a bit and mumbling. The bullet nicked the bone, taking out a chip and bruising it. Bone injuries are painful, and his body feels it even while he sleeps." He looked at Anne. "I saw no sign of the wound festering, but it needs watching. Sherbourne said you have sickroom experience, Lady Anne. If it's not an imposition, you might sit with him for a spell later this evening. His valet has worried himself to exhaustion, and I sent him to bed. He may not stay there long, although I believe Sherbourne slipped laudanum into his pint of ale. Lord Sherbourne is with him now, but he has also had a long day."

"I shall do so willingly. No imposition at all."

With the doctor's blessing to support her, Anne waved off the protests when she went up to the sickroom an hour later to find both Talbot and Sherbourne there. Talbot looked about to collapse. "You will be useless to his lordship without sleep," she scolded. "The doctor told you to go to bed. You'd be wise to heed his advice." She turned a determined look on Sherbourne. "And you. Someone has to carry on with the inquiries and whatever else you two are doing. You cannot do that and be here too. Allow me to help. I can sleep all day tomorrow if I wish."

"Is it proper for you to be here alone?" the valet asked.

She frowned at his troubled face. "Honestly, Talbot, no sensible person could think my virtue to be at risk from an unconscious, wounded man. I shall leave the door open, and my maid will be within my call. Every propriety will be met."

Having been thusly chastised, both men left without further protest, yet Anne knew their acquiescence was due more to fatigue than anything she had said. She sat beside the bed with a satisfied smile, glad to be doing something useful. Her smile faded as she leaned forward to study her patient. His eyes were closed, dark lashes lying against his pale skin. He looked vulnerable, and she had never before imagined him that way. Sweat lightly beaded his forehead, and she felt his brow and hands. Reassured he wasn't feverish, Anne pulled off one of the blankets and the top cover. The men had simply overdone it. It was July, for heaven's sake.

She opened a window in hopes of finding a breeze to clear the stuffy room, and she dampened a cloth before returning to the bedside. Once she had wiped his forehead and face, she settled into the comfortable wing-backed chair until he might need her.

At a gentle tap on the door, she turned her head and found Lady Barnett giving her an inquiring look.

"How is he?"

"Sleeping better, I believe. It was too warm in here. I dispensed with some covers and opened the window."

The older woman nodded. "Before I retire for the night, is there anything you need?"

"There is a book in my room…on the side table. If Jenny could bring it…"

"I will send her with it. She must stay the night, you know."

"Yes, of course," Anne murmured. "I will have her make up a pallet. I want to give Talbot and Sherbourne as long a rest as possible."

"If you get too tired, my dear, do not hesitate to send for me. It would not be my first sickroom either."

"I shall, of course, but I can sleep tomorrow."

Lady Barnett smiled indulgently. "Oh, to be young again. But the offer is there if you find yourself in need."

She had not been gone more than a few minutes before Anne's maid arrived with the book and an armful of bedding. Jenny made up a pallet in the dressing room, and at Anne's insistence, was soon asleep.

Anne varied her time between reading, wiping the viscount's brow, and quietly pacing the room upon occasion to stretch her legs and stay awake. She spoke to him softly when he tried to turn in his sleep and jostled his arm, the pain making the muscles in his cheeks ripple as he clenched his teeth. His breathing eased about three in the morning, and he dropped into a deeper sleep.

As the birds began to sing outside the window and dawn lightened the sky, Anne stretched and closed her book, setting it aside. She glanced at the bed to find the viscount looking at her.

"Good morning, my lord," she said with a smile. "How do you feel?"

He frowned, clearly perplexed. "What are you doing here? Where is Talbot?"

"He and Sherbourne were exhausted. The doctor and I sent them to bed."

He tried to sit up, and she slipped a pillow behind him.

"Have you been here all night?" he asked.

She took a step back and cocked her head. "Yes, but Jenny is sleeping in the dressing room. Do not tell me you are going to scold about the proprieties too."

"No." A smile played across his lips. "I was just thinking…since we spent the night together…you might call me by my Christian name."

"We did *not* spend the night together," she said firmly.

"Oh, I beg to differ. You just told me we did."

"Well, yes, but—Oh, stop it," she said, stifling a laugh. "Yes, I suppose I can call you Lucien if you call me Anne. Only in private, mind you."

"Granted, Anne." He said her name softly, making her breath

catch, and she was relieved to hear the click of the adjoining room door behind her, bringing a timely interruption.

"I thought I heard voices," Talbot said. He was still in his nightdress, hastily tying a robe. His hair stood on end. "My lady, I beg your pardon. I had not meant to sleep so long."

"No reason to fret, Talbot." Anne's lips quirked at his appearance. "I daresay I had the trouble-free hours. He slept throughout the night like a babe. Now he is awake, you must deal with his complaints and demands."

"Must you slander a wounded man too weak to defend himself?" Lucien demanded, but even his valet struggled not to smile.

Anne cut off a chuckle as Jenny popped out of the dressing room. The maid was carrying her bedding. "Good morning, my lady. Lord Ware, Talbot." She bobbed a curtsey, clearly unsure what to do next.

"Good morning, Jenny. When it is convenience, please have tea brought to my room. I will be with you shortly."

Anne stayed long enough to help Talbot change the bandage. The bleeding had stopped. His lordship...Lucien...grimaced but uttered not a sound as they lifted his arm and pulled off the bloody linen. The wound didn't look as bad as she'd imagined. Morehouse should be pleased with the viscount's progress.

"Why didn't someone wake me?" Sherbourne could be heard coming down the hallway. He stopped at the door and grinned at sight of his partner, relief pouring across his face. "Well, you look a great deal better than when I last saw you. A woman's magic, eh?"

While Lucien was telling him to mind his manners, and they were trading banter as men who know each other well are want to do, Anne slipped from the room. With Lucien awake and in good spirits, despite his drawn face, she realized just how tired she was. It had been a long night. She returned to her bedchamber, changed into her night clothes, and without taking time to touch the breakfast tray Jenny had brought, she climbed onto the soft, flock-mattress bed and sank into dreamless sleep.

Chapter Thirteen

"They did what?" Lucien jerked up in bed, banging his arm. "Bloody hell." He flinched at the jolt of pain but continued to stare at Sherry.

"I knew you wouldn't like it, but they are a plucky bunch. And they came back with information we didn't have before."

"Such as?"

"Faegan is not Faegan. Claims he came from Ghent, fleeing Napoleon's forces. She gave me his original name, but I was so astonished at what they'd done I was only half listening. I knew you'd want to talk with her regardless."

"Immediately," Lucien said. "Rothe will need that name."

"Not this morning, your lordship," Talbot interjected. "Lady Anne will be abed after sitting with you all night, and you need to rest."

"I feel better," Lucien insisted.

"Doctor Morehouse said two or three days."

"He said two," Lucien corrected. "And the good doctor is batty, if he thinks I will lay about that long."

"Did I hear someone threatening—in a very disparaging way—to disobey my orders?" Morehouse asked cheerfully as walked into the bedchamber. "I must say, my lord, I am relieved to see and hear you doing so well. Let us have a look at that arm."

Morehouse not only looked at the injury, but for the next ten minutes, he poked and prodded and asked Lucien questions about how he felt. At the end he seemed satisfied, gave Talbot his instructions, and made a sling for Lucien's arm. He gave his patient a last stern look. "Stay in bed. If you continue to do as well, you may get up for short periods tomorrow. You lost too much blood running thither and yon before tending to your arm, but you will recover nicely…unless you get up too soon. If you fail to heed my instructions, it could take weeks rather than days."

"He'll stay abed," Sherry said. "We shall see to it. If Talbot and I cannot prevail, I wager Lady Anne can."

Morehouse smiled. "Knowing women, I suspect you're correct."

Lucien started to cross his arms, stopped when pain shot down his injured arm, and glared at his partner. "You would not do that."

"You think not?"

"Traitor."

Morehouse and Sherry only chuckled.

After the doctor left, Talbot took the bloodied clothes to be cleaned or tossed, and Sherry rode into the village to nose around for anything he might learn about their inquiries or activities at Harwick House. Lucien sank back into the pillows. Despite his earlier protests, he was tired, and while pondering over recent events, he soon dozed off.

• • •

He woke mid-afternoon and convinced Talbot to help him out of bed long enough to freshen up and change out of the bloody nightshirt. He finally sank into a chair while Talbot shaved him, and he didn't protest when his valet insisted he get back into bed.

Drat this bothersome weakness. But a short nap revived him, and when Sherry came in he was eager to discuss his partner's activities.

"Have you driven Talbot to bedlam yet?" Sherry asked.

"Not yet. I wasn't as ready to get up as I thought."

"I don't have much to cheer you." Sherry pulled up the chair Anne had used all night. "Constable Jones is a fop if I ever met one, blustering, puffed up. He will be no help unless he stumbles upon something by accident. I tried to talk with Jane Mawbry's mother about the argument they had, but she shut the door in my face. I stopped at the Ellis home. He wasn't there, but his wife is very pleasant. She had only nice things to say about Jane. She one thing she could add was another villager had reported Jane had a new fellow just before she disappeared."

"That could change things. Her wretched mother thought so too, but I gave it little credence. She kept saying Jane had run off with *some man* with such spite I thought she had made it up to discredit her daughter. Perhaps I discounted it too quickly."

"Maybe not. Mrs. Ellis didn't know if the villager's story was true or not, but she insisted Jane wouldn't have run off with someone she'd just met. Called her a good girl despite her mother's poor example."

"Did you ask if Jane had worked for the Harwicks?"

Sherry jerked his head around. "No. Did she?"

"I have no idea. I'm looking for any similarities between the two girls. According to Sir George, many of the villagers have worked up there at one time or another, although no one stayed long."

"I shall ask around." He cocked his head at Lucien and rubbed his chin. "Are you thinking the same people plotting against the Crown are responsible for killing Lucy and maybe Jane?"

"Devil it, Sherry. I don't know what to think. We have no proof Jane is even dead. I look at the facts one way, and it seems improbable, but then I wonder how likely it is that one small village could have so much trouble that is not connected."

"One thing I didn't hear—there was no talk in the village of revolutionaries or complaints about the Crown," Sherry said. "If the Harwicks are dissidents, they've been very discreet. Oh, I got the Faegan fellow's original name from Miss Barnett—Lacroix, if we can rely on anything said by that band of scoundrels. I sent it to Rothe and also urged him to inquire into the Cluetts. From what Lady Anne and Miss Barnett told me, Mrs. Cluett did much of the talking for everyone."

Lucien nodded absently. "Who could confirm whether or not there was another man in Jane Mawbry's life?"

"Her former fellow, maybe, the one in the army?"

"Watts. I feel confident he would have told Whitehall anything he knew when they asked about Jane."

"Are there other relatives we could ask?"

"A married sister, I think. Moved away. From what I've heard they didn't write or visit. You might try the blacksmith in the village. A smart and talkative man. I would bet my team of grays that not much happens around the village without it coming to his ears. He first told me about Jane. Maybe he knows her friends or who this mysterious man might be...the things her mother couldn't be bothered to know or refused to tell us."

"I will talk to him as soon as I can. He might also know if she worked for the Harwicks."

Lucien flopped back against the pillows. "I loathe being stuck in this bed. It feels as though we're turning and twisting, getting nothing except tiny pieces from here and there. And none of it fits together."

A knock at the door elicited a resigned sigh from Lucien. Who was it now? "Yes, come in," he called.

Lady Anne poked her head around the door, and Lucien sat up.

"Am I interrupting?" she asked. "Lord Sherbourne said you wanted to speak with me."

"Absolutely, I do. Come in. When we talked earlier, you must have forgotten to mention your trip to Harwick House."

"To the contrary, I did not forget. The time did not seem a good one for you were in no shape for an argument. Besides, I told Lord Sherbourne everything of importance." She looked from one man to the other. "Shall I come back later?"

"No, this is an excellent time. Will you not sit with us?"

"Take this chair," Sherry said getting up. "I should be going."

"Actually, I would like you to stay, Sherry, in the event we hear something we haven't heard before." Lucien cocked his head at Lady Anne who was eying him with reluctance. "Lady Anne?"

"If this is to be two against one..."

"I promise it is not. I have no right to scold you."

"Nor reason," she said, finally sitting down. "While our visit to

Harwick House may have been...unusual under the circumstances, it was neither improper nor dangerous."

Sherry pulled another chair to the far side of the bed.

Lucien smiled at her defensiveness. "I suppose you felt it was necessary. Since the deed is done, I am more interested in what occurred during the visit, what was said, and in particular, what you observed."

"Very well, my lord." She gave him a faint smile and settled in, folding her hands in her lap.

Lucien listened carefully as she went over everything in great detail. When he was silent at the end, she said, "If none of that is important, you should talk with Margret about the time she spent alone with Mr. Ramsey."

"Oh, no, it is not that. I would never distrust your observations," Lucien said. "I was just wondering where all the pieces go. I may, however, speak with Miss Barnett separately. Ramsey may have revealed something she forgot to tell you."

"You will both keep the *amorous incident* a secret from Sir George, I hope?"

"If I can. And Captain Wycliff? Has she not told him either?"

"I think not. He was upset just about the visit, and she feared his reaction might be too extreme."

"No doubt," Sherry said. "In his place I would be taking Ramsey to task."

"Exactly what she does not want. Miss Barnett defended herself. We are not as helpless as some of you think."

"It's not that," Sherry said, somewhat affronted. "It is a matter of honor. Ramsey's actions were an insult to her and to any man paying her court or providing protection."

"They are not engaged," Lady Anne said with asperity.

"It doesn't matter."

Lucien cleared his throat. "We have digressed, and no matter how long this continues, I doubt you will resolve your differences to anyone's satisfaction."

"Do you agree with him?" Lady Anne asked, staring at Lucien.

Somewhat annoyed by her persistence, he answered more bluntly than he would have otherwise. "I might have given Ramsey the option of leaving the country in lieu of running a sword through his black heart."

Lady Anne's eyes widened. "Surely you jest, my lord."

Lucien sighed, refusing to be draw into a quarrel. "Shall we get back to your observations? You felt Ramsey and this fellow calling himself Faegan were showing unusual deference to Mrs. Cluett. Can you elaborate?"

After holding his gaze an additional moment, she gave a quiet huff. "It was not just those two, but that is where I first noticed it. Then I realized she subtly controlled the room. Not only by doing most of the talking but everyone glanced at her before responding or deliberately did not look at her when they should. Oh, I am making a muddle of explaining it."

"Not at all," Lucien assured her. "I can picture such a scene."

"Are you suggesting she is the leader?" Sherry asked.

To Lucien's surprise, she hesitated. "She could be, but they do not admire or respect her. I have seen that look before from servants who feared they would be blamed and reported to a cruel master."

"Then perhaps they work for her," Sherry said.

Anne spread her hands. "I am just not sure."

"Or for someone else," Lucien said thoughtfully. "She may represent someone above her. To use your words, a cruel master. Someone they have reason to fear."

She turned her head to him in a flash. "Precisely. I could not quite put my mind to it, but you have stated it correctly. No one wanted to challenge her for fear she would report their behavior to another."

"Dash it, Lucien." Sherry sat forward and tapped his boot on the floor. "We have another conspirator to find. That makes seven of the devils."

"But Mrs. Cluett is the key. She could lead us to him. What do we know about her? Do we even have a first name?"

Lady Anne pursed her lips and slowly shook her head. "I do not recall hearing it, but she referred to her husband as Andre. That is, if he is her husband. I observed no familiarity between them. Even in loveless marriages, husband and wife know simple, obvious things about one another. He tried to place a drink in her right hand, when she is clearly left-handed."

Once again, Lucien was amazed at the small details Lady Anne's mind recorded and could produce later when they were needed.

"Ah, that is quite revealing," Sherry said, seeming to be much struck by this detail. "One would almost think they were strangers. I wonder if anything they have said is the truth."

"Well…she is no lady," Lady Anne said.

"Not a grand lady, no," Lucien agreed. "Certainly not of the peerage."

"Not a lady at all. I am surprised you of all people did not notice, Lord Ware, unless she was dressed differently when you met. Small things were wrong with her attire. A morning dress when it should have been a half dress. Boots instead of shoes. Either she is not used to polite society, or she is very eccentric." She shrugged. "I wondered if the entire household were frauds, but I saw no such obvious mistakes by the others."

"Those seem but minor issues," Sherry said doubtfully. "Are you certain you are not making too much of it? Maybe she spilled something on the more appropriate gown, and she forgot to change her boots after taking a walk."

Anne looked at him with sympathy. "Spoken like a man. A woman raised among the Quality would not forget to change her shoes, and a lady travels with more than one of each style of gown. And there was her speech. Rather halting at times, as though choosing her words, and twice she used a cant word from the stables. She corrected herself, but I'd say she rarely converses in polite society."

Lucien shifted on the pillows to ease the pressure on his arm and reviewed his own introduction to the guests at Harwick House. Other than Mr. Harwick, Mrs. Cluett had been less talkative on that occasion.

He had noted a strain at that time. Was she the one who had recognized him and was afraid he would know her in return? Small woman, reddish-brown hair, if he remembered right. "I confess I paid her little mind. I was studying the men, wondering if one of them had struck Lucy with such force to shatter her skull. But now that we suspect the work of French agents or sympathizers in agitating the locals—" He stopped at Lady Anne's startled look and gave a wry smile. "Yes, my lady, your earlier suspicions came uncomfortably close to the truth."

"Truly? French agents again?" she asked incredulously. "Are they everywhere in England?"

"Hopefully not," Sherry interposed. "But enough that the War Office stays on constant alert to the possibility. Otherwise, we might have missed the fact that agents had infiltrated the revolutionary activities in and around London."

She turned to Lucien. "Is that the real reason you contrived an invitation to the Barnetts' house party?"

"I contrived nothing. The Harwicks' treasonous activities were unknown to me until Sherbourne arrived two days ago. If my memory serves me well, Miss Barnett extended the invitation because she thought solving Lucy's disappearance would be an amusing diversion."

"Oh, I thought… Well, yes, I suppose she did."

Anne looked away, making Lucien wonder just what she *had* thought. Perhaps that he accepted the invitation because of her? Not entirely wrong, but not the only reason either.

While he was deciding if he should say anything more, she turned to Sherbourne. "How did you discover the Harwicks were part of this rebel conspiracy?"

"A trusted informer reported to Whitehall that he heard the Harwicks mentioned at a rebel meeting in London. Rothe recognized the name when he saw it again in Lucien's message regarding the missing governess."

Lady Anne sighed. "So what now?"

"Can you recall evidence of rebel activity?" Lucien asked. "An odd word, an unusual reaction to something said?"

Anne frowned. "Only the warning looks, the hesitant answers. I felt they were hiding something, but it could have been anything. I particularly noted the warning look Mr. Ramsey received from Mrs. Harwick when he and Margret were leaving for the ballroom. He was certainly a chatty one, and it crossed my mind at the time that she was afraid he would say something he should not."

"Unless she knew how he treats women," Sherry said with a flash of irritation.

"Oh. I had not thought of that."

"You said that the visit ended abruptly," Lucien said thoughtfully. "Were you asked to leave?"

"Oh, no. Nothing that obvious. The atmosphere was less than cordial, but Lady Barnett made the decision to leave. No one escorted us off the property. No one even came to the door to see us off. The only person I saw was their older stable boy hanging around the carriage." She suddenly lifted a finger. "I'm not certain I mentioned it before, but Mr. Faegan, that is Lacroix, who allegedly only spoke French, understood English better than they said. He was listening closely and even responded when Mrs. Harwick slipped up and spoke to him in English."

"Perhaps it is a simple matter of not speaking English well enough to converse in it. On the other hand, a French agent would want to stay out of the conversation as much as possible."

"Confound it." Sherry plopped back in his chair. "How is Whitehall supposed to gather information for us if we cannot be certain of names or locations?"

"Rothe will know it could all be lies. The best we can do is send him what we have—such as detailed descriptions of each person with Lady Anne's help— and let him sort it out."

"I wish I could do sketches for you," Lady Anne said, "but my drawing skill is sadly lacking."

Nearly an hour passed before they were satisfied they had adequate descriptions and behaviors recorded on paper. At that point, Lucien finally gave in to Talbot's insistence, took some foul-tasting concoction, and rest his head on the back of the bed with one arm over his brow.

Sherry picked up the papers and stood. "Rothe will be grateful to have these. If you two can keep Ware out of trouble for a while, I shall take these to Whitehall." This earned him no more than a snort from Lucien. "I would be grateful, Lady Anne, if you would make my excuses to Lady Barnett. I shall not return until long after dinner."

"Of course. May I ask a favor in return? Please do not mention my name to Lord Rothe. I would rather he not repeat his offer of employment. I am happy to help you and Lord Ware like this, but I have no wish to be an agent or employee of the War Office."

Sherbourne cocked a brow. "He knows you are here."

"Even so, less said, the better."

"I can do that, but it won't work." Sherbourne grinned. "I recommend avoidance as your best strategy."

"I shall certainly try." Lady Anne rose, smoothing the folds in her gown and glanced at Lucien. "You are obviously tired, my lord, and I have letters to write. My mother gets worried if she does not hear from me regularly. Lord Sherbourne, I shall walk down with you and inform our hostess of your expected absence before I forget."

"Thank you." He picked up his hat and turned to Lucien. "If you're awake when I return, I'll stop in to report whatever Rothe has to say."

"I hope to see both of you tomorrow," Lady Anne said.

"Please do visit again, my lady," Lucien said. "With Talbot and Sherry giving me grief, I will be desperate for better company."

Lady Anne gave a small laugh. "I shall attempt to meet your expectations."

With a jaunty nod of his head, Sherry followed close behind as she exited into the hallway.

"A fine lady," Talbot remarked, as he came forward from the back of the room.

"That she is." *That she surely is.*

Chapter Fourteen

After the long afternoon spent with Sherbourne and Lady Anne, Lucien slept through most of the evening. Talbot brought up a tray about the time others were preparing for bed, and Lucien had just finished eating when he heard Sherry's footsteps on the stairs.

"Ask him to step in," Lucien urged Talbot. He listened to muffled voices as the two men conversed in the hall.

Talbot returned alone. "He will be in as soon as he shakes off the dust."

"He said nothing else?"

"No, my lord. He looks tired."

Because he is doing the work of two. Lucien sighed. The long nap had revived him, and with the discomfort in his arm fading, he was impatient to get back into action. He would be getting up tomorrow regardless of what anybody said. There was much to discover, and he felt a nagging sense of urgency.

Sherry strolled in fifteen minutes later in his night robe. "Sorry about the informality. I confess bed never looked so good, but I have news that could not wait. Ah well, I suppose it could, but you would no doubt never let me hear the end of it if I didn't tell you immediately."

"So, tell me. Quit blathering about."

Sherry gave a weary chuckle and dropped into a chair.

Talbot crossed to a sideboard. "Brandy, my lords?"

"Yes, thank you, Talbot. I see the longing in Sherry's eyes. Then, do go to bed. I shall call if I need you."

The valet gave his master an assessing look. "Very good, my lord." He tidied the sideboard before disappearing through a connecting door.

"Now," Lucien said, as soon as the door closed, "tell me what you've learned."

"I hardly know where to begin so much has happened." Sherry scratched his head. "Harwick House, I suppose. Rothe had already gathered a bit of background for us, but with the ladies' added information and the descriptions, they were able to weed out the irrelevant. Marcella Cluett is an actress from Edinburgh, long thought to be a French sympathizer, and she's not married. The War Office was not aware she was in England. Her alleged husband Andre is a total unknown. Mr. Faegan did flee from Ghent, but his family name is neither Faegan nor LaCroix. It is Artigue. His family escaped just one step ahead of the hangman for a variety of criminal activities. No political interests noted in the past, so he may be in this for the blunt. And finally, nothing on Ramsey. The name is so common that Rothe is not optimistic, but he is still looking."

"A good start, and all of it interesting," Lucien said, studying Sherry's face, "but I can tell something else has really disturbed you. What's happened?"

Sherry finished his brandy in one swallow. "A bloody mob of rebels set off explosives at a counting house in Clerkenwell this evening. This was far beyond the normal lawlessness seen in the eastside. Rothe says the mob was organized, and from what I saw afterwards, I agree, although the aftermath was rather chaotic. The street was filled with smoke, women and children crying and running around. Two young lads were covered with blood."

"Casualties?"

"Only two when I left, but there were numerous injuries, so more could die. One small powder keg did it all, and whisperings on the streets say worse is to come." Sherry shook his head. "Rothe had his agents out all evening, listening to street talk, and Harwick House was reported as one of a handful of locations where the rebels are gathering additional munitions."

"The devil!" Lucien shot up in bed. "Guns or powder kegs?"

"Explosives, for sure, but likely both. Considering the shot taken at you, I wonder if they have some of the newest long-range rifles."

Lucien blew a hiss through his teeth. "Is Rothe planning to raid the house?"

"Not yet. Doesn't want to tip his hand too soon, and egad, Lucien, we can't go barging into homes of the gentry without more than suspicion. Rothe will hold off a few days, hoping we can turn up some proof."

"Yes, I agree completely." Lucien brushed his hair off his forehead. "If we move now and the cache isn't there, or we cannot find it, they'll disappear and gather somewhere else. We will have lost our best chance to stop this thing. I hope Rothe isn't sending more men to spy on the house."

Sherry shook his head. "We feared strangers in the area would be noticed."

"Quite true. The village is a closed community. But we do need assistance to gather the proof he wants in such a short time. Sir George and Wycliff will help, but we may need more."

Sherry sighed. "I knew you'd say that, and I cannot disagree, but bloody hell, I am uneasy using civilians."

"Console yourself with the fact Wycliff is not a civilian, and Sir George hardly lacks experience, particularly in knowledge of the area. I hope he will enlist a small number of neighbors to hold in readiness if we have to move quickly and cannot wait for reinforcements from Whitehall."

They discussed their options for few minutes until Lucien noticed Sherbourne was visibly drooping.

"High time you got some sleep, my friend."

"Yes, good idea." Sherry yawned getting to his feet. "Be sure to take your own advice, and don't stay up all night thinking about this. Oh, I nearly forgot. On the way to London I saw the blacksmith in the village and asked him about the Mawbry girl. He hasn't heard of her working at Harwick House, nor of a fellow other than the Watts boy. He suggested we talk with the Ellises, which you've already done. So no help there."

"I wouldn't say that, exactly. We know if she had a lover, he did not come from the village. But for now let us concentrate on the bigger crisis, locating those explosives."

• • •

Despite Sherry's disturbing news, Lucien slept well. He awoke nearly feeling himself again. His arm was fine until he bumped it while shrugging out of his nightshirt. "Devil it, Talbot, I am as clumsy as a clodhopper."

Talbot's audible sniff spoke louder than words, reminding his master he had advocated for another day of rest. Lucien ignored the rebuke, but even with Talbot's assistance, by the time he had bathed, shaved, and dressed, Lucien was drained of that early burst of energy. Regardless, he refused to lie abed another day. Straightening his cravat and putting a smile on his face, he went down to breakfast.

Lucien and Captain Wycliff arrived together; Sherry and the ladies were almost finished. Their enthusiastic greeting made his efforts to hide his discomfort worthwhile. His grinning response was forestalled by his host entering the room.

"Ah, good morning, Ware," Sir George went straight to the sideboard to examine the offerings for breakfast. "How are you, my lad?"

"Never better, sir."

Sir George gave a short bark of laughter. "You will pardon me if I doubt that, but you look more robust than you did. It is good to see you up and about."

"Thank you, sir." Lucien smiled, then paused, but there was no reason to put it off. "If I may be so bold to ask, sir, Sherbourne and I wish to meet with your family and guests after breakfast—in private."

Sir George heaved a perceptible sigh. "I suppose that means there is more bad news. Anything you can tell me now?"

"I would prefer to wait," Lucien said.

"As you wish. We shall meet in my study. I am certain everyone will attend as you have roused our curiosity if nothing else."

Although the breakfast conversation remained casual, Lucien's request had created an underlying apprehension that was palpable. He regretted worrying everyone, but he wanted to speak with them before anyone wandered away. No one should leave the manor until they understood the situation...and, hopefully, had agreed to the part each must play the next few days.

No one lingered at the table. As the Barnetts, Wycliff, and Lady Anne gathered to meet with Lucien and Sherborne, the atmosphere in the study was subdued, but Lady Anne was the only one who looked truly worried. Lucien suspected that was because she already knew so much.

He and Sherbourne didn't hold back. With Sherry doing most of the talking, they imparted the latest report from London. Other than a few gasps over the explosion in Clerkenwell, they listened in shocked silence until Sir George interrupted.

"Why not arrest the whole lot of them at Harwick House? By Jove, traitors, rebels, instigators of mob violence? They should all be hanged."

"While I do not disagree," Lucien said, "they are not working alone. We have to identify the other conspirators and find the munitions or arresting the Harwick group would change nothing. Someone else would step in and set off the explosives in what I assume is a well-organized plan. We must be patient enough to catch the French agents behind it all."

"Doesn't Whitehall believe the agents are at Harwick House?"

"Perhaps," Lucien cautioned. "So far it is only rumor without proof."

"I'm sure it is true," Miss Barnett said. "They are an odious lot."

"They are certainly hiding something," Lady Anne agreed. "But it doesn't prove they are traitors."

"How can I help?" Captain Wycliff asked. "My services are at your command."

"Thank you. We hoped you would feel that way," Lucien said.

"The War Office cannot assist us without tipping off the Harwick household."

Sir George nodded his understanding. "Very true. Strangers would cause a stir."

"Which brings us to a reluctant conclusion. We must look for help within the local community, from this household and neighbors you, Sir George, know are reliable."

"You shall have all the support you need," their host said staunchly. "Folks around here know how to protect their own."

Lucien nodded. "Much appreciated, sir. We should all keep in mind we are dealing with dangerous, ruthless people, and we must act accordingly. Anyone who joins us will need to bring their own firearms and be prepared to use them. They should also be mindful not to leave their own families unprotected. For the next few days, anyone living near the marsh should stay close to home. For those we cannot trust with the entire truth, we will have to rely on concerns regarding Lucy's murder." He looked at Mrs. Barnett. "If any of you ladies choose to leave the manor, even to go into the village, an armed man should escort you."

"I shall see to it," she said firmly, before her daughter or Lady Anne could raise an objection.

"Obtainimg a proper escort should not be difficult, as all of our men will be armed," Sir George added.

"I think that is it for now." Lucien turned to Wycliff. "Sherbourne and I could use your help at Harwick House. It will take at least three of us to maintain constant surveillance, scout the property for munitions, and follow anyone who leaves." When Wycliff nodded, he looked at Sir George. "If you have a moment, sir, I wish to talk further about rallying the neighbors."

"What can we do?" Miss Barnett interrupted. "Anne and I want to help. You did say you needed everyone."

Lucien smiled. "So I did. I have not forgotten you. I want you to go shopping."

"Shopping," Lady Anne said incredulously. "What do you want us to buy?"

"Anything or nothing." His smile broadened at her confusion. "I want you to be our eyes and ears in the community. I will explain more fully after I have met with Sir George. I promise."

Their host stood. "Regardless of the hour, I could use a glass of port. Anyone care to join me in the drawing room?" He swung back. "But I *do* have a question first. Are these traitors responsible for killing the governess, or do we have another madman out there?"

"I wish I could tell you, sir, but frankly, I cannot do so with any certainty," Lucien said. "For that reason, anyone in the area needs to be cautious. Unfortunately, this French-backed uprising takes precedence on my time and Sherbourne's for the moment."

"But they are suspects, are they not?" Sir George insisted.

"They are. To be precise, our only suspects at present."

"I thought so. They have brought nothing but trouble to Blinker's Marsh," the older man grumbled. Set on discussing local reinforcements, Lucien followed his host toward the door, but they were stopped by Lady Anne, Miss Barnett, and Lady Barnett blocking their path.

Lady Anne looked annoyed. "Are you trying to get rid of us by sending us shopping?"

"Not at all. Must you be so impatient?" Lucien sighed. "I would rather not involve you at all, but I was telling the truth when I said we need everyone. Sherbourne and I realized we have spent most of our time talking with villagers in Blinker's Marsh, while the dissidents could be from or staying in other villages not too far distant. Even so, investigating every village within an hour's ride would take days. However, there is one place villagers and farmers from all around regularly come to shop...and talk."

"Benchley," Lady Barnett said. "Everyone goes to the market town."

"Exactly. It is not far for you to travel. If Sir George agrees, you could visit the shops and listen to gossip, stop for tea, talk to street merchants, and find out what is being discussed throughout the surrounding countryside." He appealed to Sir George. "What do you think, sir? Are the ladies to be allowed to assist us in this way?"

Sir George gave him a look of approval, which Lucien interpreted as his host felt this was a clever way to keep the women out of trouble. "As long as they follow the rules, I have no objection. We must all do our part."

"What should we watch or listen for?" Lady Barnett gave Lucien and her husband a wry smile. "I have never been a spy before."

"Yes, you have," Miss Barnett said. "What do you think we were doing when we called at Harwick House?"

Lucien saw Sir George bristle and ignored Miss Barnett's interruption, choosing to answer Lady Barnett's question instead. "Anything about the Harwicks or their guests. Other strangers, odd goings on at night, secret meetings, lights where they shouldn't be, and of course any mention of explosives or rebels. You will do fine. In my experience, you know it when you hear it."

"We can do this," Lady Anne said. "Are we all going?" When both women nodded, she grinned. "Then we should get changed and be on our way."

Lucien held up a finger. "Please use caution. Our quarry may not only be dangerous but unpredictable."

"I have my pistol," Lady Anne said levelly.

Lucien's brows lowered. "I sincerely hope you will not need to use it."

As the women dispersed to their rooms to change, Lucien stopped Lady Anne at the bottom of the stairs. "Take care, my lady. It would be wise to stay together, and don't forget to take an armed footman to, um, I don't know, carry your packages."

She tilted her head. "I shall do so, my lord. But dare I suggest you also should be more careful of your person?" She gave a pointed at his arm. "I see you have abandoned the doctor's sling. Try to remember you are not fully recovered."

"You sound like Talbot," he said with a grin.

"High praise, indeed. He is a very wise and worthy man. I must go. We have a long day of shopping ahead." She lifted her skirts and swiftly climbed the stairs.

Lucien smiled and watched her for a moment before making his way to the drawing room. Wycliff and Sir George were drinking port while Sherry explained the role the neighbors might play. "Lucien and I cannot predict how swiftly this situation might flare up, but it's unlikely we will have time to await reinforcements from Whitehall. We need a reliable force standing in reserve."

"They may not be needed," Lucien added as he joined them in the chairs by the windows. "But it is best to be prepared."

Sir George nodded. "I heartily agree." Lucien could tell his host's mind was already considering the best choices among his near neighbors. "I know a handful I would trust with this, but most of them are my age. They can shoot, but they are not brawlers."

"Let us hope it does not devolve to that point," Lucien said. "With this weakened arm, I would not be much use myself. What I had in mind was a small band of armed men on horseback."

Sir George set his drink down. "Then I shall be off to make the arrangements. We should be ready by early afternoon. Maybe we can help you look for the storage site."

"Excellent thought. A search of the surrounding countryside for natural caves, abandoned sheds, or recent digging," Sherry suggested. "Best you stay well away from Harwick House until summoned."

Chapter Fifteen

With a cloudless sky overhead and the July heat not yet oppressive, the Barnett women and Anne climbed aboard the coach for their shopping trip to Benchley. Anne and Margret were excited, and even Lady Barnett was eager to be included in such mysterious doings as espionage. As they entered the town at a sharp clip three-quarters of an hour later, the marketplace bustled with activity. Shop banners waved in the breeze, hawkers announced their offerings to entice people to gather, and street vendors—costermongers, tinkers, and the like—sold wares and services of all kinds. The atmosphere held a hint of festivity.

The ladies decided to start with the regular, established shops, reasoning that the owners and clerks were local residents and more likely privy to town gossip. Of nearly equal interest to them, however, the indoor shops held larger inventories of fetching hats, exotic scarves, and a myriad of other accessories to tempt any fashion-minded female. Anne immediately spotted a hat shop, and they spent more than forty minutes inside, examining and trying on the latest arrivals from London. The young woman tending shop was friendly and willing to talk about the town and its inhabitants. She knew who the Harwicks were but not their guests, suggesting a certain amount of secrecy, but it wasn't anything Anne considered helpful. When they walked out of the shop, Margret had a new blue hat in a bandbox she handed off to the waiting footman, but the purchase was all they had achieved.

"We shall need to move more rapidly, if we want to cover even half the town," Lady Barnett said as they resumed their walk down the street.

"Perhaps we should split up," Margret suggested. "You might go into the tobacco shop for papa's favorite cigars, and I see a linen-drapers shop that looks very tempting."

"What a good idea. I shall inquire at the pawn shop for a snuffbox for my brother, which, of course, I do not have, but the proprietor will not know," Anne said.

Lady Barnett looked doubtful, "Did Lord Ware not tell us to stay together?"

"Well, yes, I suppose he did," Anne admitted, knowing full well he had been most emphatic, but there was something in her that resisted such directives. "But none of us will be far away, and other people are all around us. We are entirely safe."

"Being a man, he would not realize how long shopping takes," Margret added. "Otherwise, I am confident he would have allowed such a slight adjustment under these conditions."

They discussed it for another minute or two before deciding to separate for one hour. In that time each of them was expected to visit at least two of the permanent shops, and they would meet again for early tea at the Benchley Inn clearly visible to all at the end of the street. The footman would remain on the street, keeping an eye on them all.

Anne cut across the dusty road, dodging both horse and foot traffic. She slipped into the pawn shop, smiled brightly at the proprietor as she recalled her last timid entrance into a similar establishment just before last Christmastide. What a difference her acquaintance with Lord Ware had made. A previously unnerving task had now become an opportunity for adventure.

"What can I do for you, my lady?" the portly, balding man asked. "Looking for a pretty trinket?"

"A snuffbox for my brother."

"Ah, yes, my lady. I have several from which to choose. Jewels or engravings?"

"I am not certain. May I see both?"

"Of course, of course." The proprietor scurried around, opening and closing drawers, and gathered a dozen specimens, laying them on a velvet cloth in front of her. "Lovely, aren't they?"

"Very nice, but I need a closer look." She handled each one, inspecting them in detail, chatting about local events and people. She was just about to bring up the Harwicks. but as she picked up the seventh snuffbox, a rather gaudy silver object covered in gemstones, she paused and frowned. Where had she seen it before…rather recently? "How ornate," she said turning it over. "Have you had it long?"

"Oh, no, it was just acquired."

Ah, yes, of course. She had seen the snuffbox in the hands of one of Lucien's suspects.

"I am certain I've seen if before," she said aloud. "Yes, at Harwick House a few days ago. I am surprised anyone would give up such a lovely piece." Although she knew the answer, she wanted to keep the proprietor talking. "Which of their guests was it? Mr. Ramsey or Mr. Faegan?"

"Neither. Lady Cluett brought it in. It belonged to her husband."

Anne hid her surprise. Well, well. *Mrs.* Cluett appeared to have elevated her status to Lady Cluett, and why was she claiming it belong to the man posing as her husband? Anne could picture in her mind how it had glittered in the hands of Mr. Faegan—of course that wasn't his name now, but she refused to run through his list of aliases. In any event, she had witnessed him taken a pinch of snuff during their visit.

"Oh, yes, I recall now. Did she say why she was selling it?"

"Uh, yes, but I'm not sure…you see, her reason was rather personal." His tone said he was dying to tell her.

"Oh, goodness. Is the poor dear in debt?"

"No, no, no. Nothing like that." An anxious look crossed his face. "I would not want you to mistake anything I have said to imply that."

"Then perhaps you should explain." Anne waited with an arched brow, and he heaved an exaggerated sigh of resignation.

"Very well, I shall tell you, but you must not repeat it. The box was given to her husband by a rival for his affections, a local widow lady. Lady Cluett wished to be rid of it."

"Ah, completely understandable," Anne said. A falsehood, no doubt. Did the residents of Harwick House lie about everything? But hardly significant to Lord Ware or the War Office. She gave a casual laugh. "I wonder if her husband has noticed it is missing."

"I wouldn't know," he said rather stiffly. "The gentleman she was with—whom I took to be her brother—found it as humorous as you do."

Curious now, Anne pursued it further. "Which gentleman was it?"

The pawnbroker sighed again, but clearly anxious not to lose a sale, he said, "I heard her call him Andre."

Stranger and stranger, Anne thought. When she and the Barnetts had visited the house, Andre was the first name of Mrs. Cluett's alleged husband. And now he was her brother? But Anne let it drop. It should not surprise her that the "Cluetts" were not who they said they were. Yet that didn't explain why the woman would sell Faegan's fancy snuffbox. "I wonder why she sold it now," Anne muttered aloud.

"I believe they are leaving town."

Anne's gaze shot to the proprietor's face. "What did you say?"

He leaned back, startled by her keen interest.

Anne reassured him with a soft smile. "I do not want to neglect calling to say goodbye. Did they mention how soon?"

"This week. Friday, I believe."

Good heavens. Two days from now. Were they moving the hidden explosives to a new location? Or did they intend to use them that soon? Lord Ware must be informed without delay.

"Oh, my, I shall have to visit her soon. Meantime, I am running late to meet my party for tea at your lovely hotel. I shall think about the purchase and return tomorrow. Thank you."

Ignoring the proprietor's disappointed face, Anne left the store and looked up and down the street for the footman. He was standing outside a fabric store, and Anne found Margret inside, surrounded by samples of silks and lace. She pulled her friend aside and kept her voice low. "May I send your footman to Lord Ware with an urgent message?"

"Of course you may. What have you learned?"

"Come outside." Anne nearly dragged her out the door, leaving an astonished clerk behind who—considering the piles of expensive fabrics—must have been envisioning a large sale.

Anne reported what she'd learned to Margret and Timothy, the footman, at the same time. She pressed two coins in his hand. "Obtain a horse at the stables and find Lord Ware or Lord Sherbourne as quickly as possible."

"But my lady, I was told to stay with you."

"This is an emergency," Margret said. "There are three of us. We will be fine. Go now."

He still looked doubtful, until Margret glared at him. "Father would not take it well if I told him you had disobliged me."

"Yes, ma'am." He took off running for the stables, and the two young women made their way toward the inn. They stopped at two of the costermongers, chatted them up while looking over their wares but learned nothing useful. The transient vendors were willing enough to talk, but as anticipated, they knew little about local gossip.

Still enthused by Anne's successful visit to the pawnshop, she and Margret repeated everything to Lady Barnett when they met as arranged for early tea.

"You should not have sent Timothy without asking me," Lady Barnett said. "What will your father say?"

"It was urgent, mother. You know it was. There was nothing else to be done," Margret pleaded, and Lady Barnett sighed.

"I suppose it is too late to worry about it now."

"I knew you would understand." Margret smiled, although that wasn't at all what her mother had said, and changed the subject. "Why do you suppose she sold the snuffbox? Her story was an obvious lie."

"None of the Harwick party wore much jewelry," Lady Barnett said. "What they did have were inexpensive paste pieces."

"Very true. I suppose that is why I noticed his fancy snuffbox," Anne said. "It stood out."

Margret held out her hand, turning it slightly so her own rings caught the light. "Their rings *were* plain, lacking sparkle, and their gowns were hardly of the latest stare."

"Sounds like a lack of funds." Lady Barnett took a sip of tea.

"Well, of course, you are correct," Margret said. "They spent all their money on explosives."

"Margret, dear, lower your voice."

Anne glanced around. Although no one was paying attention to them, the mood at their own table changed. Margret's blurted words reminded them of the deadly business they were about.

"I am sorry." Margret dropped her voice to a whisper. "But the you-know-what must cost dearly. The snuffbox could be the only source of funds they had at hand. Perhaps they needed money for their trip or to buy more…uh, stuff."

The conversation had added urgency to their errand, and no one dallied over their tea. They paid their fare and were back on the street within minutes. Mid-afternoon was approaching, and they decided that each of them would continue on their own. It was the only way they had any hope of finishing their task before the shopping day ended at dusk.

As arranged, they once again met at the Benchley Inn late in the day for lemonade. They were hot, thirsty, and getting tired. Shopping was not as much fun as it had been.

The Inn was busier at this more fashionable hour, and Lady Barnett sank into a chair with apparent relief. "Thank goodness you found a table. I have not shopped like this for years. My feet will soon give out. Have we learned anything new?"

Anne and Margret both shook their heads.

"Harwick House isn't well-liked," Anne said. "Locals consider them to be pinch pennies and terribly snobbish. Not a surprise but unhelpful." She shrugged and lowered her voice. "As for any rebel talk, I heard the normal grumblings about high prices, low wages, but I wouldn't consider that revolutionary."

"I heard the same," Lady Barnett agreed.

"Me too." Margret took a sip of lemonade. "Ooh, that's good.

We're almost done, in any event. There are only a few shops left."
She cast an appreciative eye at the packages surrounding her
chair. "I have some excellent purchases I'm eager to show you
when we get home, but without a footman, my arms are getting
tired of carrying them around. I wonder why Timothy hasn't
come back?"

"He has been gone a long time," Lady Barnett agreed.

"Do you suppose he could not find them?" Anne asked,
suddenly worried. "But wouldn't he return to tell us? Perhaps
they needed him for something else. After all, we still have the
coachman. They might even have sent him to London with the
message so they could keep watch on the others."

Margret grinned. "Timothy would love that. An adventure he
could brag about for years to come."

With their feet rested and their spirits revived by lemonade,
they set out for one last effort.

"Twilight is not far off," Lady Barnett warned." We must leave
by then. Since Timothy is not here, I suppose one of us must go to
the stables to find our coachman."

"Heavens, no," Anne said, looking around for a likely lad.
Choosing a child of perhaps eight, she gave him a coin to find the
Barnetts' coachman and have the carriage meet them at the Inn in
an hour and a half.

"Yes, ma'am. Thanks."

He scampered off, clutching the coin.

"All done," Anne said with a smile, opening her parasol as she
stepped into the street. "I shall see you then. Let us hope this final
effort will bear sweeter fruit."

Since Margret and her mother had agreed to cover the
remaining established shops, Anne made her way through the
street vendors and temporary stalls, admiring fruit and breads,
flowers—starting to wilt this late in the day—and stopping while
two local women haggled over the price of a beaded reticule. She
attempted to engage the women in conversation, but they were in
a hurry to complete their purchases and get home.

As she moved on, Anne's attention was caught by a familiar-looking figure disappearing around the street corner just ahead. Was that not Mr. Cluett? She glanced around the street, studying the thinning crowd, hoping to spot Lord Ware, Sherbourne, or Wycliff following him. Surely that had been the plan to follow anyone who left Harwick House. Had he slipped away? Could she have been mistaken?

She hurried to the corner, anxious for a longer look at the figure. Indeed, a gentleman was striding down the side street, and it certainly looked like Cluett from the back; the right age, height, and color of hair. What was he doing in Benchley? Could the explosives be hidden here? On the other hand, maybe he was meeting someone…such as the French agent Sherbourne had called the seventh conspirator.

Anne wavered, pondering what she should do. She was to meet Margret and her mother soon. They would be alarmed if she wasn't on time. But what if she could identify the last traitor? Or find the location of the munitions?

She bit her lip. Perhaps there was time enough to do both. She could follow him and discover what she could in the next half hour—where he turned off the main streets, what part of town, the street, maybe even the house. It would be something to report to Ware and Sherbourne, a place for them to start looking.

Giving a curt nod to herself, Anne set out in pursuit.

Chapter Sixteen

Lucien crept through the brush, followed by Sherbourne and Wycliff. They stayed behind the tree line and stopped frequently to listen for sounds of activity. So far they had seen nothing of the Harwicks or their four guests. The only signs of life had been the neighing of horses and occasional voices from the stables. Finn was positioned where he could see the length of the manor and still watch the front entrance for arrivals and departures, but Lucien had not yet heard the bird signal agreed upon if anything significant was happening.

Despite an hour searching for a root cellar, poking into thickets, and inspecting each open space in the woods for evidence of recent digging or a newly made path, they'd found no evidence of hidden powder kegs or other munitions. Upon completing their examination of the immediate surrounding area, the three men returned to Finn's position.

"Anything?" Lucien asked.

"Nothin' 'cept the head groom, Thom. Came outta the kitchen and went to the stable."

"We didn't have any luck either," Sherry said, dropping onto a fallen log.

Lucien squatted beside Finn and stared at the house, wondering where everyone was. Of course, it was not yet eleven. Even in the country many households didn't stir until midday.

His gaze moved to the two small storage sheds behind the stable and its attached carriage house. They had not yet attempted to explore them. Both sheds were closed up, and the newer one was locked with chains. *Safeguarding explosives?* The proximity to the stable made it difficult to take a look. Although the head groom was the only occupant sighted so far, they'd heard other voices, including a coachman and at least two stable boys.

Risky or not, the buildings had to be done.

Lucien gestured to Sherry. "Let's make a try at the sheds. Wycliff, if you'll cover us…" The two men ran across the open area and flattened against the rear of the older of the two structures. Sherbourne moved on to the second shed while Lucien peered through the cracks between boards: a shovel, some pots. He shifted to another spot: shelving with a few small bags, more tools for hedge and flower maintenance—nothing but a gardener's shed.

He looked around the corner, and seeing none of the house or stable inhabitants had appeared, he joined Sherbourne behind the small building with the chain locks.

"Could you see anything?" Sherry whispered.

"Gardening tools."

"No luck here. Slats aren't letting in enough light to see what's in there. I could pick the lock holding the chains, but not out in the open like this."

"Then we wait for dark."

They returned to the woods, where Wycliff and Finn were crouched behind the first line of large trees.

"Everything is so quiet," the captain said. "What do you suppose they are doing?"

"Sleeping, plotting. Who know?"

"Or they aint there," Finn said.

"There is that," Sherry agreed. "But I'm not about to knock on the door and find out. I'll search the locked shed after dark, but I've been thinking—it's small to hold many powder kegs. More likely it's the large garden tools—wagons, barrows, and the like."

"What do we do about the stables?" Wycliff asked. "Dark won't help us. The stable hands will be sleeping near the horses or in with the carriages."

"I'd bet on the stable hay loft," Lucien said. "In any event, no one should be in the carriage house now, and I saw a window I could boost Finn through…if we're really quiet." He turned to his small groom, who weighed less than eight stone. "Are you willing? A quick look for powder kegs, weapons, or a trap door we'd need to explore later—and out again. Four or five minutes, no more."

"Aye, m'lord. Y' know I be game." Finn gave him a toothy grin. He frequently grumbled that Lucien had too many adventures without him.

They left at a crouching run and reached the back of the carriage house without anyone raising an alarm. Nonetheless, Lucien waited several heartbeats to be sure, his hand in the pocket with his pistol. When nothing stirred, he eased up to peek in the window. Other than the door into the stable—which was closed—he couldn't see much beyond the first coach.

"Looks clear," he mouthed. "Ready?" At Finn's nod, Lucien retrieved the knife he kept in his boot and pried the window, pulling it outward when he felt the hinge give. He nodded to Finn, made a step with his linked hands, and lifted the smaller man to the high window ledge. Finn quickly slipped inside. Then Lucien waited, listening for sounds of discovery or footsteps coming around the building.

Minutes passed—more than Lucien had allowed, and he was starting to worry when he heard a faint scrabbling sound and looked up to see Finn wiggling head-first from the window. Lucien grabbed his shoulders and helped him down, putting a finger to his lips when Finn started to say something. He eased the window shut and nodded toward the woods. They crossed the short distance once more without discovery and joined Sherbourne and Wycliff.

Sherry cocked his head. "Well?"

Finn frowned, looking at Lucien. "'Taint there, gov. Nary a box or bag around the carriages or in the beams, 'cept the harness you'd expect."

"And no trap doors," Sherry clarified.

"Naw, I looked real good."

"If something doesn't happen soon, I may fall asleep," Sherry grumbled.

"Since we can't do much except wait for them to make a move, I thought I would do a bit of scouting farther from the house by horseback," Wycliff said.

"I may join you." Lucien stood. "That lets you take a nap, Sherry, if you can do it with one eye on the house. And Finn can keep an eye on you. If anyone leaves, one of you needs to follow."

"Right by me," Sherry said, settling down as if he might actually take a nap. "Wake me when the scoundrels have been captured."

Lucien laughed softly, and he and Wycliff made their way back through the woods to where they'd left the horses.

For the next few hours he and the captain rode over the hills, through ravines, and across open fields. They rode in increasing circles outward from Harwick House to a distance of two miles, inspecting creeks, hunting huts, rock piles, and anything that looked unusual. All to no avail. They had turned back to rejoin Sherry and Finn when Lucien heard his name called.

A man on horseback, riding hard, raced toward them, kicking up a cloud of dusk. Lucien and Wycliff galloped to meet him, and Lucien recognized one of Sir George's footmen.

The lad halted his horse abruptly, sending clods of dirt flying. "My lord, Lady Anne sent me with a message."

"Well, out with it," he urged.

"She said the Harwicks' guests are leaving on Friday. She thought something might be happening sooner than expected."

"How does she know this?" Wycliff demanded.

"Don't know, sir. That's all she said. The ladies had been all over Benchley, talking to everyone."

"Very good," Lucien said. "Have you told Sir George?"

The lad shook his head. "I was told to find you or Lord Sherbourne."

"Then ride now and tell Sir George. Who is with the ladies?"

"Uh, no one, sir. Well, the coachman. I, uh, tried to tell…"

"You need not explain," Lucien interrupted. "I can imagine, but someone needs to go to Benchley as soon as possible."

"Yes, my lord, I'll see to it." The lad's eyes gleamed with resolve as he reined his horse around and galloped toward Barnett Park.

Lucien frowned. "I had hoped to slip inside Harwick House tonight to nose around, but someone must ride to London and apprise Whitehall of this new information. They were not expecting movement this soon."

"I can do it, if you tell me who I should approach."

"Ask for Lord Rothe, second floor in the War Offices. Tell his secretary you have a message from Simon Grey. That should get you in immediately. Sherry, Finn, and I will remain near Harwick House unless someone or something unexpected draws us away."

Wycliff nodded. "I should be back in two or three hours."

Lucien gave a wry smile. "Unless Rothe has other ideas. He has a habit of seizing anyone available for his own pursuits."

The captain wheeled his horse and waved with a grin. "I'm used to commanding officers."

• • •

"Running out of time, are we?" Sherry eyed Lucien with a jaundiced eye after hearing Timothy's message. "I'm wondering if sitting on the house is going to pay off. Not a hint of movement so far, not unless you count the maid that passed one of the upper windows two hours ago. I haven't even heard the children. You don't suppose the household has already departed, do you?"

"Blasted Frenchies," Finn muttered.

Lucien frowned in thought. "You know, the children were not around on my last visit. I wonder if they were sent away so the others could clear out more quickly when the time came. But somebody must be here with the head groom and coachman still in the stables."

Sherry raked a hand through his hair. "You're probably right, but I'd like to know for sure."

"What about the carriages?" Lucien asked Finn. "I saw one. Were the others inside?"

"Aye, guv," the groom said perking up. "They was there. Four of 'em."

"I had forgotten you were in there," Sherry acknowledged. "So, either they're in the house, or left on foot or horseback. They should return by dusk."

"Shadows are lengthening. Servants will light the house soon and show us who's home and where. As soon as the shadows deepen near the house, I plan to inspect the cellar." Lucien nodded toward the locked shed. "Even with darkness that shed sits in the open, visible from both house and stable. Is it worth the risk to get inside?"

"I'd be all for ignoring it, if it weren't for those chains. Why secure a shed like that unless you're protecting something?"

Lucien shrugged. "I guess we should hope for a moonless night."

With little left to talk about after so many hours of surveillance, they waited in near silence another thirty minutes. Night sounds seemed loud—an owl hooted, frogs could be heard in the marsh. A horse whinnied from the stable. Finn lay on the ground, one hand propping up his chin, the other drawing marks in the dirt with a stick. Sherbourne stared morosely at the stable from his perch on the fallen log; Lucien leaned against a tree, keeping his eyes on the house. Lights began to appear in the mansion—lighting up more rooms than a servant staff would need—and Lucien felt relief that at least some of their quarry were still inside.

Sherry got up and stretched. He shifted impatiently, scuffing the dirt with his boot. "Isn't it about time to do *something*?"

Lucien straightened from the tree. "You won't get any argument from me. It's dark enough. I'm heading for the cellar door on the far side. I shan't be long."

"You can't go alone," Sherry said indignantly.

"No, not alone. Finn is coming. He is small and nimble, better at getting around in small places than either of us." Lucien watched Sherry's jaw tighten like it did when he was preparing to take a contrary stand. Lucien forestalled it by placing his hand on his partner's shoulder. "If something goes wrong out here...or in there, you are the best man to deal with it. And while we're gone, sort out how to get into that shed without getting caught." Lucien motioned for Finn to follow him, and they disappeared into the bushes before Sherry could make an objection.

Even though Lucien moved slowly to avoid notice, it only took a few minutes to reach the old cellar door he'd spotted earlier. It was warped and worn as though it not been used or maintained for many years. Lucien hoped it was unlocked or the lock and hinges were so old they could be broken without undue noise.

"Stay close," he whispered to Finn. They darted across the rear gardens at a running crouch, then slipped from tree to bush until they reached the side of the house and squatted next to the foundation. Lucien crept up to the cellar door and ran his hands over it. He smiled in the dim shadows. It's condition was worse than expected. The boards were rotten. He tested the latch. When it failed to move, he pried the nearest board with the knife from his boot. The wood splintered and shifted. Painfully aware of each creak, he pulled it loose, reached through, and pushed up the wooden bar that had secured the door from below. This time the door opened. He held it up for Finn to slip through, then followed, easing it back into place behind them.

The dark was oppressive. Nothing tickled his senses except the earthy smell of a dirt floor, coal dust, and damp musty walls. Rats scurried nearby. Lucien dug in his pocket, pulling out a piece of broken candle and a small pocket tinderbox he had brought back from the war—and used more times than he cared to count.

The small light produced revealed Finn crouched no more than three feet away. The groom made a sour face as a startled rat dashed for cover.

Lucien cupped his hand around the flame to restrict its range, hoping the small glow and whiff of smoke would not betray them to any two-legged creatures upstairs. "Let us be quick," he whispered and started forward.

They had entered the west half of the cellar, between the coal storage at the end and the kitchen storage/wine cellar in the center. A stairs from the upper floor descended to the wine storage. A solid wall divided this half from what would be the male servants' quarters on the east side. If explosives were stored under the house, it would be in this area, most likely in or near the coal storage. But he already had doubts he'd find the munitions there. The cellar door would have been the logical entrance for such things, and it had not seen recent use. The coal chute was an improbable alternative. Still, he had to be sure.

He started across the room holding the candle aloft to direct its light onto walls and into corners. Voices and footsteps from overhead brought him to an abrupt halt, and he grabbed Finn's arm. Shielding the light with his hand, Lucien was ready to blow it out if the upper door opened. He stood immobile, Finn hovering by his side. Lucien tried to make out what was being said above them, but the words were indistinct.

After what felt like hours, in reality no more than two or three minutes, the sounds receded. Lucien and Finn exchanged a look of relief.

With Finn slithering between broken shelves and furniture and then climbing over larger bags and trunks, they explored every dark corner. Seeing several wooden boxes stacked under the cellar stairs, Lucien crossed the room, past the wine racks and stored liquor until he could see the boxes held nothing except more wine. He turned back then froze at the sound of boot steps overhead. They came straight to the cellar door.

"Hide, and stay quiet. No matter what," Lucien hissed to Finn. He doused the candle and pressed his knife into Finn's hands before shoving the small man into the shadows under the stairs. Lucien hunkered close to the wall. There was nowhere else to go.

The door to the cellar stairs opened. Loud, booted footsteps started down, preceded by the bobbing glow of a lantern. Lucien pressed closer to the wall and narrowly missed stepping on a rat underfoot.

Sucking in a tense breath, he held his position and watched as the boots and legs of a man appeared on the steps. Finally the lantern light revealed the fair-haired figure of Mr. Ramsey. As

Harwick's guest reached the bottom of the stairs, he looked neither right nor left but went straight to the shelves of wine.

As least Ramsey had not come down looking for intruders, Lucien decided. He was on a domestic errand and probably unarmed. Loath to shoot a defenseless man or bring the household down on him by the sound of gunfire, Lucien bent his knees and felt around the dirt floor for something to use as a weapon if needed. His fingers closed on a lump of coal. Not much of a weapon, but if Ramsey spotted him, their escape might well depend on putting out the lantern light. Lucien eyed the target and wondered if he still had the throwing skills of the young lad who'd plagued the shrews on his uncle's estate.

Agonizing moments passed before Ramsey finally made his wine selection and turned to go. Lucien remained just outside the circle of lantern light and kept his breathing shallow. As Ramsey reached the steps, Lucien's hopes rose that they would avoid discovery.

But the pesky rat that had nearly tripped Lucien chose that moment to scuttle across the floor, the small noise from its claws drawing Ramsey's attention. He turned his head to look, lifted the lantern to illuminate the area, and caught Lucien in its glow. They stared at one another for an instant of suspended time, before Ramsey's startled exclamation. "You! What the hell—"

Lucien heaved the chunk of coal.

His aim was off. Instead of striking the lantern, the coal hit Ramsey in the face. Yet, it had the desired effect. Ramsey dropped the lantern, the glass shattered, and the last thing Lucien saw before the cellar plunged into darkness was Ramsey leaping toward him.

They collided in the dark, the impact toppling them both to the floor. Wrestling and punching, they rolled in the dirt. Ramsey grabbed Lucien's injured arm, wrenching and twisting it as though he knew it was a vulnerable spot. Lucien punched with his other arm and successfully broke the hold, but Ramsey grabbed his hair and slammed his fist against the side of his face. Lucien hit him in the gut this time. The other man groaned, and Lucien rolled free.

But it was already too late. Voices and lantern light spilled down the stairs, and Charles Feagan/Artigue leaped into the fray before Lucien could regain his feet. The newcomer kicked Lucien in the ribs and stomped on his arm. The sharp pain drew a gasp from him, but Lucien kicked out, tripping Artigue and dumping him to the ground. Lucien shot to his feet, ducking and backing away at the report of a firearm.

"Stop this, all of you," a feminine voice demanded. "Simon Grey, that shot was a warning. You only get one."

The Cluett woman. Addressing him as Simon Grey left little doubt they knew of his spy activities on the Continent. He still had to try.

"I bow to your superior weaponry, ma'am, but you have mistaken me for someone else. I am Viscount Ware."

"Maybe now, but in Paris you were Simon Grey." She descended another step, the pistol unwavering. "Don't you recognize me, *mon ami*? But of course you don't. I was posing as a lady's maid at the time. Beneath a gentleman's notice."

The voice was vaguely familiar. Lucien narrowed his eyes, studying her. Light dawned. "With brown hair braided and pinned up. Lisette's abigail. Jeanne, was it not?"

Mrs. Cluett smiled, but it didn't reach her eyes. "*Mais qui*. I see by your face that you begin to understand." Her lips curled. "Have you blamed her all this time? More fool you."

Lucien was momentarily speechless. Was she saying her mistress had not betrayed them? He had been so sure…although it shouldn't have mattered. Lisette Armand had merely been an aspect of his job, a pawn in the spy game—at first. But their mutual attraction had turned into something real, or at least a beginning. Then he and Sherry were betrayed—exposed as English spies—and Lisette was the only one he had told. He'd thought her guilt confirmed when she had married a French officer a few weeks later. All this time…it had been the bloody maid.

"I should have known," he finally said.

"Yes, you should." Her eyes glittered with malice. "Lisette was besotted. She would never have betrayed you."

"She married soon enough."

"To save herself. You left her behind, and she was tainted by the connection. Marriage to a French lieutenant was her only way out."

"Have we not had enough talk?" Ramsey asked in impatience. "Just shoot him."

"Not here, you fool," she said with a scathing look. "He will be missed, and someone will come looking—even constables or the Horse Guards from London. I want no blood or other evidence to be found. We need more time." When he gave a derisive snort, she narrowed her eyes at Ramsey, sending a clear message.

More time, Lucien repeated to himself. Enough for Sherry and the others to locate those powder kegs? He hoped Finn was taking this all in from his corner hiding place and would be able to repeat every detail…if he got out of there.

"What shall we do with him?" Artigue asked, speaking English well enough, even though his pronunciation was greatly affected by his native tongue.

"Lock him in with the supplies. When we load them, we will get rid of him."

"Why not now? We could easily hide a dead body in the woods." Ramsey seemed determined to get Lucien off his hands.

"Not in this weather. A corpse would attract animal life and make it easy for searchers to find." She waved the pistol in Lucien's direction. "Now, stop arguing and do what I tell you. Tie him up. Look around outside to be sure he came alone, then put him in the cave."

Cave? Lucien hadn't seen a cave in the vicinity. But he wasn't interested in being dumped inside one. If he was going to make a bid for freedom, now was the time. As Artigue and Ramsey closed in, stepping briefly between him and Mrs. Cluett's pistol, he made a break for the old cellar door. He had calculated his odds without considering the wine bottle still in Ramsey's hand. It shattered against his skull.

• • •

Lucien woke to a throbbing head. He opened his eyes and squinted in the sparse light. He lay in dirt and scattered straw, trussed up like a pig, his wrists and ankles tied with jute rope and his body wedged against stacks of wooden boxes, powder kegs, and burlap bags. He turned his head carefully and discovered he was not in a true cave but a storage area dug under an overhang of the creek that fed into the marsh pond. It had been built high above the water. The munitions had been set on boards, and a heavy bed of straw placed under and around them to absorb any seeping moisture. The entrance was covered with more loose boards, and from what he could see between the boards, foliage had been placed on top to conceal it.

He tested the rope ties and found little give. Squirming around, he peered at the boxes, looking for metal pieces, anything sharp that might cut his bindings. Even a nail he could use to yank and pull on the ropes might do. But he saw nothing on the ones in his view. The powder kegs were smooth and useless for his purposes. He wiggled and scooted closer to the bags and used his teeth to pull one open. Lead shot. Bags and bags of musket balls and small shot for pistols or rifles.

So what was in the wood boxes? Spotting one that had been opened, he braced his good shoulder against the boxes and pushed upward with his bound feet, raising his body, then twisted to land hard on his knees. He looked over the edge of the box, squinting to see in the poor light. *Bloody hell.* Fire balls—hollow cannon balls that when filled with gunpowder and a wooden fuse made crude bombs. He'd seen them used on the battlefield. Normally shot out of heavy artillery, they could also be thrown with deadly results-- brutal weapons that tore apart human flesh.

Haunted by flashes from the past, Lucien's breath quickened. Sherry had said Rothe suspected there were several secret stocks of munitions, and this cave alone held enough to blow up several buildings and massacre dozens or hundreds of people on a crowded street. Several well-placed fire balls might take down vital parts of Whitehall, or Parliament, or the palace itself.

Lucien closed his eyes, determined to quell his runaway imagination. The government buildings were so closely guarded that getting a large amount of explosives near them would be difficult, although not impossible. Of greater vulnerability were the unguarded theatres, the pleasure gardens with their large crowds, the ships moored near the docks, and possibly a hundred other places.

Lucien gritted his teeth. Fretting about what *could* happen was a waste of precious time. He had to figure out a way to stop it— which began with getting out of here. What he wouldn't give for his knife right now.

He turned his head and resumed his search of the man-made cave, looking for a tool dropped in the dirt or even a sharp rock that would cut or fray his bindings—preferably before Ramsey and the others returned for the munitions...and to kill him.

Chapter Seventeen

Anne kept her parasol angled down to hide her face. She had left Benchley's market street and was following Mr. Cluett on a dirt side road. Since few people were walking there, and even passing carriages were scarce, she stayed well behind. He walked briskly, with purpose, and abruptly turned another corner. Anne quickened her step for fear of losing him, and at the intersection, she looked in the direction he had gone and gasped in dismay. The little-used dirt street, hardly more than a path, had only four cottages on one side—and it was empty. *Where was he? Inside one of the houses?*

She walked slowly, scrutinizing each cottage from beneath her parasol. The only activity she saw was two small children playing near a shed behind the third house.

The road ended at the woods after less than a three-minute walk. A path led into the trees, and some instinct told her that was where Cluett had gone. She stopped at the entrance and stared ahead, but she couldn't see far. A sharp turn only a few feet from where she stood hid the rest of the path. Reluctant to give up without knowing what Cluett was doing, Anne slipped her hand into her reticule to feel the comfort of her small pistol and swallowed the uneasy lump in her throat. If she did not go soon, she'd lose any chance of following him. She hurried forward.

But Cluett was not around the turn, and another curve looped around a pile of stones. She picked up her pace, nearly running now.

Oh, mercy! Anne stifled a shriek and jumped off the path behind a tree. She had nearly run into the clearing where Cluett was talking with another man no more than a dozen yards ahead. After a moment, she took a cautious peek. Wasn't that the stable hand from Harwick House? He must have brought a message or perhaps was taking something back to the manor. It would have to be small, because she saw nothing in their hands. Perhaps it was a message too important to write down. On the other hand, were they meeting away from Harwick House because they had something to hide from the others?

Anne wished she could hear what was being said, but if she moved closer, she'd be noticed for sure. She stole another look just in time to see the stable boy leave and Cluett turn back in her direction.

Anne took off at a run. Unless she moved quickly, he was going to see her, and if she exited the woods, she'd be too exposed on the little Benchley road. So where was she to go? Breathing hard more from fear than exertion, she pushed her way behind a growth of bushes and put a hand over her mouth to quiet her heavy breathing.

She heard his footsteps approaching and held her breath. They passed without slowing. She listened as his steps receded, then let out her breath and waited another minute or two, giving him time to turn the corner toward the main part of the village. Stepping out of hiding, she returned to the path and hurried toward town. The Barnetts would be looking for her by now.

As she came around the stone pile, she cut off a startled cry and stepped back. Not fast enough, as Cluett lunged forward and gripped her arm.

"I knew I heard someone. Lady Anne, isn't it? Why are you following me?"

"Unhand me, sir. You are much mistaken. I was exploring the village while my companions finished shopping, noticed the path, and wondered where it went."

"I do not believe you." His voice held a hint of menace, and he tightened his grip until it hurt.

Anne kicked his shin and swung her reticule at his head. When it connected, he loosened his hold and she pulled away, retreating a safe distance before stopping and turning to face him. She slipped her hand into her reticule, found the handle of her pistol, and lifted her chin.

Running wouldn't help—he would simply chase her down. "Keep your distance, Mr. Cluett. I do not appreciate your ungentlemanly behavior or your tone of voice."

His face twisted in a fierce scowl. "Then you should mind your own business."

"I was until you accosted me." Despite her rising fear, Anne kept her voice steady. "You are very much mistaken if you believe your affairs are of any concern to me." She adopted a haughty tone. "You are a married man, sir. What interest could I have in you?"

"Exactly what I want to know."

He strode forward again but Anne did not allow him to get more than a couple of feet before she pulled out her flintlock. "Be on your way, Mr. Cluett. I know how to use this."

He came to an abrupt halt. His expression underwent several changes—anger, disbelief, calculation—and he settled on an apologetic smile. "I did not mean to alarm you, my lady. I can offer no excuse for my lapse in manners other than I have had a very bad day. Pray accept my humble apology." He gestured at the woods around them. "Surely this is no place for a lady to be on her own. May I escort you back to your companions?"

Anne gave a short, humorless laugh. "I have no need for assistance. Certainly not from a man who would bully a woman." She lifted the pistol a little higher. "Please leave now...back through the woods, sir."

He hesitated, his eyes growing cold, and his conciliatory expression slipped for an instant.

"I am a very good shot," she reminded him softly.

He gave a half-bow. "Very well, my lady. I beg pardon if there has been a misunderstanding." He circled carefully around her and walked back into the woods.

Misunderstanding, my eye. As soon as Cluett was out of sight, Anne ran out of the woods and walked through the village streets at a most unladylike pace. She had no doubt Cluett would harm her if he could. Her hands were shaking, and she kept looking over her shoulder. She finally remembered she was still clutching the pistol and stuffed it in her bag before someone saw it. Drawing in a breath to collect herself, she slowed to a walk as soon as other people were in sight.

What a terrible miscalculation she'd made! She had thought Cluett rather mild-mannered on prior meetings, but today he had shown her a truly frightening side.

When she was reached the street that led into the village market, she began to relax...until she thought about what he might have done if she hadn't had the pistol. She shook off that unpleasant image and turned her mind to something more productive. What had Cluett been doing that made him act that way? Was he afraid she'd seen him talking with the stable hand? Maybe seen something pass between them? Or had he intended to go elsewhere in Benchley and didn't wish to be followed? Perhaps to the location of the powder kegs... although that might be unlikely with so many villagers about.

Well, somebody else would have to sort out the answers. She would not be hanging around to get herself into further trouble—not this time.

Approaching the stables on market street, she was delighted to see the Barnetts' coach hitched and ready to go. Her throat tightened at the sight of several agitated people standing around it. Anne hurried forward, and Margret saw her.

"Annie," Margret called, lightly running toward her. "Where have you been? We were worried something was wrong."

"It almost was," Anne admitted as Margret took her hand and pulled her toward the carriage. "Am I that late?"

"Anne, dearest." Lady Barnett's tone held a mixture of relief and reproof as she poked her head from the coach. "Are you all right?"

"Yes, ma'am, I am so very sorry I kept you waiting. What a bother I am to have worried you." Anne was genuinely remorseful. She had not intended to cause the deep concern etched on the kind woman's face. "It was just that I saw—someone." She broke off as she realized they could not have this conversation on the street. Anne climbed into the coach, followed by Margret.

"Who did you see?" Margret asked as the coach pulled away.

"Mr. Cluett, and I wanted to know why he was here, so I followed." She stopped as Lady Barnett gaped at her.

"Good Heavens, child."

"You went after such a dreadful person by yourself?" Even Margret looked appalled. "Oh, Anne, how could you?"

"I had not thought to go far, only to see where he went, to identify which house he was visiting so I could tell Lords Ware or Sherbourne. But, well, he just kept walking, and I kept thinking I would go just a little farther..." She trailed off to several moments of silence.

"I am sorry for worrying you," she added. "Truly."

"Well, I *do* understand, my dear," Lady Barnett said, a motherly smile covering the remaining touch of asperity in her voice. "We all want to help, but we must not act foolishly. Thank heavens you are safe. Now, let us go home before Sir George turns out the militia to find us."

"So, where did Cluett go?" Margret asked, impatiently. "Did you discover what he was doing in Benchley?"

Anne settled her skirt around her and sighed. "That is the worst of it. I did not learn a thing, except he met with Harwick's stable boy. I could not hear what they said, and even worse, I may have given away our suspicions of them." She went on to relate her confrontation with him. "He was terribly angry and suspicious." She left out the more alarming aspects for Lady Barnett's sake.

"He threatened you?" Lady Barnett sniffed indignantly. "Such uncivil behavior. Whoever these people are, they are certainly not Quality."

"He was rather uncivil. When he became too insulting, I offered to shoot him."

"Shoot him?" Lady Barnett stared at her. "Do you carry a pistol?"

"Not always. But I have had it several months now. It fits nicely into my reticule."

"Oh, my dear," Lady Barnett said faintly.

"I think it is very enterprising of you," Margret declared. Her face lit with avid interest. "May I see it?"

"Absolutely not," her mother said. "No pistol will be brandished about in this coach." With a visible effort, she calmed her tone. "But I suppose it is fortunate you had it, Anne, on this particular occasion. No telling how unruly he might have become."

"Why did you start carrying it?" Margret asked curiously. "It is most unusual, and you've never before mentioned it." She sounded baffled, maybe slightly hurt, that Anne had not shared such an interesting habit.

"Let's just say I have learned from past experience to be prepared." She gave Margret a look indicating it was not a story her mother needed to hear. She rarely talked about her encounter with the gang of thieves last Christmastide, and she did not wish for Lady Barnett to think she was a hoyden who got into serious scrapes all the time.

"Later?" Margret mouthed behind her hand when her mother wasn't looking.

Anne nodded, but she hoped she could distract Margret from the subject. She'd prefer not to discuss today's events either. There were moments—such as the leer on Cluett's face before she produced the pistol—that she was reluctant to think about, much less describe. Instead, she asked Margret about her purchases, and they spent the rest of the ride discussing fashion.

They arrived at the manor just about dusk and learned the others had not yet returned. According to the butler, Sir George was still recruiting neighbors, Captain Wycliff had gone to London on an errand, and presumably Lords Ware and Sherbourne continued to keep watch at Harwick House.

The ladies went upstairs to change for dinner. Jenny had just helped Anne into a white gown with blue and green embroidery and pinned her hair when they heard raised voices in the front hall—not a row, but some kind of alarm.

"What could have happened now?" Jenny asked, opening the door to the hall.

A distraught male voice—clearly servant class—could be heard demanding to see Sherbourne, Sir George, or the captain.

Anne rose hurriedly and went to the head of the stairs. Lord Ware's redheaded groom was shouting at the butler.

"What is wrong?" she called down. "Perhaps I can help."

The groom's gaze shot up to her. "They got 'im, m'lady. He be captured. They takin' 'im somewheres to kill 'im. Someone gotta do somethin' real quick." He paused long enough to drag in a breath.

A band tighten around her chest. "Who's been captured? Is it Lucien, I mean, Lord Ware?"

"Aye, lady, the master. And he be unarmed 'cause he give me his knife and lost his pistol in the fight."

The little man looked like he might start weeping, and Anne swept down the stairs. She gripped his arms to steady him, her own composure better now. "Finn? Isn't that your name?" He nodded and she went on. "Just tell me plainly what has occurred."

"Yes'm, ma'am. But somebody gotta go…right now." His gaze searched the hallway as though he might find help hidden in the shadows. "Where be Master Sherry?"

Anne frowned, her fear deepening. "I thought he was with you and Lord Ware at Harwick House."

"He was, but I couldna find 'im, not after the master was taken. He's not here? Oh, 'pon me mother's soul," he said in a voice of doom. "They musta got 'im too!"

"Finn! Tell me how this happened." Anne didn't realize her own voice had risen until the drawing room door flew open, and Lady Barnett and Margret emerged.

"What's going on?" Margret scowled at the groom in confusion. "Did you say someone was taken? Taken where?"

"I dunna know, miss," Finn's voice quavered.

"Not now, Margret. Can you not see he needs a cup of tea?" Lady Barnett interjected. "Or maybe a pint of ale." Apparently grasping that Finn was presently unable to give a coherent story, she placed a motherly hand on his shoulder. "Let us go to the kitchen. Now, young man, you must calm yourself, or we will never understand what needs to be done." She steered him down the hall to the back stairs that descended into the kitchen. Anne and Margret followed close behind.

"Ye be right 'bout that, ma'am." Finn's eyes darted around, his urge to take immediate action clearly foremost in his thoughts. "But I be sore afraid for the master. They gonna kill 'im I tell ya—"

"Yes, I understand, but the more we understand what has occurred, the faster we can do the right thing." Lady Barnett's soothing tone finally had its effect on him, and Finn fell silent with a heave of his shoulders.

Anne and Margret's impatience was curbed by Mrs. Barnett's stern look, but her handling of the matter proved to be exactly what was needed. Once Finn downed half a pint of ale in one swallow, he regained his color and was able to explain that he and Lord Ware had been caught searching the cellars of Harwick House and that Ware had ordered Finn to hide and go for help as soon as he could. "He 'most got away, but the others come, and the master he be bashed on the head with a bottle of wine."

Finn's voice tightened as he described his search in the woods for Sherbourne. "When I couldna find 'im, I figgered he be here and run all the way."

"Was it not the plan to follow anyone who left Harwick House?" Anne asked gently. "Sherbourne may be following someone. We should not despair over his capture yet. Let us send out riders to apprise Sir George of the situation. Mean time, we shall begin searching for Lord Ware as soon as I change into riding clothes. Will someone send word to the stable to saddle my horse?"

"No, Anne, certainly not," Lady Barnett said decisively. "We must wait until the men come home. You cannot go charging up there alone—and certainly not without knowing where they're holding his lordship. You could make matters worse."

"But ye cain't wait," Finn insisted, squirming in his chair. "I heared 'em say they'd kill 'im."

At the sound of men's voices from overhead, Anne leapt from

her chair and started toward the door, calling, "Sir George? Lord Sherbourne?"

Thank heavens. Someone was home. Heavy booted footsteps ran down the hall, and Sherbourne bounded down the stairs and into the kitchen. The groom nearly tackled him.

"Finn, thank God," Sherbourne exclaimed gripping his shoulders. "Why the devil did you leave? I have been imagining the worst. Where is Lucien?"

"Oh, Master Sherry. Frenchies got 'im, an' they gonna kill 'im."

That was the third time he'd said it, and Anne felt a chill in her heart at every repetition.

"*Bloody hell.*" Sherbourne seemed unaware of having uttered the vulgarity in front of the ladies, and none of them said a word to correct him. Anne watched him struggle to grasp the situation. He dropped into a chair as if the air had gone out of him and stared at Finn. "Tell me everything."

In starts and fits, prodded by Sherbourne, Finn did his best to recall the details of events in the cellars. "After the others come, there be a good bit of talkin'."

"About what?" Sherbourne asked, leaning forward.

"Somethin' about Paris, and Simon Grey."

"Good lord," Sherbourne moaned. "That's bad news for sure."

Anne's palms grew clammy. From his reaction, she assumed someone at Harwick House had recognized Lord Ware from his spying days in France, someone from the French side of the conflict.

But Finn neither understood nor cared about the past. He was riveted on Lord Ware's immediate peril and much taken by his master's lack of weapons. "Shouldna give me his knife," Finn lamented. "I was gonna stick that Ramsey fella for 'im, but them others come tearin' down the stairs."

"It's all right, Finn," Sherry said, fully in command of himself now. "You did exactly as he instructed. We can take it from here."

"I brung his pistol. I stepped on it after they all went back upstairs. Lost in the fight, me thinks." He pointed to the firearm he'd laid on the table. "He aint got nothin'"

"I understand, but don't worry. Lucien has been in a lot of scrapes. He will somehow come through. Count on it."

Anne studied Sherbourne's face, wondering if he truly believed that or was just reassuring Finn...or maybe all of them, including himself. It sounded as though Lucien was bound by ropes with nothing to rely on except his wits. And no amount of cleverness would cut those bindings. She closed her eyes, chiding herself for her doubts. She should not underestimate the viscount.

When Finn got around to the point in his story where they were moving Ware somewhere outside the manor house, Sherbourne struck his fist on the table. "That's what Faegan was doing! The scoundrel has much to answer for when I get my hands on him."

"How do you mean?" Margret asked.

"He lured me away, so they could move Lucien," he said bitterly. "And I fell for it." He seemed to fall into a dark mood.

"But how?" Anne prodded.

"Oh, sorry. He left the house acting furtive, and took off on his horse, whipping the beast into a rapid gallop. Like a dunderhead, I followed him."

"But that was the plan," Anne said. Both Sherbourne and Finn were blaming themselves for Lucien's situation. "Was it not agreed you should follow anyone who left?"

"Common sense should have told me that was exactly what Faegan wanted. And I certainly should have recognized the trick when all he did was ride to the village, stop a few minutes at the tavern, and ride back. I could kick myself." He shook his head and heaved a sigh. "When I got back and Lucien wasn't waiting, I still failed to tumble to the truth. I wasted several more minutes before getting worried enough to circle the house looking for him. Confound it all." He ran a hand through his hair.

"So, how did you know something was wrong?" Margret asked.

Sherbourne was telling his story to them as if talking to himself, going over the details in his head, and he kept leaving out parts. Thus, Anne and Margret kept prodding him with questions.

"The cellar door was busted open. Lucien would never have left it like that for them to find if he had gotten clear."

"I done that," Finn said, hanging his head. "Got out an' ran. Forgot t' door."

"It doesn't matter. Once Lucien was discovered, the need for secrecy was over. He will be right proud of what you did, Finn."

"Ifn we find 'im, 'fore it be too late."

"We will, but we need a plan. According to what you saw, we know at three of the conspirators are in the house—Mrs. Cluett, Faegan, and Ramsey. The Harwicks, Mr. Cluett, and the seventh conspirator—the presumed French agent—could be there, but we cannot be certain."

"Mr. Cluett was in Benchley," Anne interrupted. "I saw him."

"Doing what?" Sherry asked sharply.

"I don't know exactly."

"Anne. Tell him what happened," Margret insisted.

Sherry turned to Anne. "Anything that might help us find Lucien?"

"No. It was nothing, really."

"Then it will have to wait. I want to hear about it…after we find Lucien. So what else do we know that might help us locate him? Lucien and the powder kegs are in a place Mrs. Cluett referred to as the cave. I know of no such place. Possibly it's a hidden cellar under that locked shed, but we cannot waste time searching the entire Harwick estate again." He lifted a brow. "I suggest we gather reinforcements, storm the house, and force them to release him."

"Will that not provoke a fight? They have firearms," Lady Barnett said with concern. "They are not going to allow you to just walk in and take him."

"What is the alternative?" Sherbourne shrugged as though the threat of such a fight was nothing to him.

Anne caught her breath at his attitude but supposed to a man who had been in the war it might seem that way. To her, the prospect of a battle with firearms and the resulting injuries or deaths was terrifying. She saw the same dread on Margret's and Lady Barnett's faces and suppressed a shiver.

"It is a calculated risk," Sherbourne said. "But I am not leaving my partner in the hands of those devils."

"I'm goin' with ye," Finn declared. "I knows how to use a popper."

"Good man."

Within minutes, Sherbourne, Finn, and two armed footmen were prepared to leave when Sir George and Captain Wycliff walked in together after meeting up in the stable yard. They were swiftly apprised of Lord Ware's plight.

"We were just leaving," Sherbourne finished.

"You'd do better with more men," Sir George said. "I have eleven able-bodied neighbors just waiting for orders."

"How soon?" Sherbourne demanded.

"Twenty minutes, maybe less. I can send the footmen and grooms in different directions to quickly get them the word."

Sherbourne weighed the proposed delay against the greater chance of success by confronting the conspirators with a large force and nodded at Sir George. "Do it. Finn, get up to Harwick House. Let me know if anyone goes in or out of the house." He pulled a pistol from his pocket and handed it to Finn. "Use it if you have to protect yourself or bring us quickly." The groom sprang up and ran out the door. Sherbourne turned to the captain. "You saw Rothe?"

"I did and gave him the potential time constraints. Our meeting was interrupted by another explosion. This one on Pall Mall."

"My God. Westminster. The blackguards have struck the very heart of London," Sir George thundered.

"And moved close to the palace," Sherbourne muttered. "Fortunately, Prinny is not in residence." He looked at Wycliff and asked the question that Anne was dreading. "Casualties?"

"Not as many as might have been. The powder kegs were in a parked wagon. A few souls were lost to flying boards and debris. Upwards of twenty injured, and two horses had to be shot. When I left, the injured had been taken for care and order nearly restored."

"How horrible," Anne said aghast. "Those poor people."

Margret pursed her lips. "And these dreadful traitors at Harwick House are planning something even worse. Someone *has* to stop them."

"Amen to that," Sherry said. "But first we free Lucien."

Chapter Eighteen

Lucien gritted his teeth and continued to tug and twist on the bindings long after his wrists were raw and bleeding. To his disgust, he made little progress, maybe a slight loosening but not enough to slip free. At this rate it would take hours, perhaps days, and he did not have that kind of time. So far he'd failed to locate a sharp or jagged object he might use to fray the soft jute rope binding his wrists and ankles. He glanced around his makeshift prison once again, racking his brain to come up with something.

His pockets were empty except for the tinderbox. Ah...a possibility? When opened, its metal edges were relatively sharp—not like a knife of course, but if he could get it out of his pocket...

Precious time passed as he struggled, bending this way and that, getting on his knees next to a wood box. He leaned over the box, pressing himself against the top edge just under the tinderbox in his pocket, and pushed himself downward, moving the small metal box toward the top of his pocket.

Several minutes passed before the box finally dropped on the dirt. Sweating profusely from the stuffy air and his concentrated efforts, Lucien sat back on his heels and rested a moment. So far, so good. Toppling himself over onto the ground, he rolled around and scraped the dirt with his nearly numb fingers until he found the tinderbox. More minutes ticked away while he pried it open, grasped it in one fist and finally began to saw on his bindings.

For a long time, nothing appeared to happen. How long... he lost track. He nearly gave up at one point, but gradually the rope began to fray. Heartened by that, he doubled his efforts. By stretching and yanking at the weakened rope, he finally broke it.

Pushing into a sitting position, Lucien flexed his fingers, restoring a flare of painful feeling in them before he worked on his ankle bindings. It went faster this time, yet he kept hearing imagined footsteps in his head.

At last he was free, stomped his feet to get the blood flowing, retrieved his tinderbox for an idea already forming, and rose to a crouch. Hunched over he could move around despite the low ceiling, and he began pulling the boards away from the entrance.

He froze when he heard the dreaded sounds of a horse cart stopping outside and then two men talking. One of them he recognized as Ramsey; the other was too muffled to identify.

Devil it. All he'd needed was five more minutes.

As the men drew closer, the other man was talking. "When the others get here, load up and move everything to the Compton house." Although he spoke in English, the heavy French inflection made him difficult to understand. This must be the French agent they'd sought. But what house was he talking about? Was the word Compton? He listened closely, hoping Ramsey would repeat it.

But Ramsey changed the subject. "What should I do with the prisoner?"

"Kill him. Quietly. Leave the body inside the cave. If they find him too soon, it will ruin our plans. Whitehall would raise a hue and cry."

Ramsey gave a gloating bark of laughter. "I shall silence him with pleasure. According to Cluett, he has much to atone for."

"Do not waste time on him," the other man snapped. "Petty revenge is not worth it. Do not fail me, Ramsey. Keep our goal in mind. I am going ahead to Compton to see that everything is ready. No mistakes, *mon amie*. We are almost done."

There. He'd said it again. Sounded like Calmton, which must be Compton.

"Don't worry, Jacque. A glorious *specktacle* awaits us," Ramsey gloated. "They will not see it coming."

Jacque. Had he heard the name recently? He tried to keep listening, but he had to lay some of these boards back in place.

Ramsey must not realize Lucien was free of his bindings—not until the time was right.

"Hold on one day more," Jacque said, his voice dimming as Lucien heard the creak of harness as he mounted a horse. Then came the sound of hooves breaking into a gallop headed south toward Blinker's Marsh.

One day. Lucien hissed through his teeth. Lady Anne had been correct. So little time left, and this fellow Jacque was already on his way to set the final stages in motion.

The Frenchman's departure had one good effect: the odds for Lucien's escape had gotten better...his captors had been reduced to one. He smiled grimly, as he lay one of the last two boards in place, keeping the other as a weapon. Then he crouched off to the side and waited as Ramsey approached. He heard the scrape of brush being pulled away, then the boards removed. A dark figure loomed in the entrance.

"Hello, Mr. Grey or Ware, whatever you call yourself. Your time is up."

A scratch of flint, the smell of smoke, and Ramey's face was illuminated in lantern glow. He set the lantern down on the dirt, crouched, and half-crawled into the low-ceilinged space. Before Ramsey could gain his bearings, Lucien swung the board, catching his would-be killer across the forehead. The man gave a startled cry and fell sideways. Lucien swung again, catching Ramsey's shoulder as the man attempted to roll out of reach.

"You'll pay for that," Ramsey snarled, as he groaned and fell back.

"Not this time. Your friends are not around to save you." Lucien shoved Ramsey aside, snatched up the lantern, and tossed it on the dry straw. "Get out if you can." A blaze flared, and Lucien dove out the entrance, landing face down in the shallow creek.

The violence of the explosions shook the ground, shooting water, dirt, and stones into the air. They pelted Lucien as they came down, and he threw up his arms to protect his head as the force heaved him against the far bank, knocking the air from his lungs.

He rolled over, sucked in a quick breath, and scrambled up the bank, flinging his battered body behind a tree.

A few minutes of battlefield hell later, it was over. When the explosions stopped, he peered around the tree, then stumbled across the open space and crawled into the brush. If the other conspirators were nearby, he was in no shape to fight them off.

Only moments later, he heard the chilling sound of pounding hooves. Lucien pressed deeper into the underbrush, stopped, and remained motionless, barely daring to breathe. Had his luck run out?

"What the devil happened here?"

Lucien closed his eyes and laughed softly. *Sherry*. Lord bless him.

He fought his way out of the bushes—the branches snapping around him—to see a dozen guns pointed at him. "Looking for me?" he asked. He wasn't surprised it took a moment for them to recognize him. He was dripping wet and covered from head to boots in mud.

"Lucien!" Sherry shouted, as he dropped from his mount and ran to help. "By God, you look awful," Sherry said, actually going so far as to embrace him, dirt and all. "But I am glad to find you alive."

"I'm rather please to *be* alive," Lucien said with a grin. "Ramsey was inside the cave when I tossed the lantern, so I very much doubt if he made it out, but you'll have to move quickly to catch the others. They're leaving Harwick House today, and Ramsey was supposed to move the munitions to London. I couldn't be sure anyone was around to stop them, so I lit the powder kegs."

"All right, men. You heard him," Sir George roared. "Let's get after these devils."

"Go, Sherry," Lucien urged. "I will be fine."

Sherry gave him a swift look of assessment. Apparently concluding his partner would mend, he nodded and leapt onto his horse. "We'll be back," he yelled as he galloped after the others.

A few moments later, Finn came pelting down the path from Harwick House. "Master Lucien, Master Lucien." He skidded to a halt. "Be you a' right?" After Lucien assured him he was, Finn asked anxiously, "Can ye walk?"

"Of course, I can. I might be a bit slow at first, but give me a moment. I'm just a tad shaken."

"But you're bleedin', milord."

Lucien glanced down at his wrists. They were oozing some, but then he realized Finn was looking at the left side of his face. Lucien lifted his hand to find a stream of blood curling around his ear. Probing further, he touched a bloody gash near his temple. *Botheration*. The flying debris had left him a nasty head wound. No wonder his head hurt. "Nothing to worry about, Finn. Head injuries always bleed freely."

"Aye, but it be drippin' over them fine clothes."

He looked down at his bloody, filthy, and ripped garments. His valet would be beside himself. "Talbot can never repair them, so help me get my coat off. I might as well put what's left to use." Once the coat was removed, he stripped off his waistcoat, wadded it, and pressed the relatively clean back side against the wound.

"We be goin' back to the manor now?" Finn motioned toward Barnett Park in the distance.

"I want to see what's happening first." Lucien started to climb the path toward Harwick House but stopped when he saw Sherry and the other horsemen returning.

"Not a soul there," Sherry said disgustedly, "except a maid from the village. Not even the stable staff. The maid said the household was all packed to leave. When they heard the explosions, they tossed everything in the carriages and whipped the horses into a run."

"They can't have gotten far."

"Lucien, it's been half an hour. They are miles away."

"Three of our young bucks are still out looking," Sir George said. "But they won't catch them. Sherbourne's right, they have fled."

"And we don't know where," Sherry said, his voice full of frustration.

"Compton," Lucien said. "At least that's what it sounded like. A fellow was talking to Ramsey in a thick French accent, giving orders. He said they were meeting at the Calmton house."

"Has to be Compton Street in London," Sherry said. "We'll catch them now."

• • •

While the others rode ahead to explain the explosions to the ladies waiting at home, Lucien and Sherry talked quietly as they walked back to Barnett Park, and Finn followed leading Sherry's horse. Lucien told his partner everything Rothe needed to know—including the name Jacque, the suspected French spy—and summarized the rest from the time Lucien woke to find himself in the man-made cave. As soon as they had reached the manor, Sherry left for London to report to Rothe, dispel Whitehall's fears over the Blinker's Marsh explosion—for word of it would soon reach them if it had not already done so—and to pass on the word that the revolutionaries' were gathering at a house believed to be somewhere on Compton Street.

Despite urging from Sherry and Sir George, Lucien refused to have Doctor Morehouse called, but as soon as his partner left, he had begged time to clean up before relieving everyone's justifiable curiosity. Talbot took one look at him, sent for bath water, fussed over the head injury, and sniffed his disapproval while striping him of the offending garments.

Forty minutes later, clean and dressed in fresh attire, Lucien strolled into the Barnetts' drawing room to find the household still awake and many of Sir George's band of neighbors drinking port and brandy. They turned expectantly as he entered.

Lucien smiled at the gathering. "Looking for me?" he asked, mimicking his words from the creek. The men in the riding party laughed, understanding the quip.

"Brandy?" Sir George asked, already pouring a glass.

"Absolutely. Although I cannot stay long. I must ride to London to join Sherbourne."

"No, not tonight." Various forms of protest came from several directions, but the only one he heard was Lady Anne. "You must rest first," she insisted.

"No time, my lady. This uprising is not over. Not until we locate the rebels and the powder kegs. But I shall delay long enough to finish this very fine brandy and to satisfy your curiosity." He turned his attention to the others. "Thank you. All of you. I'd like to ask you to continue to watch Harwick House. Some of them could return, and we must capture everyone involved. As for what happened this evening..." Because he was anxious to be on his way, Lucien gave them a shortened version yet enough to satisfy their concerns. The brandy and port had mellowed the tension, and the neighbors were pleased they'd had a hand in driving the traitors away.

As soon as possible, Lucien slipped out and went to the stables to collect Finn and his curricle. When he led the team into the cobblestone stable yard, he found Lady Anne waiting.

"I came to wish you good fortune." She drew closer, her expression uneasy as she surveyed his bandages. "Are you sure you should go so soon? Your arm is still healing, now your wrists, and the head injury alone requires rest."

"I am well enough, my lady. You know I must go. And why."

"Yes." She sighed. "But take care of yourself."

The manor door opened behind them, and Captain Wycliff strode toward the stable. "Wait for me, Ware. I shall ride with you. I cannot leave this matter unfinished."

Lucien nodded. "We shall be glad to have you." When the captain disappeared into the stable, Lucien turned back to Lady Anne.

"Will you return?" she asked. "To Barnett Park, I mean?"

He smiled down at her upturned face and took her hands. "Of course. Talbot is here. I must retrieve him when this is over. And yes, I shall tell you all that has transpired." He might have said more if the captain had not chosen that moment to emerge from the stable.

"Please, stay safe," she said softly. "I…well, just stay safe."

He squeezed her hands lightly before letting go and climbing into the curricle. "I promise," he said as he loosened the reins on the horses that were prancing in their eagerness to go. "Try to stay out of trouble while I'm gone." Lucien and Wycliff left at a brisk trot and urged their horses into a gallop at the end of the lane.

• • •

Lucien and Wycliff made good time. London streets were relatively uninhabited at two in the morning, most of the upper classes not yet on their way home, the working classes already tucked into bed. As they approached Westminster, they heard a commotion ahead. Turning onto Whitehall Street, Lucien wasn't surprised to see the War Offices lit, but he immediately reined up at the sight and clamor of a crowd on foot and horseback fleeing from somewhere south of the Horse Guards. Fear and panic was written on their faces.

"What has happened?" he shouted at the streaming crowd.

A well-dressed man pulled up his horse long enough to yell, "Rebels have blown up the House of Lords."

"Good Lord. Were they in session?"

"Aye. But you'd be wise to turn around. A terrified mob is right on our heels." The rider sped away.

Salcott. Lucien leapt to the ground. "Finn, get the horses out of here. I'll make my own way home." He started to run down the street, dodging through the panicked crowd of poor and rich alike. If his father was dead…they'd never have a chance to put things right between them.

At the next cross street, he smelled smoke but was surprised at the lack of flames. A fire wagon was parked in front of Parliament. The main entrance was blocked by collapsed structure, just now being pulled away, but most of the building appeared intact.

He slowed his pace, searching the faces in the crowd. Several were familiar, and it looked as though many of the peers had gotten out before the beams gave way. He failed to see Salcott and pushed through the by-standers to reach those clearing the entrance.

A hand touched his shoulder. It was Captain Wycliff. "Your father?"

Lucien shook his head, grabbing the end of a broken beam. "Not out here."

Wycliff edged in beside him to grasp another part of the beam, and they began to work it out of the pile. As they tugged and tossed rubble aside, Lucien listened to the conversation around him and gathered bits and pieces of what had happened. Two fire balls had been thrown in different entrances, blocking them, but the guards had caught one of the rebels involved and the other ran off before further damage was done.

A small undamaged door at the back of the building was now blocked to the public and was being used to evacuate the wounded. Fires at the damaged entrances had delayed rescue efforts, and heavy smoke was still an issue. Only two casualties had been confirmed, but the chaotic situation left the fate of many unknown.

With dozens of men struggling to get the front doors open, they broke through only minutes after Lucien and Wycliff arrived. Rescuers surged forward. As he was near the front, Lucien stepped quickly through the soggy mess. The stench of smoke was strong, but the air inside was clearing enough to see what was happening. A few wounded were still inside, and a dozen or so lords were doing their best to care for them or provide support until medical assistance arrived.

Lucien still could not locate his father. "Where the hell is he?" he muttered. He asked two peers he recognized if they had seen him, but they both shook their heads.

"What about over there?" Wycliff pointed.

A half dozen men hovered around someone lying on the floor. Lucien couldn't see more than that, but he did not see Salcott anywhere else. He is fine, he told himself. Salcott is too damned tough to be taken down by a random fire ball. But Lucien's heart was beating fast.

"Who is it? Let me through." Ignoring decorum, Lucien pushed past those standing around, but the gathering was already breaking up. He stopped and stared at the back of his father's head. Salcott was on his knees. As Lucien moved closer, he saw that his father was bending over an unconscious man, his blood-covered hands applying pressure to the man's leg injury.

Lucien crouched at Salcott's side. "Can I help?"

"Carlson needs a doctor," the Earl said without taking his eyes from his task, "but a temporary tourniquet would get him by until help arrives. If you could keep the pressure on while I shift to the other side…?"

"Of course." Lucien pulled off his cravat and draped it over the Earl's shoulder before taking over. "You will need this. I've seen a cravat used in similar situations."

Salcott barely missed a beat. "Yes, I suppose you have. It should do well enough."

As soon as Lucien slipped his hands into place, Salcott moved to the far side and began wrapping the cravat above the shrapnel wound.

"I'll find a doctor," Wycliff offered and hurried away.

Once the cravat was tied securely in place and the blood flow slowed to a stop, Lucien sat back on his heels. "It is holding for now."

Salcott nodded and caught Lucien's eye. "Thank you for coming."

Father and son looked at each other, and Lucien realized the significance of "for coming" rather than "for helping." He gave a brief nod. "Where else would I be?" When all was said and done, blood was a strong bond.

With the Parliament building swiftly emptying of inhabitants and smoke, a doctor was found and soon joined them. Wycliff had even located two men with a litter. The surgeon made a quick assessment, examined the tourniquet, and gave his approval. "Fine job, gentlemen. I'll get him to my surgery where I can better work on that wound."

"Can you save the limb?" Salcott asked quietly.

"I'm optimistic," the doctor said. "Your swift action has given me that option."

"Um, well, good. Do not waste time on us," Salcott said brusquely, although a smile belied his tone. "You have work to do."

Lucien gestured at Wycliff, and they slipped away while Salcott was supervising the transfer of Lord Carlson to the litter. Now that he knew his father was safe, Lucien needed to talk with Lord Rothe.

Chapter Nineteen

Lucien and Wycliff found Rothe's door at the Whitehall War Offices shut and heard raised voices inside. "I don't think it will be long," Sloane, his secretary, said. "His lordship has been with Lord Southway for nearly half an hour."

He had barely spoken when the door opened and Southway stormed out. The young Whig opposition proponent, a stalwart fellow with a trimmed beard, brown hair fashionably swept back, and a fancy cane with a silver, horse head knob, was red in the face. He straightened and slowed his pace upon seeing Lucien and Wycliff. "Good evening, gentlemen."

"Lord Southway."

After this brief exchange, the man was gone, his obvious bad temper propelling him from the War Offices and down the stairs.

"Go on in," Sloane urged Lucien.

Leaving Wycliff in the outer room, Lucien entered Rothe's private office and found the marquess looking out the window in the direction of Parliament.

"Lord Southway giving you a bad day?"

"Ware," Rothe said turning abruptly. "After Sherbourne's report of your part in the explosion at Blinker's Marsh, I did not expect to see you this soon. Ah, yes, Southway. Never a good day with him. I do not care for the man. He habitually has a new complaint to make. Even before the dust has settled on this latest rebel attack, he comes here to censure the government for 'failing to protect its Parliament,' and I was the only one who'd listen to his grievance. Enough of him." Lord Rothe's gaze ran over Lucien's disordered attire and the blood on his sleeves. "Since I cannot fathom why you would ride from the country in such disorder, I assume you too have come from the House of Lords. Your father is safe?"

"Yes, he is unscathed."

"Some good news at last. Confound these rebels. I hear we lost two men." Rothe sounded tired, discouraged, and he rubbed a hand across his brow. The long night had already taken a toll.

"A clerk and one of the Horse Guards at the front entrance. Lord Carlson suffered a serious leg injury. Others are wounded, but I don't have the details."

The marquess nodded. "Sloane sent one of the clerks to collect the particulars for me. Considering what could have been, we escaped a greater disaster. Even the building damage was slight, easily repaired." He pinched the bridge of his nose. "Was this the rebels' big event?"

"Unlikely, sir. A part of it, perhaps—to draw our attention from other activities—but this attack wasn't large enough. It only required three fire balls—one of which they stopped from exploding—and four men, or so I heard."

"One captured, was he not?" Rothe interrupted. "Where is he? Has he been questioned?"

"Fatally wounded while setting off the second blast, sir. I believe he died before they could even get his name."

"Then that is that," Rothe said morosely. "No help at all."

"I take this as more of a warning, sir. A statement, perhaps, intended to create unrest and confusion but not a high death count. The cave at Harwick House held both powder kegs and fire balls. If there are additional stores of munitions—as you have suggested— then something much, much larger and terrifying is underway."

"I was troubled you'd say that," Rothe huffed. "Follows my own worst fears. We *have to* locate the remaining explosives before the rebels can use them."

"As soon as I change, presuming my valet doesn't murder me for ruining yet another shirt and coat, I shall be back on the job."

"Is that wise?" Rothe frowned. "You've been injured—twice, I might add."

"When else, my lord? I doubt the rebels and their French allies are going to wait while I lay about."

Rothe flashed a brief smile. "To be young and indefatigable again." His expression hardened as he returned to business. "We have been busy since Sherbourne told us the munitions were on the move...and have searched Compton Street and Little Compton without success. A heavily laden wagon of firearms was intercepted on the outskirts of town and four prisoners were taken, but none have talked. Two were shot during capture—I doubt they will survive. The others will eventually give us what we want, but it may not be soon enough."

Lucien frowned. "Perhaps I have the street name wrong. His accent was heavy."

"Sherbourne mentioned that. But it was worth pursuing. We're continuing to watch for other wagons, and the next one will be allowed to pass through in hopes our men can follow it to the rest of the rebels and their weapons."

• • •

After leaving Whitehall, Wycliff tied his horse to the back of Lucien's curricle, and they drove down Compton Street. Not that Lucien thought they'd see something others hadn't, but he still needed to see for himself. They found nothing suspicious.

"What could the Frenchman have said that sounded like Compton or Calmton?" Lucien murmured to himself.

"Chalmford?" Wycliff suggested.

"I am certain it didn't end in ford."

"Compton, compton," the captain repeated thoughtfully. "Could it have been cotton? Although I cannot imagine where that might be."

"The cotton house? Doesn't sound right. At least I don't think so." Lucien shook his head and turned the corner toward Wycliff's lodgings. "I am no longer sure what I heard. Somehow the French accent has thrown me off. My Lord, that's it." He pulled the horses to a stop. "The cursed fellow has been taught to pronounce English words, but he'd say unfamiliar names as he would in his own tongue. Where he'd say Com, we'd say Cam."

"Camden," they said looking at one another. The London parish was about two miles north of Compton Street.

"We're looking in the wrong part of town," the captain said.

"Exactly. I need to go back and tell Rothe."

"Don't worry about me," Wycliff said, jumping down while Finn untied his horse. "I shall join you if I can."

Lucien turned around, irritating a number of drivers on his hasty return to Whitehall, took the War Offices stairs two at a time, and burst in on Rothe just putting on his hat to inspect the damage at Parliament for himself.

"Ware, what the devil is it now?"

"Camden, sir. He may have said Camden." As he explained, Rothe began nodding.

"That is a large area, but I shall get men on it immediately."

Rothe strode off to consult with Sloane, leaving Lucien standing there. When he walked by the marquess on his way out, the two men were already dispatching couriers to redirect the searchers and had spread maps across Sloane's desk. Lucien wondered if Rothe, in his eagerness to organize a new search, would remember to remove his hat.

• • •

After appeasing Talbot, changing his clothes again, and eating a bit of bread and cheese, Lucien returned to Whitehall. The building was a flurry of activity. A second wagon had already been located and followed into Camden, but it had been abandoned on the street when Rothe's men got too close and were spotted. The rebels got away. It was rotten luck. But Rothe was undeterred. From the maps and city files, he had identified possible properties that might be "the Camden house." A few were on the wagon's course, and he had placed those under surveillance.

"The most likely is here," Rothe said, pointing to the map that had been moved to his office. He went on to describe an older mansion with a large coach house that had fallen into disrepair and was isolated among substantial grounds of overgrown brush and trees. "According to our records, it stood empty for eight years until a year ago when it was sold for a pittance. Neighbors say no attempt has been made to make it livable. In fact, no one had been around until lights were first seen two months ago and a few nights more recently."

"Have we looked inside?"

"Not to my knowledge. Sherbourne and a handful of men are keeping watch, but we don't want to scare the rest of these damned rebels away. If someone is there, they haven't come out, nor has anyone gone in during the last hour. But the buildings are large enough to hide hundreds of rebels and a half dozen or more small munitions' wagons, those small enough to make it through the London streets. For all we know, everyone has gathered inside, and the two wagons we saw were only the stragglers."

"How confident are you?"

"Not at all. Not until we see the proof. We have other properties being watched, but this looked like the best fit. These other places have owners or tenants in residence, and none of them are suspected rebels or dissenters. My wager is on this one." His jaw clenched. "Exactly how large was the stock of munitions in Blinker's Marsh?"

"Enough to bring down this building and Horse Guards too if the fire balls had all been armed." He gave him a count of the dozens of boxes and bags of gun powder he'd seen.

"Devil take it, Ware. I'd hoped Sherbourne had exaggerated. The two wagons we stopped had only a third of that."

"Regardless, a significant load," Lucien said with a sigh. "The rebels have plans on an ambitious scale."

"Yes."

Rothe's single word response was sobering. Or maybe it was the apprehensive tone that matched Lucien's fear of the devastation if things went wrong...if they'd made a mistake and were watching the wrong house while the traitors gathered elsewhere to launch their heinous plot. He felt a sudden need to get to Camden and discover for himself if they had been duped— if *he* had been duped. Could Ramsey and the French agent have been aware he was listening? Had they mentioned Camden only to deceive him? But for what purpose? Had they not intended to kill him?

Lucien sighed, impatient with himself for second-guessing. Rothe's men had followed a wagon into the parish of Camden. Every sign was positive, but that still left room for error. They had to get it right.

"Any headway toward determining their target?"

Rothe shook his head. "We are taking a hard look at places on an easy, direct route from Camden and at events where unusually large crowds are expected. Nothing stands out, and frankly, the places that attract daily crowds are nearly endless. Our best bet is to apprehend the explosives before they get into position, but we have ordered all constables and Horse Guards to be patrolling the town by tonight." He gave Lucien an unreadable look. "I hesitate to ask, but might Cade know something to help us?"

Lucien shrugged. "As you know, he helped us before." The Gentleman Thief, as Charles Cade, the owner of Cade's Club was known throughout London, had his own band of spies in the city. He lived by his own unique code of ethics, but had assisted them in identifying a French spy several months ago. In some strange fashion which Lucien still did not understand, he and the crime lord had formed an...understanding. "Hard to say whether that was true loyalty or a whim, sir. I assume you want me to approach him for information."

"He'd tell you, if anyone."

"I shall stop at Cade's Club when I leave here. Unless I have something to report immediately, I shall go to Camden from there and locate Sherbourne. Any message I should convey to him or your other men?"

"Captain Wycliff left only minutes before your arrival. I told him most of what I knew, so they should be up on the news. Just remind them we *must not* allow the revolutionaries to bring this off."

. . .

Lucien entered Cade's Club, a posh gentlemen's meeting house, with serious misgivings. Charles Cade was not an acquaintance he had intended to pursue. The man was an unrepentant criminal, running gangs of thieves and cutthroats. And yet, there was something about him and his mysterious background as the alleged by-blow of an aristocrat who grew up in the rookeries, that intrigued Lucien. Perhaps he felt a twinge of admiration for the urchin who had scraped his way up from the streets to grudging acceptance by society.

Due to the late hour, the crowd was thinning, only the hardened gamesters remained, and Lucien quickly spotted Reginald, the house manager. Lucien had never heard the man's family name.

"Viscount Ware," the man lifted a brow. "I am surprised to see you here so late."

You are surprised to see me at all, Lucien thought. He never patronized the club. "I need to see Cade. With some urgency," he added.

Reginald seemed to assess him. "I believe *Mr.* Cade has gone home, but I will find out." He was back within minutes. "Indeed, you are too late, sir. He has retired."

"Thank you, Reginald. I shall seek him out at his home."

The manager frowned. "I would not recommend it."

"Noted, but my errand is pressing." Lucien turned away.

"Sir, I really…" Reginald's voice held a token of alarm as though Cade might hold him responsible for the middle-of-the-night intrusion.

"No reason for alarm, my good man. Cade knows how impetuous I am."

"Ah, sir. I said he had retired, but he has not gone home."

Lucien stopped in mid-stride and swung around. "If not home, then where?"

Reginald took a deep breath. "Is this so important as to risk his vast displeasure?"

"A matter of utmost urgency." Lucien came back to give the man a hard look. "Out with it. Where can I find him?"

"He has a suite of rooms here, my lord, but we have orders not to disturb him."

"I am sure you do, but this is an exception. I will take responsibility."

"As though that would matter," Reginald murmured. "Very well. I shall ask if he will see you."

The manager was gone longer this time. Indeed, twenty minutes passed. Lucien was beginning to think his request was being disregarded when Reginald finally appeared. "He will see you in his office. Right up those stairs."

"I know the way." Although Lucien had been brought through the rear entrance by Cade's thugs on his prior visits, he was confident he'd recognize the owner's private office at the top of the stairs. Indeed, it was hard to miss with a well-dressed brute standing on each side of it.

As Lucien approached, one of the men tapped on the door, opened it at a response from inside, and said, "He's here, sir."

Lucien couldn't hear Cade's response, but it must have been affirmative. The bodyguard pushed the door open.

Cade's office was much as Lucien had last seen it—a spacious and stylish study from the polished cherrywood furniture to the Persian rugs on the floor. The only change was the man himself. Instead of the impeccable dress of an elegant gentleman, Cade had chosen to meet with him in his night robe—not just any robe, mind you—one of the finest silk. The dark garnet color suited him.

For a man with so much history behind him, Cade was only in his mid-thirties, and his medium height, well-trimmed mustache and brown hair, and overall fineness of manner were better suited to a gentleman than a thief. He was seated behind his desk.

"Ah, Viscount, you will forgive my dishabille, I trust. I understood you could not wait until morning." Charles Cade's pale blue eyes studied Lucien as though he could divine his mission simply by looking at him.

"I beg your pardon for intruding at such an hour, and further for dispensing with the civilities. My request is indeed pressing. We need your help."

"Surely there is time for brandy," Cade said nodding toward the sideboard. "Perhaps you would do the honors."

Well, this was unexpected, but if Cade wanted to act as though they were friendly acqaintances, Lucien could do that. He poured the brandy, handed one to the club owner, and took a chair across the desk from him, setting his hat on a side table.

"By *we*, I assume you mean Whitehall," Cade said, taking up the conversation again. "I may have helped you in the past, Ware, but I am hardly at the Crown's beck and call whenever it suits them."

"Nor do they assume so. Allow me to explain."

"Certainly. You have until I finish this brandy."

Ah, that attitude was more like the Gentleman Thief Lucien knew, always taking control of the situation. Nevertheless, Lucien had come to him with a request and must play by Cade's rules. He briefly told him about the rebels, the French agitator, the explosives, and their concerns that something big was in the wind.

Cade leaned forward, his interested caught. "I knew of the increasing unrest. Much of it is warranted in my opinion. The common people deserve better, but French interference cannot be tolerated, and I agree serious mischief is brewing." He leaned back again, looking thoughtful. "These rebel explosions have increased public outcry. Although I understand you set off the one near Blinker's Marsh."

Lucien no longer wasted time wondering how Cade knew these things, he simply nodded. "A stock of powder kegs and fireballs."

"You were fortunate to escape serious injury."

Lucien shrugged to conceal his discomfort at the depth of Cade's knowledge. Did the man know every aspect of his life?

"What is it you want from me, Viscount. I have no connections within the revolutionary cause."

"But your people see and hear things."

Cade smiled. "They do."

"We're looking for a hideout in Camden which the rebels are using to launch an attack somewhere in London tonight."

Cade's brows shot up. "Tonight? And you know neither where they are nor where they will attack?"

"That is about it."

"You indeed have an urgent problem." Cade frowned. "I am not certain I can help you. I have not paid much attention to the specific rumblings of rebellion. Do you have a list of possible rebel dens and locations they might attack?"

"Way too many." Lucien told him of the house they were watching in Camden and their other activities throughout London searching for the rebel's gathering place, watching for wagons or carriages moving munitions, and assessing places vulnerable to attack.

Cade nodded several times, showing approval of the efforts underway. "I would assume the explosives are already in London," he said at the end. "They won't chance moving them again until they're ready to execute their plan." He cocked a head at Lucien. "You feel good about this house?"

"I suppose I do, but I have not yet been there."

"I suggest you follow your instincts. Such feelings are often based on observations and connections we are not aware we have made." He took a last sip of his brandy. "I wager you've relied on yours more than once. Why not now?"

"With time running out, not much else I can do," Lucien admitted.

Cade rose. "I shall put out an inquiry and see what we get. Do not count on it. If I were running this operation, I would be keeping the details to myself until the last moment."

As you have probably done a dozen times before. Lucien picked up his hat and rose. "I appreciate your time. If you hear anything…"

"I shall be in touch."

• • •

The day was breaking, misty and gray, by the time Lucien found Sherbourne and Wycliff. They were hidden just inside the Mill Lane property, the primary Camden house under surveillance, hunched down among the brush with three other men from Rothe's unit and two officers of the Horse Guards. They had a fair view of the back of the house and the main doors of the coach house.

"Hey, partner, what took you so long?" Sherry asked

"Rothe sent me on an errand. Any activity here?" Lucien asked as he squatted beside them.

"In the last few minutes, two men have gone from the house to the coach house and back again. Hard to say whether they are part of the conspiracy or just ordinary people going about their business. Rothe wants us just to watch until we're sure everyone is gathered, but we're not seeing enough activity," Sherry said. "And why no sign of anyone from Harwick House?"

"They could have arrived well before you," Lucien suggested. "Or they may have gone somewhere else."

"'Pon rep, my friend. That's what worries me."

"Somebody's coming out of the coach house," one of the Horse Guards officers said in a harsh whisper.

Lucien peered at the paunchy man scuttling quickly toward the house. He was dressed as an ordinary tradesman, but his furtive manner suggested otherwise.

"Haven't seen him before," another man said. "That makes three. If there is more they are certainly quiet."

An hour later, they all came to attention when a fourth man emerged from the house and headed toward the front gate.

"I'll follow him if he leaves." One of Rothe's agents got up but sat down again when the man merely looked up and down the street before returning to the house.

"Acted as though he was looking for someone."

"They could be awaiting one of the wagons that was stopped,"

Wycliff suggested. "I wonder if the missing wagons will make them call if off."

No one commented, and for a while, they watched the lane more carefully. As time passed, they relaxed again. Lucien stifled a yawn. He, Sherry, and Wycliff had been up a long time and were dead on their feet.

"I'm tired and hungry," Wycliff finally said, looking at Lucien and Sherbourne. "I'd wager it is going to stay rather quiet during the day. Seems as though we would do better with a couple hours of sleep."

Sherry rubbed the back of his neck. "I admit I can barely keep my eyes open. Bed sounds good."

Lucien couldn't agree more.

"You should take advantage of the calm," a Horse Guards officer suggested. "I intend to do so. We have fresh officers arriving soon to keep watch the next few hours."

Lucien stood. "A fine idea. I should be back long before dusk, but if I'm needed earlier..."

"Someone will send word."

Chapter Twenty

Anne wandered into the Barnetts' breakfast room by mid-morning, selecting only tea and toast. She had not slept well and had little appetite. While she waited for Margret to appear, she wondered what was happening in London. Had they found the rebels? Had there been a fight? Were her friends all right? Would someone send word if they were not? She nearly choked on the thought and set down her tea.

But of course, she would know. With Lord Ware's valet still here, someone would come for him, and surely one or more of the men would eventually return...if they were able.

She left the table abruptly and went looking for Talbot. She found him downstairs, polishing Lord Ware's boots.

"My lady." He leapt to his feet. "How may I be of service?"

"Oh, do sit down, Talbot." Of course, he did not, and she went on. "If you hear anything about his lordship...and the others, of course, you will tell me, won't you?"

Talbot's demeanor softened. "They will be fine, my lady. I have been with the viscount eight years this autumn. He gets himself into precarious situations now and then, but he always comes out on the right of it."

"But you *will* tell me?"

"Yes, of course."

Anne gave him a quick smile and dropped her gaze. The conversation had been awkward from start to finish, and the exchange had only made her feel marginally better. She needed something to do, a distraction to keep busy until they had news from London.

She stepped into the garden, but a stroll among the flowers was not what she needed. She yearned to *do* something. A few minutes later she went back inside, snatched the letter to her mother from the hall table, and set out on foot to mail it. On such a beautiful day, the half-mile walk to the village would do her good.

And it did help. The fragrance of wildflowers tickled her nose, and the birds busily twittering to one another could not help but raise her spirits. The gentle breeze seemed to sweep her worries away, and she was humming to herself when she reached the edge of the village.

Blinker's Marsh, however, was anything but tranquil. Residents spoke of little else than the explosion. Several had been to the site to view the large hole, and speculation was rife over what had taken place. Interestingly enough, the Harwicks had never been popular with the locals, and the village gossips had put the pieces together with the rebel explosions in London. "I knew they were bad ones" was a recurring theme.

Anne dropped off her letter and started back to the manor. Visiting the village had gotten her thinking about Jane Mawbry. The girl's horrid mother had not only cared little for Jane's ultimate fate but had refused to tell Lord Ware why she forced Jane to leave. Mightn't that be an important thing to know?

She stooped to pluck the bloom of a Bishop's Wort growing at the side of the lane, breathing in its subtle fragrance, and walked on, still thinking about Jane. She had a couple of theories for Mrs. Mawbry's actions, but neither seemed to fit the neighbors' description of Jane's character. She sighed. Why hadn't Lucien pushed for the truth?

She smiled, knowing the answer. She had once implied he was not a gentleman, but she'd known—even at the time—that she was wrong. Civility was in his breeding, including the proper way to treat a woman, any woman, even one so lacking in feminine feelings as Jane's mother.

Anne came to an abrupt halt on the path. No such compunction was stopping her. Why not try her hand at getting Mrs. Mawbry to talk? Surely Lord Ware could not object if she gathered a few facts while he was off saving the country.

She spun around to return to the village…and stopped in mid-step. Margret would never forgive her if she wasn't included. Reserving course again, she nearly ran to Barnett Park and hurried up the stairs to wake Margret.

"Get up, sleepyhead," she said, entering her friend's bedchamber unannounced. She stopped and laughed in surprise to see Margret already up and mostly dressed. "I have an adventure for us. Please say you've eaten. I wish to leave right away."

Margret turned on the seat of her dressing table to give her an interested look. "I've had chocolate and toast. Enough for now if your errand is urgent. What kind of adventure?"

Anne's gaze slid to the maid finishing Margret hair, and she shook her head at her friend. It would not do for Lady Barnett to hear what they were about until it was done. "Not a true adventure, I suppose. Just a walk to the village on a beautiful morning. We can stretch our legs and talk on the way. It's much preferred to sitting and wondering what's happening in London."

Margret caught her friend's excitement. "Sounds delightful. Let me get my parasol," she said jumping up. "I thought I saw a freckle this morning."

"But Miss," her maid protested, "your hair needs one more pin."

"Then put it in." Margret lowered her head while her maid complied. "Doubtless it will be blown around on our way to the village, but I suppose we must try."

"Of course, Miss. As you say." The maid gave her a hopeless look. She began tidying the room as Anne and Margret hurried into the hallway.

The moment they were outside the front door, Margret said, "Now tell me. Where are we going and why?"

"To the village, just as I said." Anne smiled to herself, purposely teasing her friend

"And?" Margret prompted impatiently.

"We're going to interrogate Mrs. Mawbry."

"Are we?" Margret's eyes sparkled. "What fun. But what do you think that dreadful, vulgar woman can tell us?"

"Well...she refused to tell Lucien, um, Lord Ware, the details when he asked about her row with Jane. I feel it's important to know. Their disagreement may hold the answer to where Jane has gone. Lord Ware was, of course, too gentlemanly to force the woman to talk, but *we* are not gentlemen."

"Ooh, yes, indeed." Margret clapped her gloved hands, giving a most unladylike squeal of delight. "We shall force her to tell us the truth and refuse to leave until she does. Did you bring your pistol?"

Anne laughed. "Never you mind, silly. I don't intend to shoot her."

"It would only be as she deserved," Margret said with a frown. "I cannot imagine anything I could do that would make Mama send me out on my own."

"Nor can I, but we are fortunate in our parents. Jane was not."

On that serious note, they hurried on in silence until they reached the village and turned on the lane where Jane had lived. Anne quickly spotted the well-kept cottage of the Ellises with its cheery blue door and at the end of the lane, the one room cottage that had to be the Mawbrys' home. The latter stood sad and worn, surround by tall grass and weeds.

Anne and Margret looked at one another, then knocked on the barren wood door. It was thrown open after several moments, and an untidy woman with straggly dark hair, a stained apron, and dripping hands looked at them in evident surprise. "Well, lookee here. The quality be callin' again. Ladies this time. Whatcha want with me?"

"Are you Mrs. Mawbry?" Anne asked sweetly.

"Aye, that's me name."

"I am Lady Anne Ashburn, and this is Sir George's daughter, Miss Barnett. May we come in? It's getting very warm out here." She thought it best not to mention their errand until they were inside. No reason to give the woman cause to shut the door in their faces.

Mrs. Mawbry seemed taken aback by the request but backed up, leaving the door open. "I s'pose," she mumbled. "Though I caint figger what you be after."

"Only a bit of your time," Margret said, following Anne's example by giving a friendly nod.

Anne looked around. The house smelled of stale sweat and refuse. Clothes were draped here and there, a pile near the back door. An orange tabby stared at her balefully at the interruption of his nap. Two scruffy dogs didn't even raise their heads. The kitchen was piled with what she assumed were dirty pans, and vegetables covered the table. They appeared to have interrupted her cooking, which might explain the stains on her apron, although most seemed old and dried.

"Aint no place to sit, so you best state your business." Mrs. Mawbry wiped her hands on her apron, leaving fresh streaks of red juice.

"It's about Jane."

Mrs. Mawbry flung up a hand and turned away. "Mercy me, not her again. I shoulda known. I already told his lordship all I know. Yer wastin' yer time. And mine."

"Why did you send your daughter away? What had she done?"

"Who told you that? Reckon it's my business, not yorn." She sniffed indignantly.

"Lord Ware is trying to find her," Margret said. "Do you not wish to know where she is? If she is all right?"

"Don't matter to me. She run off."

"We know she did not," Anne said firmly. "You threw her out after a disagreement. If we are to help Lord Ware find her, you must tell us why."

"Won't make no difference. Shameful she was. Why you want to find her anyhow?" Mrs. Mawbry was suspicious...and on her guard.

"Because she is *missing*," Margret said in exasperation. "If you think there is something in it for us, you are mistaken. We are only concerned about her welfare, to know she is safe."

"If she weren't, I woulda heard. As I said Janie's my business, not yorn."

Anne thought Mrs. Mawbry was much too fond of the word

business. Maybe the repetition was one of those nervous habits. She *was* nervous. Surely she wasn't embarrassed to tell them the truth. That would be the height of irony.

Anne sighed impatiently for Mrs. Mawbry's benefit. "I will only ask you once more...what happened to Jane? If you refuse to tell us, we will be forced to draw our own conclusions."

The woman parted her lips, showing her yellowed teeth in a crooked smile. "And what be they, nosey miss?"

"That you rejected Jane because she was carrying a child."

Mrs. Mawbry's face turned red, her breast heaved, and she sagged onto a stool at the table. Anne felt a moment of elation that she'd sorted it out, but her satisfaction was quickly replaced by horror for the situation Jane had had to face alone.

Margret gasped. "I should have thought of that. Oh, dear me." She turned accusing eyes on the older woman. "And you turned her away?"

"She were goin' to her fancy man. I knowed it." Mrs. Mawbry's shoulders began shaking, and Anne realized to her shock that the vulgar woman was crying.

When she heard the first blubbery sob, she muttered, "Heaven forbid," and hurriedly offered her handkerchief. She stooped beside the older woman. "Why are you crying? I thought you didn't care."

"Course I care. She's kin, aint she?" Mrs. Mawbry snuffled into the lacy handkerchief. "I was so mad at her. She coulda had a better life." She swept a hand gesturing toward herself. "Look at me. I was purdy once...but I was with child at fifteen, and he who done it took off 'fore the child was born. Trouble like that wears on ya."

Anne frowned, still reluctant to feel sympathy for this woman. But goodness. That history would make this pinch-faced woman only in her thirties. Anne took a closer look while Mrs. Mawbry wiped her face with the dirty apron. The woman's pride in her former looks was not false bragging. Her bone structure was good, and she had not totally lost what once had been a fine figure. Even now, a bath and a hair wash would make a huge difference. But

Anne could not change the life of this woman who was old well before her time, nor would Mrs. Mawbry welcome the attempt.

"Tell me about Jane. Who is this fancy man you mentioned? Is he the father of her child?"

"She wouldna say. I heard her upping her porridge and guessed why. She cried and cried, but wouldna tell me nothin'. But Harwicks' footman come once bringin' her a note from that fancy man stayin' at the big house. I knowed it weren't nothin' about a job, like she tried to tell me."

"Which fancy man?" Margret asked.

"That yellow-haired devil. Always eyein' the village girls."

"Ramsey," Margret said, disdain twisting her lips. "She is not with him. That we know for sure. He had been staying with the Harwicks, and now he is dead—from the explosion."

"Good riddance," the woman spat between her teeth. She dabbed at her red-rimmed eyes. "He had no business dishonoring my girl."

With the woman recovering, Anne straightened and stepped back. "Why did you send her away?"

"I tol' you—I was so mad, but I dint mean it. I woulda tried." She spread her hands wide. "But I cain't take care of Janie—an' not an infant too."

"Why won't you help Lord Ware? Don't you want to see them? Know how they are?" Margret demanded, clearly unmoved by the woman's tears.

"Course I do, but if the father dint want 'em, I feared to hear they both be dead—just like Lucy."

Margret gasped, and Anne couldn't think what to say. My heavens, if that's what she thought, why hadn't she gone to the authorities, and welcomed Lord Ware's inquiry? Anne eyed this wretched female who despite her flaws was still a mother, and Anne tried to appeal to that. "What if you are wrong, and she isn't dead?"

Mrs. Mawbry shook her head and wiped her eyes. After a moment she got up and walked to the kitchen table. "I got work to do."

Anne glanced at Margret and lifted her hand in a helpless motion. They had the truth they came for.

Leaving the woman chopping vegetables, Anne heaved a sigh of relief as they stepped outside. If Jane and her child were alive, Anne fervently hoped they never returned to that wretched house. Mrs. Mawbry had nothing of herself to offer.

Grabbing Margret's arm, she made a beeline for the blue entry of the cottage next door. Lucien had said that Daniel and Mattie Ellis had befriended Jane. She wanted to hear what they'd say about Mrs. Mawbry's latest story.

Mrs. Ellis opened the door. She too was wearing an apron, but what a contrast—spotlessly clean, white with a row of dainty blue ruffles at the bottom. Her brown hair was neatly pinned up, and she offered a warm smile.

"Oh, my, Miss Barnett. I apologize for my appearance," she said, whisking off the apron and patting her hair. "I've been baking bread. Are you looking for my husband?"

"Sorry to intrude on your day," Margret said. "This is Lady Anne Ashburn. We wished to talk with you and your husband about Jane."

"Oh, yes, do come in. I'm happy to answer anything I can, but Mr. Ellis isn't home, and I don't expect him until this afternoon. Have you news of Jane?"

"Not yet. Lord Ware was called away for a few days on another urgent matter, but I'm sure he will have something to report very soon."

Anne cringed inwardly at Margret's casual assurances. Promising what they couldn't control might only end in more heartbreak. "I know he is doing his best," she said, forestalling any further promises. "Perhaps we can talk in the kitchen while you tend to your baking?"

"Well, goodness, I'm not quite sure it's proper to entertain guests over my stove." Mattie Ellis's smile was contagious. "But if you don't mind, I really should get the next batch into the oven." She led them through her tidy cottage and into a small kitchen in the rear. The smell of freshly baked bread greeted them, and Mrs. Ellis hurried to retrieve two beautifully browned loaves from the oven.

She offered tea, which they declined, and then lifted a cloth from a bowl of bread dough. "So, how may I help you?"

"We've just spoken to Mrs. Mawbry," Margret explained. "She told a different story than she had given Lord Ware."

Mrs. Ellis nodded as though she was not surprised. "Was it helpful?" With her hands skillfully kneading and shaping loaves of bread, she listened as they related Mrs. Mawbry's admission that Jane was pregnant and her conviction that Ramsey had forced himself upon her.

Mattie paused in dismay to shake her head, her eyes misting. "Forced her? Oh, my goodness no." She brushed at her eyes, leaving cheeks smudged with flour, then grabbed a towel and wiped her hands, her baking temporarily forgotten. "Poor dear Jane. If only the child had come to me."

"So you think it is true?" Anne asked gently. Why couldn't this understanding woman have been Jane's mother? How different things might be.

"I suppose it is. It would be just like Bessie Mawbry to react in anger, spouting off in such a harsh way. And Jane might be ashamed to reveal her condition to us—not that she *should* be ashamed, lord bless her, whether she was seduced by a sweet talker or was given no choice. But she would not go to a man like that for help. Jane she has too much good sense."

"Is there anyone she might have approached?"

Mattie Ellis sighed. "Talk with Sadie Pratt, the midwife. If Jane was with child, then…it's possible Sadie would know."

"We shall do that. Take heart, Mrs. Ellis. If Jane did not tell the father, he would have no reason to harm her," Margret said encouragingly.

The older woman's face lit with hope. "Does that mean you think she is still alive?"

"It's possible, is it not?" Margret said, suddenly uncertain.

Anne stepped in. "If she didn't turn to him—or you—and her mother threw her out, then she may have gone into the city."

"Oh, my. I suppose that is possible," Mrs. Ellis said softly.

The three women exchanged uneasy glances. Getting away from Blinker's Marsh did not necessarily mean Jane or the babe had survived. The city offered many pitfalls, and it could be unforgiving.

Mrs. Ellis broke the awkward silence with forced cheerfulness. "Well, if anyone can make it, I'd put my wager on Jane."

Anne and Margret chatted quietly as they walked along the dirt roads of the village. While they believed Bessie Mawbry had told them the truth and Mattie Ellis had offered new insight, neither was heartening. It appeared the midwife, Sadie Pratt, might be their last hope.

• • •

Miss Pratt lived in the back rooms of a small boarding house on the west edge of Blinker's Marsh. She was a large-boned woman with a cheerful demeanor and a full-throated laugh. She grew silent for a moment when Anne asked about Jane Mawbry.

"Now why would you be asking me about Janie? 'Course I knew her. It's a small village."

Not wanting to besmirch Jane's reputation, Anne approached the subject cautiously. "Then you must know she is missing. Do you know any reason she might have left or where she may have gone?"

"Why are you asking me? And what is your interest? I must admit I find it odd that two ladies of the Quality are asking about her."

"We fear she may have gotten into trouble," Margret said carefully.

The midwife frowned. "She's been gone quite a while. What caused your concern at this particular time?"

"Well, recent events—"

Sadie frowned, then her brows shot up. "Oh, mercy me. Are you telling me the bones could be hers? I thought it was the governess."

"It was," Anne said quickly. "We are attempting to learn if there is a connection between her disappearance and Jane's."

"You think Jane is dead?"

"I hope not." Anne studied Sadie's face. "Will you help us? Or rather Lord Ware? I assume you heard of his inquiry into Lucy Drayton's death—that led him to Jane's disappearance."

"I see." Sadie let out a sigh, heaving her substantial bosom. She motioned them to chairs in her parlor. "A woman in my work is expected to keep quiet about what she knows, but given the circumstances, I will help if I can. Would you care for tea?"

"Thank you, but we cannot stay long," Anne said. "We only have a few questions. Did Jane come to you with a...shall we say delicate situation?"

"A pregnancy, you mean." Sadie lifted a brow. "No, but I may know something that would help you—if you promise to be discreet with the information."

"Of course. We have no wish to harm anyone's reputation," Anne said. Margret nodded in agreement.

"Very well. The local women come to me for a variety of female ailments. It's not that Doc Morehouse isn't a capable practitioner, he is, but it's easier to share female matters with another woman. And in a small village, a visit to Morehouse raises speculation. The short of it is that Jane came to me late one night—bleeding and frightened. She'd been brutally ravished, but she wouldn't talk about it or tell me who hurt her."

"Not even a hint?"

"No. She was too afraid. I thought at the time that she had been threatened. But this happened weeks before she went missing. One event may have nothing to do with the other."

"Unless that's when she became pregnant or he assaulted her again," Margret said.

"Yes."

"She didn't come back?"

Sadie shook her head. "No. I only treated her that one night... but I did give her the name of a man in London, known only to me as Dr. Jay—in case there were complications of any kind. Although a man, he is sympathetic to the plight of women and far removed from the gossips of Blinker's Marsh."

Anne resisted asking what kind of help he'd provided in the past. This was likely one of those times when the less she knew, the better.

"Where could I find Doctor Jay? I promise not to get him in trouble, but I'd like to know if Jane met with him. Perhaps he can tell us she is alive and well. What a relief that would be."

"To us all. Very well, I shall entrust you with the only address I have. It's a London shelter, but I must warn you, I heard it shut down a few months ago." Sadie rummaged in a desk, drew out a paper, copied the address, and handed the note to Anne. "If you learn anything, please send me word—good or bad."

Anne assured her they would, and they said goodbye. As they turned their steps toward home, Anne and Margret talked over what the midwife said. Although they'd known the girl was with child, they had assumed she'd had a secret lover. Neither of them had honestly considered she had been brutalized and raped.

What misery she had endured.

"Ramsey may have killed her to conceal his horrid deed," Margret said.

Anne gave a short, bitter laugh. "Why would he bother? Such a man would not care, and who would take the word of a poor village girl over his? The gossips would blame her, thinking she was just like her mother. There has to be more to Jane's story."

But what could it be? The chances of finding her or even learning her fate had grown dim. Nonetheless, Dr. Jay's name *was* a new line of inquiry, and as soon as the rebel activities were quelled, she would ask Lord Ware to keep trying.

"You do believe the captain and Lord Ware—and Sherbourne are safe, do you not?" Margret suddenly asked.

"Oh, Margret, you too?" Anne said turning to her with a

sympathetic look. "I have asked myself that question a dozen times today. It is so hard not knowing or being able to help. With the Harwicks gone, I cannot think of anything useful we could do."

"I fear I'm not brave enough to go back to Harwick House. Not after they shot Lord Ware, captured him, and then the explosion… It all gives me the shivers, but I cannot quit thinking about it." Margret was quiet for a moment as they came in sight of Barnett Park. "I wonder who Jacque is? Faegan, or whatever name is, might have the accent, but I cannot imagine him giving orders, can you?"

"Heavens, no. That wimp."

"So where has this other fellow been. Strange we have not seen him before."

"I suppose plotting against England is a big job," Anne muttered.

Margret giggled. "Oh, Anne, how droll you are. But truly, no outsiders have gone in or out. How was he keeping them informed of everything?"

Anne frowned. "I wonder. Maybe we missed something."

"Such as?"

Anne merely shook her head, but she was already pulling the events of the past week from her memory. Nothing jumped out at her as significant until she came to her confrontation with Mr. Cluett in Benchley—or rather his meeting in the woods with . . . *Jack, the dark-haired stable boy who only grunted or mumbled when spoken to.* She pictured the oddly hostile look on his face when she and the Barnett ladies were leaving Harwick House on that first visit. Jack, Jacque. She drew in a sharp breath. Could it be that obvious? How dull-witted she had been.

Margret turned at her friend's gasp. "What is it?"

"Jack, the Harwicks' stable boy, may also be Jacque, the French spy."

Chapter Twenty One

Despite his exhaustion, Lucien didn't sleep well or long. He was haunted by dreams of explosions and screams of innocent women and children. He rose from bed with a sense of urgency well before midday and was on his way to Whitehall within the hour.

Rothe sprang to his feet when Lucien walked in. "Has something happened?"

"No, sir. Not to my knowledge. I was about to ask you the same. I went home shortly after dawn and thought I would stop to hear the latest before returning to Mill Lane. Have we made any progress?"

"Not much." The marquess eased back into his chair and brushed an idle finger across his lips. "It has been quiet today—too quiet. I keep going over everything, hoping the cursed rebels have not planned some disaster we have not considered."

"Well, sir—"

"No, no," Rothe interrupted, waving his hand. "I do not require you to reassure me. None of us know what will happen. We are spread out across the city, watching, waiting, but we cannot be everywhere."

Rothe's frustration was understandable. Lives and property were at risk. But that nagging instinct that had brought Lucien safely through the war told him the Camden house *was* the key to disrupting the rebels' plot, and he was anxious to return there.

"If I can do nothing for you, sir, I shall ride north."

"Good, good." Rothe heaved an audible sigh. "If nothing changes between now and five, I want you and the Horse Guards to enter the Mill Lane property at that time. We cannot delay beyond that. If the rebels are not hiding there, we will have an hour or two to shift our forces elsewhere."

And where would that be? Lucien thought. But he didn't ask it aloud.

• • •

Lucien arrived at Mill Lane, Camden, to find Sherry there before him. Along with two officers of the Horse Guards and two of Rothe's other agents, his partner was hunkered in the same position on the west side of the estate. Two other positions were covered on the north and east, and mounted officers of the Horse Guards were stationed deeper in the woods and across the road on a neighboring property.

Nothing else had changed except the weather. An early dawn mist had given way to sunshine before Lucien left his townhouse. Now the clouds had gathered again, the hot air turning sticky. Crouching in the brush, fighting off insects, was not pleasant.

"Did you get much sleep?" Lucien asked his partner.

Sherry shook his head.

"Nor did I." Lucien raised his voice to be heard by the others. "I stopped by Whitehall on the way here. Rothe says to hold our position until five. If there is no activity by then, we go in and see what is there."

Most of the men just nodded. They all knew time was running out and were eager to take action. "I wish we'd do it now," one of them muttered. "What the devil are we waiting for?"

Shrugging, Lucien settled in to wait. It wasn't his job to explain Rothe's orders. He too was impatient, but he understood the need to capture everyone and not leave behind a scattered band that would simply reorganize.

Time dragged. Nobody stirred from the house or coach house, and tension mounted as there was little to do other than swat flies.

Captain Wycliff failed to return, and Lucien wondered if Rothe had sent him somewhere else. Or perhaps he'd had enough—he wasn't officially assigned to the War Office—but somehow Lucien didn't think that was the answer.

Lucien shifted his feet and stretched. Two more hours before the Horse Guards were to arrive en masse. That left plenty of time to worry they were making a mistake.

He came to alert at the sound of an approaching coach and four. It entered the front gate and pulled up to the coach house. The driver's hat was pulled low, concealing his face. The coach house doors opened, and the coach drove inside.

"Finally some action," Sherry whispered, a grin on his face. "You can't tell me that was not suspicious."

"I dare say our wait is nearly over."

Tense minutes past before the coach house doors opened again. Five horse-drawn wagons with canvas covering the cargo pulled out and stopped as dozens of men—heavily armed by the occasional musket barrel glimpsed under coats too bulky for the weather—came out of the house and climbed aboard. Another dozen men openly carrying rifles or muskets sat astride the teams of horses.

The air bristled with tension. A sudden pistol shot from the woods startled everyone. A rebel on the lead wagon fell to the ground, and pandemonium erupted. Horses plunged while their drivers yelled and applied the whip, urging them forward. Weapons appeared everywhere, and the rebels returned fire.

Lucien cursed at someone's precipitous actions, then he and the other men sprang into action. Gunfire came from the other two surveillance positions, and mounted Horse Guards burst from the woods and raced to block the front gate. Two of the wagons rolled through before the gate was closed, and one of them was stopped in the street by the Horse Guards who'd been hidden across the street.

The rebels trapped behind the gate poured off the wagons like rats abandoning a ship, distancing themselves from the powder kegs and fireballs that might be ignited by a stray shot. Many sprinted for the coach house to take refuge inside or to snatch up anything they could use as a weapon once their pistols were empty. Wagon two blew up with a deafening roar, scattering debris everywhere.

Lucien took shelter behind the trees, picking his shots with care. Panicked and injured horses, terrified by the yelling and the gunfire, whinnied and kicked up clouds of dust. Wagons were overturned and splintered, wooden boxes spilled and cannonballs rolled across the cobblestones breaking off wooden fuses and spilling gunpowder.

When nothing else exploded, shouting, swearing men on both sides seemed to run everywhere, swinging clubs, boards, fists, or empty musket stocks, or just trying to take cover and stay alive. The early volley of bullets and the wagon explosion had left dead, wounded, and dying men in the midst of a raging battle with no one able to respond to their pleas for help.

Lucien, Sherry, and most of their companions escaped serious injury in those beginning moments, but they were greatly outnumbered and exposed. And from the safety of the coach house, the rebels were reloading and starting to fire again.

"Let's take cover in the house," Lucien yelled. Sherry nodded, and they sprinted for the back door, followed by other agents and some of the Horse guards now on foot. Lucien stopped to help an injured rider, half dragging him to the back door, where others grabbed and pulled him inside. Lucien looked back and saw a man shouting orders in French and heavily accented English, urging the rebels to retreat into the coach house.

"Come on, Lucien," Sherry called from inside the residence. "Get in here."

"One moment." Lucien crouched beside the door and studied the rebel leader. He recognized the voice as the Frenchman talking with Ramsey outside the cave, and he looked vaguely familiar. Lucien was trying to place the face.

"Lucien, what the devil are you waiting for?"

"Coming." He ducked inside just ahead of a volley of musket fire. The Whitehall forces now under cover had an opportunity to reload, and the exchange of shots between house and coach house turned into a standoff. Lucien knew the odds were on his side. The sound of gunfire would bring the local constables, and the mounted Horse Guards in the streets would have sent word to Whitehall, asking for reinforcements. All Lucien and his men need do was wait.

The rebels must have realized it too. A sharp crack of shattering glass heralded a breakout of men leaping from the coach house windows, slipping out the side doors, running into the woods, or scattering toward the surrounding properties.

"After them!" Sherry shouted. "Show them how Englishmen feel about traitors!"

Chapter Twenty Two

Since Anne and Margret had eaten little before their walk to the village, they eagerly sat down for a what some called nuncheon around one in the afternoon. They'd been telling her parents about their morning activities and the note Anne had sent to Whitehall. Although Anne doubted that knowing Jack was actually Jacque would be helpful at this stage of events, she didn't want to assume that was true and be proven wrong. Not knowing where Lucien, Sherborne or the captain might be, she had written to Rothe as soon as they got home. She was just finishing a biscuit and tea when noises from the stable yard sent her and Margret running to the window.

"Young ladies," Lady Barnett scolded. "Show some decorum."

"It's the captain," Margret announced, a smile lighting her face. "Surely he has news for us." Then she demurely returned to the table as though she had not been anxiously watching the windows for his return.

Anne joined her at the table, although she smiled at Margret's pretense. She would probably do the same if it had been Viscount Ware. After all, a lady cannot appear too eager.

"Excellent," Sir George said. "Perhaps I should speak with him in private."

"Papa," Margret protested. "You would not do that. We are all keen to hear the latest news from London."

"No, I suppose I would not dare." His eyes twinkled at her, then he turned toward the door as Wycliff entered. "Captain, please join us. Have the traitors been captured?"

"Not yet, sir. Ladies," he said, acknowledging the others before taking a seat at the table. He accepted a pint of ale and related what he knew. "Whitehall is continuing surveillance at Mill Lane throughout the day, so I imagine Lord Ware and Sherbourne returned to Camden some hours ago."

"Did they receive my message about Jacque?" Anne asked.

"What message?"

When she explained about the note she'd sent, he shook his head. "Sorry, but I have no knowledge of it. I have not seen Rothe nor Ware since very early this morning."

"Oh, well, I doubt it matters any longer."

Wycliff turned his attention to Sir George. "I saw none of the Harwick household in town, which may not be significant, but I worried they might return home and become a danger to the neighborhood."

Sir George's brows lowered. "I have seen no activity, but I suppose they might have returned during the night. Shall we ride over there? If anyone is there, we can nab them and save Whitehall the trouble." He pushed back his chair. "I shall send our footmen to gather the neighbors."

"I would like to take the path through the woods and look first, sir." Wycliff set his ale aside and rose. He glanced at Margret as he headed toward the door. "It will only take a few minutes."

In reality, half an hour passed before he returned to find the family and Anne waiting for his report. Sir George had changed into riding attire, and two footmen had been ready to ride for the last twenty minutes.

"Well?" Sir George demanded the moment Wycliff appeared in the doorway.

"Somebody is there. It might only be the servants—perhaps they've returned to pack those things left behind—but surely a master or mistress is there to supervise."

"I would think so," Lady Barnett said. "Yet, I cannot believe those horrid people would have the effrontery to return."

"Don't you fret, my dear. We shall soon have them under lock and key." Sir George grabbed his coat lapels to emphasized his determination. "While the footmen gather our neighbors, we can rouse Constables Jones from the village."

"I saw a wagon and a heavy travel coach, but most of the riding horses are gone," Wycliff said thoughtfully. "It may only be the women. Perhaps we should take one of our ladies in a carriage to assist with transporting any females we find."

"I will go," Anne said immediately.

Margret chimed in, "And me."

"I shall do whatever is needed," Lady Barnett added.

Wycliff smiled. "Such courage, my ladies, but I truly believe only one is necessary to maintain the proprieties."

"I very much wish to go." Margret gave him a winsome look.

"I spoke up first," Anne countered. "And I have experience in such things."

Margret put her hands on her hips. "How does getting abducted make you more qualified?"

Wycliff attempted to intervene. "Ladies, anyone with the slightest acquaintance could see you are both well-suited to the task, but…"

"Oh, let them both go," Sir George said, saving Wycliff from making a choice that was sure to make his life uncomfortable. "As long as they promise to stay in the carriage—which shall remain at the foot of the lane until we know the situation is under control— they should be safe." He eyed them both. "Well, do I have your promises?"

Of course they agreed, and forty minutes later, seven riders, including Constable Jones, accompanied the ladies' carriage as they left Blinker's Marsh winding toward Harwick House. As planned, the coach stopped at the bottom of the hill.

"I can ride on alone and see if we're going to face resistance," the captain offered. "No reason to risk everyone."

"I am coming with you," Sir George said. "It will be safer for two."

"You're certainly not leaving me behind," Constable Jones blustered.

"We're all going," said a neighbor, echoed by the others.

Wycliff shrugged. "So be it." He turned his horse, and they galloped toward the manor.

Anne and Margret watched from the carriage window as the men dismounted in the courtyard and split up, two of them circling the house toward the back door. The rest of them approached the front entrance and went inside without knocking. Minutes passed and nothing was seen or heard.

"What are they doing?" Margret asked, biting her lip.

"It's taking an unduly long time," Anne agreed. "I'd say they found someone, but we haven't heard shooting, so that is good."

Sir George finally stepped outside and gestured for the coachman to bring the carriage. When the horses halted in front, Anne and Margret climbed down without waiting for assistance.

"What has happened, Father?" Margret asked. "Is everyone all right?"

"Yes, yes, of course, my dear. We had a bit of bother, but it is over now."

"Who did you find?" Anne asked.

"The Harwicks and Mrs. Cluett. Harwick resisted until Constable Jones hit him with his baton, and Wycliff had to take a pistol away from the Cluett woman, but all is sorted with no harm done."

"Are you taking them to jail?" Margret asked.

"For now. Treason is a hanging offense."

"Oh." Margret had plainly not thought of the serious consequences.

Anne slipped her hand into her friend's. "Hanging is an awful thought, is it not? But the explosives they had were intended to kill hundreds of people."

"Yes, you are right. They deserve whatever comes to them," Margret said rallying. She looked up at her father. "Did they tell you where the other men are, or the plans for the attack?"

"No, but I believe they will in time." Although Sir George's tone was nonchalant, Anne had no doubt the inquisitors would not give up easily.

The front door opened, and Harwick came out first, his wrists fettered by manacles, followed immediately by Constable Jones.

Then Mrs. Cluett, similarly restrained. Captain Wycliff had hold of one of her arms. Mrs. Harwick, not in handcuffs, as she'd offered no resistance, was accompanied by one of the neighbors. Another local man ran to the stable to get Harwick's horse. He would be riding surrounded by the men; the two women would go in the carriage with Anne and Margret.

When the female prisoners were loaded and Anne and Margret settled across from them, Captain Wycliff stuck his head in the door. "Do you have your pistol, Lady Anne?"

"Certainly I do." She moved the folds of her skirt to reveal a small barrel. "I shall not hesitate to use it if the occasion should arise."

"Very good." He turned a stern gaze on the prisoners. "Ladies, mind you do not cause trouble. Your journey will be short, as it is not far to Benchley, where you will be confined until trial and a court decides your fate."

Benchley, Anne mused. Not a lengthy trip but there would be time enough for her purposes. She had questions that needed answering.

"Will you not remove these chains for the ride? What could I do confined to a coach?" Mrs. Cluett asked, leaning toward the captain invitingly. "They are most uncomfortable."

"Your discomfort is only beginning," Wycliff said coldly. "Wait until you see the prisoner cells." He closed the door and gave a nod to the coachman. The carriage moved forward with a sudden jerk.

Mrs. Cluett's lips tightened, and she stared stonily out the window; Mrs. Harwick kept her eyes on her lap. Anne and Margret exchanged a look and by tacit agreement let the silence grow for a few minutes.

"What happened to Lucy?" Anne suddenly asked. "Who killed her?" When neither woman answered, she went on. "I know both of you could tell us. Consider what the truth would mean to her parents. What do you have to lose?"

"What do we have to gain?" Mrs. Cluett asked bitterly.

"Is that all you can think about? Yourself?" Margret asked

scornfully. "If you are not confessing this additional crime because hope the court will be lenient on a woman, forget it. No Englishman is likely to forgive your treason, but Anne and I would at least think better of you if you showed a little compassion."

Beatrice Harwick choked off a small sound. Tears trickled down her face, and she raised a lace handkerchief to dab at her eyes. "I am not a bad person, truly. Jacque caught Lucy listening at the door when we were first planning the attacks."

"Shut up, you fool," Mrs. Cluett snapped.

"Why? He's the one who got away, isn't he…while we are going to prison? You said no one would know. We are in so much trouble, and I…I do not want to burn in hell."

"Oh, bollocks." Mrs. Cluett looked at her with scorn. "It's too late. We are going to hang, and your hands are drenched in blood. Nothing can save your soul."

Mrs. Harwick caught a strangled breath, staring at her companion in horror. "How can you say that?"

"Because it is true. Not even your God will forgive you."

"Stop tormenting her." Anne glared at the Cluett woman. "Allow her to make her own peace. She cannot do worse than you have." Anne shifted her gaze to Mrs. Harwick. "Jacque pretended to be your stable boy, did he not? Is he the French agent behind all of the bombings?"

Mrs. Harwick wiped at her eyes again and nodded. "Yes, Jacque Mercier."

"He will kill you for this," Mrs. Cluett spat. "You condemn us all, but Jacque is who you should fear. He will find you and take pleasure in ripping out your cowardly heart."

Appalled by the woman's cruel words, Anne picked up her pistol. "That is enough, Mrs. Cluett. If you keep threatening her, you may not make it to prison." She gave the woman a hard stare, hoping she would not call her bluff. If she did, Anne would have to ask Captain Wycliff to move her to the open top of the carriage.

Margret supported Anne's harsh words without hesitation.

She shoved Mrs. Cluett's feet. "Get away from her." Margret kicked her feet again when she didn't move and kept it up until the surly woman slid closer to her window.

"Where is the Frenchman now?" Anne asked. "Where is he taking the explosives?"

"London, but where I do not know. Jacque kept the final details to himself." Mrs. Harwick shrugged. "I suppose he did not trust anyone."

"With good reason," Mrs. Cluett muttered.

Anne studied Mrs. Harwick's face. She believed the woman was telling the truth, and there wasn't a good reason to continue questioning her. She would doubtless talk freely to the constables when she was alone, filling in any details they required, and Anne was loath to push the Cluett woman into violent behavior that would require Capt. Wycliff's assistance. Was pride influencing her decision? Yes, maybe, but in truth she already had the answers she needed.

Indeed, she did. A smile touched her lips as she settled back in her seat. Anne would have much to tell Lord Ware about the death of Lucy and how he might find Jane. Putting a stop to the rebellion was up to him.

Chapter Twenty Three

"Get the scoundrels! No one gets away."

Following Lucien and Sherbourne, Whitehall agents and Horse Guards poured from the Mill Lane house in pursuit of the fleeing revolutionaries. Haze and a strong scent of expended gunpowder hung over the courtyard, stinging Lucien's nose and eyes. He swept his gaze over the scene and caught a glimpse of the French agent among the abandoned wagons. He was using them for cover as he worked his way toward the front gate. Popping up behind the last wagon, he sprinted forward, leaped over the broken gate, and cut across the road. Running hard, he headed deeper into the city in the general direction of the Thames and Westminster.

"This one is mine," Lucien yelled and chased after him. Barely keeping his quarry in sight, he followed the Frenchman through a second crossroads and then they plunged into a densely populated section of town. The man made a sudden turn down a lane between two large houses onto a street of row-style townhouses.

Of a sudden, the threatening skies opened and rain came down in waves. Lucien was soaked in seconds, slipped in the mud, and lost sight of the Frenchman, only spotting him again as he darted through a courtyard to reach the parallel street. At first Lucien was relieved this surface was paved with cobblestones, but it was slicker than the dirt road that had caked his boots with mud.

As both pursued and pursuer became winded, they slowed their pace but kept on street after street, jogging or sometimes sprinting around corners and following twisty lanes.

When they crossed Tottenham Road, Lucien realized they were angling across to Covent Garden. Was it possible the Frenchman was not attempting to get away but was headed toward the intended location of their attack? Was he hoping others had escaped and would join him? Perhaps he thought one of the wagons had gotten away.

Good lord, could other rebels be on the way to meet him? And if Covent Garden was their destination…the popular garden with its large market, public houses, brothels, and the theatre would be a tempting choice for those with maximum death and mayhem in mind.

Lucien grunted as he stumbled while jumping a large puddle on Drury Lane. When he regained his balance, he'd lost sight of the Frenchman again. He hesitated only a moment before turning into the nearest entrance to Covent Garden.

The heavy rain had cleared some of the center space normally teeming with buyers visiting the hodge-podge of stalls and sheds in the market. But no one had gone home. Waiting for the rain to stop, men, women, and children had crowded under archways and columned entrances or inside the shabby stalls that offered some respite from the storm.

As quickly as it had started, the heavy rain stopped and turned to drizzle. Lucien spotted the Frenchman jogging through the market, shoving his way between those hardy souls who were already venturing out from shelter. Moving quickly to intercept him, Lucien was still several yards away when the Frenchman glanced back. The two men locked gazes for an instant, and Lucien realized who he was—Jacque and the Harwicks' s stable boy, the one who acted painfully awkward or simple, were one and the same—and they had overlooked him.

Jacque broke eye-contact first and dashed toward the nearest building, Madame LaBelle's, a four-story brothel. He entered the establishment without slowing his pace, and Lucien bounded up the steps after him.

Lucien's first glance took in the red brocade, three scantily clad women, but no Frenchman. He cocked his head, looking upward toward the sound of rapid footsteps on the stairs to the upper floors. Uncertain it was his quarry, he asked the women the one question sure to get a response, "Where did the French traitor go?"

"Up the stairs." The women pointed. Lucien climbed rapidly, followed by cries from the three women, "Let 'im pass. He's after a Frenchie!"

Lucien sped past closed doors and took the next flight of stairs. A few doors opened on the next floor to see what all the commotion was about, closing again when they saw Lucien and heard the women shouting.

Three flights, four…where the devil was he? Lucien slowed and walked the length of the last floor, ready to start opening doors until he spotted a ladder into the attic. He scrambled up the slats, cautiously lifting his head to peer into the space above. Hearing an ominous rustle, he ducked down as a bullet hit the beams overhead. He took out his own pistol and waited for a second shot in the event Jacque was using a double-barreled flintlock. When nothing happened, he cautiously hauled himself upward into the attic, rolling across the floor and rising into a crouch.

Still no second shot. The room appeared empty except for the large trunks along the back wall with extra bedding stacked on top. Three dormers with windows looked out upon Covent Garden, and the panes had been knocked out of one.

Devil it! The blasted Frenchman had taken to the roof.

Lucien stuck his head through the broken pane to take a look at the roof. He couldn't see Jacque, but the dormers were set back enough to allow plenty of space to step onto the roof. Holding his pistol in one hand, he eased through the widow, and squatted behind a dormer.

The roof was wet and slippery from the continuing drizzle, and Lucien shifted his feet carefully. He glanced below and saw that more of the Garden's patrons had come out of shelter, and several of them were pointing toward the roof. Great, just great…all he needed was an audience.

He raised himself to view the rest of the roof, hoping to spot Jacque, and spied the barrel of a rifle poking from behind the third dormer. *Bloody hell.* The fellow didn't have a rifle when he entered the building. He had always planned to come to this roof and had the rifle waiting. How did that fit with mob violence and powder kegs? Was it just an added bit of terror...or something else?

The sudden discharge of several muskets from below caused him to drop flat to the roof. Bullets buried themselves into the dormer above him. Who was doing the shooting? Sliding across the roof edge, he took a cautious look below—and swore in surprise.

Bedlam had broken out. People were running from a mob armed with muskets and clubs—apparently more of Jacque's band of rebels. Lucien strained to make out what the mob was shouting, confused by the mixture of protests he heard, from denunciation of Prinny to support for Bonnie Prince Charlie. Anyone with a cause or any complaint and every madman in London must have been invited to Jacque's big event. Lucien clenched his jaw. The Frenchman's invitation must have failed to mention to planned to set off enough explosives to kill them all.

At least that part of his scheme had failed. Jacque had lost the explosives for his big finale. So why was he here?

As Lucien started to pull back from the edge, he stopped, a grim smile tugging at his lips. Jacque had miscalculated the English temperament. Those loyal to Crown and country had turned on the mob, firing their own pistols, throwing vegetables from the marketing stalls, and plummeting them with umbrellas, fancy canes, or anything else at hand. The rioters found themselves outnumbered, and then a unit of the Horse Guards charged through the main entrance from the direction of Bow Street. The mob began to scatter.

Lucien's smile faded as he spotted a familiar figure below. What the devil was the Prime Minister doing there? Jenkinson, Lord Liverpool was hurrying across the Market, escorting his wife to the Russell Street exit onto Bow Street, obviously seeking safety from the authorities. Their path would take them directly below Lucien . . .

And Jacque with a rifle.

Fear tightened Lucien's chest as he realized Jacque's true reason for being there. The explosives weren't only intended for mass murder, they were a cover for the assassination of Prime Minister Jenkinson, Lord Liverpool.

The sound of a rifle hammer being cocked carried across the roof, and Lucien leapt to his feet.

"Curse you English dogs." Jacque popped up from the third dormer aiming the rifle at Liverpool.

Lucien fired his pistol. His shot barely touched the Frenchman's arm, but it was enough that Jacque flinched, jerking his shot off its mark. He spun toward Lucien and fired again. Lucien had already dropped to the roof, but ironically, the rifle misfired in the damp, misty air. Spewing a string of curses in French, Jacque heaved the empty firearm toward Lucien and took off running, slipping and sliding toward the far end of the roof.

Lucien went after him, more slowly, mindful of the treacherous surface. What was Jacque up to now? Did he honestly think he could escape? Lucien stopped and stared at the scrambling figure, realizing the Frenchman was going attempt a leap from this roof to the next. "You will never make it, Jacque."

The Frenchman looked back. "A better death than hanging."

"A fate no less than you deserve. Treason, mob riots, assassination...but why the devil did you murder two women from Blinker's Marsh?"

Jacque's forehead wrinkled, seemingly perplexed, then he smiled. "Ah, the pretty governess, you mean. I think I shan't tell you. But two *jeune fille*? Non. Not Jacque." With that, he turned and took a running leap off the edge. He landed on the other roof with inches to spare and might have made good his escape in better weather. His feet slipped sideways on the wet surface, he tottered, his arms flailing, nearly recovered, then slid over the edge and plunged four stories...without uttering a sound.

Lucien ran to the roof edge overlooking the Market and hunted for the figure of Lord Liverpool. The Prime Minister and his wife were no longer in sight. Hoping they had made it safely to Bow Street, he hurried down the ladder to find out.

As he arrived at the Bow Street station three minutes later, Lord Liverpool and his wife were emerging from the building escorted by two armed men. "Lord Liverpool," Lucien called as the Prime Minister handed her ladyship into a waiting coach. "A word, sir."

Liverpool lifted a questioning brow but took a few steps to meet him. "Viscount Ware, is it not? Salcott's heir."

"Yes, sir. I apologize for hailing you on the street like this, but I *must* speak with you. If we could step back inside the station."

"Now? We have just come from the Market and— "

"I know, sir. I was there. I only need a moment."

"Very well." Liverpool turned to the armed men. "Stay with my wife. I shall return shortly." He eyed Lucien as the station doors closed behind them. "What is this about? My wife is upset, and I need to get her home."

"Sir, I interrupted a French agent with a rifle aimed at you only minutes ago. How did he know you would be there? Do you come here the same day of each week?"

Liverpool's face went from impatience to disbelief, then he paled. "We come once a week but rarely the same day. It depends on my schedule, what is playing at the theatre…" He broke off. "See here, Ware. Are you certain about this?"

"Absolutely. I was ten feet from him."

"Where is he now?"

"Dead, but I am not convinced this is over."

"My wife…I—"

"She should be safe here, sir. I'm concerned what happens when you leave. Who knew you were visiting the Garden today?"

"My office clerks. My household servants." He rubbed his chin in thought. "Oh, dash it, Ware. I spoke of it in a parliamentary meeting on Wednesday because they suggested we meet again today."

Lucien's hopes plummeted. "A large meeting?"

"No, only six other than myself. We are working to change certain portions of the Opposition Bill."

"I will need those names."

"Your father was there, Darby, Spencer, Southway, Tomey, and Martin."

Three Whigs, three Tories. Well, he could eliminate his father. And perhaps Lord Darby. He knew little of Spencer beyond his name. The three Whigs were not friendly toward the current government, but that did not mean they would condone assassination.

Liverpool glanced toward the door, clearly impatient to be gone. "If that is all you need, my wife is waiting. I trust you will eventually give me a full accounting?"

It was more an order than a question, and Lucien nodded. "Absolutely, sir. As soon as I have the answers."

"I shall look forward to it." Liverpool hurried away, more worried about his wife than the thwarted attempt on his life.

Lucien returned to the Market, thinking rapidly. How should he handle this? If a member of Parliament was behind this—which appeared possible—the political implications were enormous. He should take his suspicions to Rothe and let him handle the sensitive pitfalls.

"Lucien, what happened up there?" Sherbourne ran up, out of breath. "I saw you on the roof with the Frenchman. He had a rifle, and I think he fired it. With all the noise I couldn't tell, then you went down, and I couldn't see you. Egad, my friend, were you harmed?"

"Not a bit. I need your help, Sherry. I have a tiger by the tale." Lucien quickly explained what had transpired on the roof. "He was waiting for Liverpool. He couldn't have known the Prime Minister would be here today, unless someone close to Liverpool told him."

"That's it. Now Cade's message makes sense." Sherbourne dug in his pocket and handed Lucien a folded note. "One of his thugs found me half an hour ago and gave this to me for you. I apologize for reading it, but—"

"No need," Lucien interrupted. "What does it say?"

"That two people had been overheard at the Pelican discussing an assassination. A dark-haired Frenchman with a heavy accent, and an English gentleman carrying a cane with a silver horse head."

Lucien stared at his partner, realizing what it meant. "*Bloody hell!*"

"You know who it is?" Sherry asked.

"I do. *Bloody hell,*" he repeated, softly this time. "I surely do. Lord Southway, leader of the opposition bill."

• • •

Lucien went straight to Whitehall and reported to Rothe, informing him of the assassination attempt and Lord Southway's suspected part in it.

"The politics of this are not to my liking, sir."

Rothe's face looked like a thunder cloud. "Nor mine. I will handle it. The bloody scoundrel. I shall see to it with pleasure."

Lucien made a hasty retreat and returned to the ranks of those chasing down the rebels. Even with the combined efforts of Whitehall, the Horse Guards, and Bow Street, it took most of the night to capture the remaining revolutionaries and clear the three bloody scenes. The French agent's body was carried to Whitehall by Rothe's command. The marquess wanted to see for himself the face of a man driven to such brutality.

Once the rebellion was under control, Lucien and Sherry spent the rest of the night accounting for the conspirators from Harwick House. Finn met them at Whitehall around midnight and drove them from one location to another to examine bodies and groups of prisoners— from Covent Garden to Church Road, where the escaping wagon had been overtaken, then to the house in Camden, and back to Whitehall where they'd viewed the prisoners at the Horse Guards.

The located Mr. Cluett on a wagon of wounded. He would lose an arm but probably live long enough to face English justice. The man who had gone by the various names of Faegan, Lacroix, and Artigue was found in a pile of corpses inside the Mill Lane coach house. Counting Jacque and Ramsey, four of the seven main conspirators were dead or under arrest.

The possibility the other three might escape punishment did not sit well with Lucien or Sherbourne.

It was well-nigh dawn when they gave up the search as futile and stopped at War Offices one last time before heading home. They found Rothe had been in a meeting for over an hour, and Mr. Sloane could not even estimate when it might end.

"We shall talk with him tomorrow."

"I will tell him. Before you go, this might interest you." He showed them the accounting of human loss he had just received: nineteen dead, twice as many injured. Most of the dead were rebels who perished at Mill Lane or during the capture of the escaped wagons. Five of the rebel mob died in Covent Garden, and a middle-aged man and woman had been shot in the mob's initial blast of musket fire. Of the agents and Horse Guard among the wounded, one had already died and three suffered crippling injuries.

"It could have been worse," Sloane said with a weary sigh.

And indeed he was right. If the Frenchman's plans had not gone awry, the death toll would have been unbearable and the government thrown into turmoil.

Lucien and Sherry were set to leave Whitehall when Rothe's office door opened, revealing several high-ranking members of Parliament. Lord Rothe glanced at his two agents, gestured they should wait, and came to meet them.

"We have reached an agreement on Lord Southway," he said. "I thought you deserved to know."

Lucien suppressed a weary protest, aware he might not like what he was about to hear.

"It may not feel like justice to you," Rothe said, correctly reading Lucien's expression, "but we cannot afford for the government to look weak by revealing Southway's treason—not in the face of tonight's uprising. We gave him the option of exile in Australia, and he accepted. He will sail tomorrow."

"Good riddance," Sherry muttered.

Lucien nodded. "Yes, I agree. I understand the need for secrecy." Southway didn't deserve the mercy he was being shown, but he knew Whitehall and the palace would breathe a sigh of relief to escape such a thorny scandal.

Sherry and Lucien descended the stairs in silence. Southway's punishment wasn't their only source of frustration. His fate was out of their hands, but they still had to find the last three conspirators.

"How could they have gotten away?" Sherry demanded. "I kept an eye out for them every chance I got."

"I doubt if they intended to participate in tonight's riot. After all, they knew about the bombs. It is more likely that Harwick stayed behind to accompany the women out of the country."

Sherry swore softly.

Dirty and close to exhaustion, they nodded to Finn and climbed into Lucien's coach. As the carriage started to move, Lucien slumped against the cushioned seats, rubbing his face with both hands.

"What a night."

"I plan to sleep for a week," Sherry said. "Maybe longer. How about you?"

"Wish I could, but I need to collect Talbot from Barnett Park."

"You could send for him."

"So I could, if I had not promised Lady Anne I would return with the latest news."

"Lady Anne, eh? She won't be much happier than we are that the Harwicks and Jeanne, er Cluett, whatever she calls herself, got away," Sherry grumbled. "I suppose they've reached France by now."

Lucien yawned. "Hardly seems right, does it?" In truth, he was too tired to worry about it tonight…this morning. The sun had been up at least two hours, and all he could think of was his bed. "Maybe fate will bring them back within our reach one day."

The only response from the opposite seat was a gentle snore. Sherbourne was asleep.

Chapter Twenty Four

Lucien woke to the sound of his butler's footsteps crossing the bedchamber. When the curtains were pulled back letting in a shaft of bright sunlight, he raised his forearm to shield his eyes. "Good God, Hughes, don't tell me it is morning already."

"It was morning when you came home, my lord."

"So it was." Weary to the bone yet covered with blood and grime when he arrived, Lucien had insisted on bathing, nearly falling asleep in the tub, before climbing into bed and drifting into sleep...only minutes ago, it felt.

"Sorry to wake you, but your father has been downstairs for almost an hour now."

Lucien sat up with a jerk. "The Earl! What does he want?"

"I could not say, my lord, but he seems most anxious about your health."

"My health?" Realizing he was repeating everything Hughes said, Lucien shook his head to clear the fog of sleep and swung his legs over the side of the bed. "Nothing is wrong with my health. What time is it?"

"Nearly one o'clock. I fear the Earl heard of yesterday's events—indeed, all of London has heard by now—including alarming rumors that dozens of the Crown's men were killed and wounded."

"Curse it! Why do these gossip-mongers never get it right? I suppose he thought I was among the carnage."

"I assured him you were not."

Standing in for the absent Talbot, Hughes offered to shave him, but Lucien waved him off. He was perfectly capable of shaving himself, had done it for months at a time on the Continent, but he rarely did for himself at home. It distressed Talbot too much.

He quickly dispensed with his ablutions and put on the cream-colored breeches and dark blue coat Hughes had set out as suitable for his planned trip to the country. He pulled on his shiny Hessians and glanced at the waiting butler. "So where is he?"

"Small parlor, my lord, drinking your best sherry."

Lucien smiled. "For an hour? He should be mellow by now." He walked out and descended the stairs.

The Earl of Salcott was pacing the room. He stopped and turned as Lucien entered, his gray eyes, so like his son's, held a question as he took in Lucien's tall form. Lucien conceded that he and Salcott were very alike in appearance, aristocratic features, dark hair, and his father had even retained much of his youthful athletic build. But there the likenesses ended. Father and son stared at each other.

"I see you have avoided serious injury."

Lucien crossed to the sideboard and poured himself a sherry. "I am unscathed by yesterday's violence. Did Hughes not tell you?"

"He did, but I wanted to see for myself. I heard it was a bloody awful affair."

"It was." Lucien nodded. "Nowhere near the numbers of casualties being reported—but it was a dangerous situation. The French agent who incited it all had intended the streets to run red with English blood. And he nearly succeeded."

"I heard about Liverpool and Southway."

Lucien lifted a brow. "Oh…where? I thought Liverpool had insisted it be kept quiet."

"From the Prime Minister himself."

Lucien nodded. His father was highly trusted in political circles. "Did you approve how the matter was resolved? I had no part in the decision. Southway was treated lightly in my opinion… but I am not a politician."

"They chose a political solution," Salcott conceded. "Perhaps justice as you perceive it was not served, but there was little else they could do. Exposing Southway's treason to the public might create more anti-government outcry than we already have." He pursed his lips as if deciding what to say. "Is this rebel activity the reason you disregarded my letters?"

Lucien looked up in surprise. "I have been out of town for several days. The mail has piled up. I apologize for being remiss in my correspondence. Was there something important?"

"Not urgent. Some regular estate matters, but I was concerned I had not heard from you. I was not aware you intended to leave town."

He gave his father a searching look, wanting to ask why the sudden interest in his affairs, but he opted for a less provoking response. "Did Grandmama not tell you she had set me a task?"

The Earl waved a careless hand. "She said something about a missing girl, but I did not understand it would take you away from London...or that it would put you in the way of being shot."

Lucien suppressed a grimace. "How did you hear about that?"

"I picked it up somewhere. You know how servants talk."

Not mine, Lucien thought. So where had Salcott come upon that piece of gossip? "'Twas nothing, sir. I was never far from town—Barnett Park near the village of Blinker's Marsh. Do you know it?"

"Sir George's home. Yes, I have been there. Years ago. We're old friends."

Lucien lifted a brow. "I was not aware of the acquaintance." But now he knew where Salcott had learned of the shooting...Sir George had sent word to his 'old friend.'

"I fear it is my fault you are unaware of a great many things. Sir George's friendship is only one of them." Salcott's voice had changed, holding a hint of regret.

Lucien steeled himself, fearing it was too late to forestall the inevitable awkward conversation regarding their long estrangement. Since Rothe had chosen to apprise Salcott of Lucien's work for the Crown, they had circled around raking up the past for several months. But today of all days?

The Earl cleared his throat and surprised Lucien by saying, "We need to talk...sometime soon. The past months—and a conversation or two with your grandmother—have made me realize how unjust...I may have been." He straightened himself. "I shall not get into any of that now. I am sure you have things that need to be done."

"I do, actually." Lucien relaxed a bit and gave his father a wry smile. "Rothe may be satisfied with my work, but Grandmama will not be if I don't bring her more complete answers regarding Lucy Drayton than I have given thus far."

"May I ask what you have learned?"

Lucien tilted his head. "Do you truly want to know?"

"I do. I would help if I can."

Lucien was taken aback by the offer, but he tried not to show it. Instead, he invited his father to sit and told him the story of Lucy Drayton from beginning to end, and even mentioned the disappearance of Jane Mawbry. "I still haven't discovered if the two matters are connected. I believe Jacque killed Lucy—although I don't yet know why—but he denied knowledge of the other girl. I intend to keep digging until I have the answers or I have run out of ideas."

He waited for Salcott to dismiss such undertakings as unworthy of a gentlemen, but the Earl surprised him again.

"Misfortune to the young is particularly disturbing, and more so when families are left without explanations. I dare say, it would be difficult to walk away from such grief."

This level of compassion was more than Lucien had previously credited to his father. Perhaps both of them had made unfounded assumptions about the other.

"If the Frenchman killed the Drayton girl," the Earl continue. "Perhaps your prisoner—ah, Cluett, wasn't it? —can tell you why."

"Yes, I should have asked him last night. I haven't the time to go back today...but soon. In light of Jacque's denial, I am more concerned about Jane Mawbry. If there is a chance she is alive..."

"You believe the Frenchman?"

Lucien shrugged. "What had he to gain by denial?"

"Yes, I see your point." Salcott pursed his lips again, a gesture Lucien recalled when as a young child he had watched his father work at his desk. "If she is alive, she may not want to be found—not if she was taken up by some scoundrel or works in a brothel."

Prostitution was a sad but common ending for wide-eyed country girls who came to the city for work and fell into the hands of ruthless men or smooth-talking purveyors. "Those who know her believe she would never go down such a path."

"If she were my daughter, I too would believe that," Salcott said. "She may not have had a choice."

"I know, and her wretched mother has no interest, but there are others, friends, who want answers, no matter how distressing."

"And they deserve no less. Perhaps we can discover the truth together."

Lucien chuckled. "Sir, I hope you are not suggesting we visit all the brothels in town—an exhausting prospect."

Salcott's lips twitched in response. "Hardly that, my boy. I was offering to make more respectable inquires. I serve on the boards of one hospital and two shelters for unfortunate women."

Lucien looked at him in astonishment. "You amaze me, sir."

His father gave a rather resigned shrug.

Yes, there was a great deal they did not know about one another.

"I'm going to Blinker's Marsh today," Lucien said. "If I learn anything that might speak for or against such an inquiry, I shall send word. Thank you for the offer."

Looking rather pleased, Salcott gave a nod and rose. "I must be going. I wish you success in your endeavors. Do let me know if I can provide any assistance."

"I shall. Good day, sir."

"And to you, son."

Salcott's footsteps echoed on the stairs.

Lucien stared at the doorway, listening to his father's indistinct words with Hughes as he retrieved his hat. The Earl appeared to be reaching out, but was it not too late? The boy Lucien had been had waited long years for his father's attention and approval; the man he had become had made his own way.

Shaking his head, Lucien puts thoughts of Salcott aside and

walked out of the parlor, calling for his breakfast. He had things to do today, including a pleasant conversation with Lady Anne to share events since they'd last been together.

• • •

Within the hour, Lucien was driving his curricle through town headed for Blinker's Marsh with Finn up behind. The small carriage would be crowded bringing Talbot and their bags back, but the day was too pleasant to be confined inside a coach. A breeze ruffled Lucien's black hair, and there were just enough clouds in a blue sky to hold the worst of the heat at bay.

London streets and walkways buzzed with crowds, and progress was slow in the more commercial parts of town. He picked up snatches of conversation from pedestrians, most of it about the mob riot in Covent Garden. The incident would likely remain the center of gossip for weeks to come unless even more shocking events occurred to engage the public mind.

He had thought to stop at Whitehall, but Westminster was swarming with Londoners taking advantage of the break in the weather, and he changed his mind, turning off Piccadilly and taking the back streets out of the city. In no time, he was passing through Blinker's Marsh and then pulling into the cobblestone stable yard of Barnett Park.

Lucien leaped down and turned toward the house as Captain Wycliff strode from the side entrance.

"So this is where you've been," Lucien said. "I had wondered."

"I was concerned for their safety." Wycliff clapped his shoulder with a grin. "Good to see you in one piece. Bits of news about a mob riot and shootings at Covent Garden trickled into the village, but we weren't sure how much was true. We've all been worried, knowing that you and Sherbourne would be in the midst of it."

"As you see, I am well. As is Sherbourne. Covent Garden was indeed the final scene of a very long day."

"I am keen to hear it all, and we have a rather interesting tale of our own."

Lucien jerked to a halt, laying a hand on Wycliff's arm to stop him from entering the manor. "What happened? No one has been hurt?"

"Nary a scratch. But let us go inside. The ladies and Sir George are anxious to know the truth behind the rumors."

Lady Anne and Miss Barnett met them in the hallway. Anne's pale blue gown brought out the color of her eyes, and he smiled at her.

"What kept you?" Miss Barnett grabbed his arm and drew him toward the drawing room. "We're having tea, and we are ever so eager to hear…well, everything! We've heard there was a mob in Covent Garden. Were you there?"

"Margret, we might let him sit first." Anne's laughing eyes met his, her look a bit mischievous. Whatever story she had to tell must having a good ending. He relaxed for the first time in days.

"Oh, yes, of course. I did not mean to be impatient."

"It is I who should apologize for my tardy arrival," Lucien said. "I can only plead the exhaustion of an eventful day and night. And I cannot stay long."

"Surely you will stay for tea," Miss Barnett protested.

"Yes, of course, and I promise a full account of events before I leave." As he settled into the drawing room with the Barnetts, Lady Anne, and Wycliff, he realized how sorry he was to be leaving the household. Not only because of Lady Anne, but he had become quite comfortable with the family. They were most congenial. He set down his cup of tea and proceeded to relate the recent events in London, skimming over the gory details of blood and death, and not mentioning the close calls. Nor did he say anything about Lord Liverpool. Perhaps he would tell Wycliff and Lady Anne in private, but the assassination attempt must never become public knowledge.

"So it *was* Jacque Mercier, the stable boy," Wycliff declared. "I paid him no mind."

Lucien frowned. "You already knew about Jacque? How?"

"Anne figured it out," Miss Barnett said, beaming at her friend.

"Mrs. Harwick confirmed it and supplied his family name. She also said he killed Lucy," Lady Anne added.

"Did she, by Jove. Well, you found out more than I did. When did you talk with her?"

And so he heard the story of the capture of the last three conspirators at Harwick House, of Anne and Miss Barnett's interrogation of the two women in the carriage, and even Miss Barnett's rather glowing account of Anne threatening Mrs. Cluett with a pistol.

Lucien laughed, but his admiration for Lady Anne moved up another notch.

"Did you learn how Lucy died?"

Anne nodded. "We did. Lucy overheard them plotting the details of the rebellion, even the powder kegs, and Jacque caught her trying to sneak out and notify authorities. He bashed her in the head with a candlestick from the hall, and she fell to the bottom of the servants' stairs. The rest of them cleared out her room and buried the body."

Lucien shook his head. "What a sad end. I am in awe of your persistence to complete Lucy's story. The Draytons will have the consolation of knowing she died attempting to help her country." He turned to look at the Barnetts and Capt. Wycliff. "You have my admiration for your courage throughout recent events. You have left little undone, and I thank you."

"You have not heard everything yet," Miss Barnett said, looking at Anne. "Go ahead. Tell him about Jane Mawbry."

He lifted a brow. "Don't tell me you found her too?"

"Well, no, but we couldn't just wait and worry," Anne said, "so we ask a few questions in the village."

"Who had I missed?"

Lady Anne tilted her head. "It wasn't a matter of having missed her...we had a chat with Mrs. Mawbry unhindered by your gentlemanly manners."

He nearly choked on a laugh. "Did you threaten to shoot her too?"

"No, of course not. She is neither a criminal nor traitor, just a terrible mother."

"But Anne made her cry," Miss Barnett said rather gleefully.

"I did not intend it. I merely told her I thought Jane had been in a delicate way, and she started sobbing." Lady Anne and Miss Barnett continued with further disclosures—Mrs. Mawbry's suspicions of a "fancy man" from Harwick House, and Mattie Ellis's suggestion they speak with the midwife, Sadie Pratt.

"So we went to see her," Miss Barnett said. "And she revealed Lucy had come to her after she was beaten and, um, forcefully seduced."

"That happened several weeks before Jane disappeared," Anne said. "But Sadie had given her the name and direction of a Doctor Jay in London, in the event there were *complications*."

"Jacque may have killed Lucy, but I wouldn't describe him as a fancy man," Lucien said.

"No, it was that odious Mr. Ramsey," Miss Barnett said. "Jane's mother had mentioned his yellow hair in particular."

"Then Ramsey must have murdered Jane," Wycliff said.

"Maybe not," Lucien said. "Jacque not only denied harming Jane, he acted as though he'd never heard of her."

The room grew quiet.

Wycliff frowned. "Surely he would know."

"She may still be alive," Anne said with hope in her voice. "And went to London looking for Dr. Jay."

Before retiring for the night, Lucien found an opportunity to inform Wycliff and Lady Anne of the attempt on the Prime Minister's life. Both were shocked at this unexpected development and understood the need for secrecy.

"I see how the truth might stir further rebellion," Lady Anne said. "Of a certain, we do not need that."

"And the threat has been eliminated," Wyciff added.

"Indeed." Lucien sighed, still not satisfied with Southway's punishment. "The man behind the plot is on what I trust is a long and unpleasant journey to Australia. I can only hope the inhabitants of those lawless colonies will deal with him accordingly."

Chapter Twenty Five

When Lucien departed Barnett Park early the following morning, his curricle was over-loaded with Talbot, Finn, and several bags. Captain Wycliff rode alongside, returning to his own town lodgings. Lady Anne would be leaving the following day, as her cousin Georgina and Aunt Meg had concluded their visit with Lord Bennington's parents and were returning to London.

The Barnett family and Lady Anne came out to see them off, but since they all planned to meet again at a ball on Friday, goodbyes were not prolonged. Lucien promised Lady Anne he would call upon her earlier if he learned anything notable regarding Jane Mawbry.

Once he dropped Talbot and the bags at the townhouse, he went to Whitehall. As anticipated, the building was still buzzing with the aftermath of yesterday's events. Despite the unfortunate deaths and injuries, the incident had been concluded to the Crown's satisfaction, and the atmosphere was one of quiet satisfaction.

Rothe looked up with a smile when Lucien walked in. "Have you heard the last of the Harwick House conspirators have been arrested?"

"Yes, excellent news. I just came from Barnett Park. Captain Wycliff and the locals did excellent work. You should consider attaching him to our unit."

The corners of Rothe's eyes crinkled with humor. "One ahead of you, Ware. I already sent a message asking him to meet with me."

"I have another detail obtained by Lady Anne Ashburn and Miss Barnett. The Frenchman's family name was Mercier. Jacque Mercier."

"Ah, yes. Lady Anne sent a message yesterday identifying a stable boy called Jack as the French agent Jacque. I tried to get the message to you yesterday, but events were already underway. I am pleased to know his full name. I keep a file on these spies, living and dead." He raised a brow at Lucien. "Lady Anne is a remarkable woman. Any chance she will change her mind about working for us?"

Lucien shrugged. "She did not mention it to me. You would have to ask her."

"I might just do so."

Rothe's eyes remained on him another moment as though he expected a more candid response, but Lucien maintained an indifferent expression. He was opposed to Anne working for the War Office, placing herself in constant danger, but he had no right to speak for her. He asked about the prisoners instead. "Any luck in getting details from the Harwicks or Cluetts? I'd sure like to know where they got the powder kegs."

"As would I, by God. It's early days, but the Harwick woman seems eager to tell us anything to escape the hangman's noose."

"Will that work for her?" Lucien asked. "Do you intend to recommend leniency?"

"Perhaps. Do you object?"

Lucien shrugged. "I leave that to you, sir."

Midday had passed by the time he left the building. Since Parliament convened around four each afternoon, Lucien went straight to the Salcott mansion so he would not miss his father. He had decided to accept the Earl's offer of assistance in finding Jane Mawbry. If the young woman was still alive and in the city somewhere, it would take a stroke of unusual luck to find her unless they could locate her name in medical records or talk with Dr. Jay. While Lucien and Sherbourne could visit shelters or talk with Londoners in the streets or shelters, they'd be repeating the work already done by constables, night watchmen, and Bow Street runners. His father had access to people and places that Bow Street and even Whitehall did not.

Lucien walked into the Earl of Salcott's study unannounced. His father was perusing papers that looked like legislative proposals and notes on pending bills. "Lucien, pour yourself a drink and one for me if you don't mind. I shall just be a moment. I have to be prepared to oppose Colby this afternoon before he gets us into a third war."

Lucien lifted a brow but said nothing to distract his father's concentration. He knew how seriously Salcott took his responsibilities in the House of Lords. He poured two glasses of brandy, set one on the desk, and stretched out in a chair.

Salcottt jotted a note to himself and laid his papers aside. "I did not expect to see you so soon."

"I have further information that supports the premise Jane Mawbry may have come to London. And the partial name of a doctor." He stretched out his legs and relaxed in the familiar sights and scents of the study. The shelves of large books, the smell of brandy-soaked cigars. As a very young boy, he hadn't fully understood that something was seriously wrong between him and the Earl, and he'd looked up to the man behind the desk as the epitome of everything brave and powerful. Not all of his childhood memories were bad, he realized with surprise. He looked up to find Salcott waiting patiently for him to go on. "There is reason to believe she came to London because she was carrying a child. Will you help me look for her?"

"Certainly. What do you need?"

"Access to shelter files, hospital records."

The Earl pursed his lips. "Such an undertaking will require time. The shelters I help oversee will be easy, but the others… However, I am acquainted with members of other boards or know those who are. Will a day or two be soon enough?"

"Perfectly fine, sir. She has been gone two years. Two more days is unlikely to make a difference."

"Missing since July of 1810, am I correct?" Salcott shoved a blank paper across the desk. "If you'll write her name, age, and a description, I shall get it to the hospital boards and the heads of any legitimate shelters or charity houses. Of course, the brothels are unlikely to cooperate, but the shelters often know the names of the street girls working in their parish."

"I appreciate whatever you can do, sir." Lucien quickly wrote the details he had on Jane, then looked up. "Oh, I almost forgot to give you the name of the doctor. It's a long shot, but Jane was referred to Dr. Jay. He was working through a shelter on Bridge Street, which I understand has closed. Perhaps someone knows of him."

His father looked thoughtful. "Jay might be an alias or an initial, but I shall ask around."

Lucien took another sip of brandy. "I have the last piece of Lucy Drayton's story—confirmation that Jacque Mercier was her killer. I thought I'd speak with Grandmama. How is she today?"

"Doing well. She is not as sturdy as she was, but nothing is wrong with her wits. I told her we have discussed your progress, and she is eager to know what you've discovered."

"I wish it was better news." Lucien set his drink down and stood. "She will have heard I'm in the house by now, so I shall not tarry. Good luck with Lord Colby." A smile tugged at his lips. "I have no doubt you will prevail." He bowed, exited to the hall, and bounded up the staircase to the Dowager Countess's sitting parlor.

• • •

Lucien spent the next hour relating Lucy's story and answering his grandmother's many questions. She wanted to hear every detail, no matter how distressing, and he had to make some selective refinements in his head.

At the end, she dropped her hands to her lap, gently shaking her head. "That poor child. She must have been terrified. What a lonely death." Her eyes were moist, and she quietly dabbed at the corners before looking up. "I know I should not welcome anyone's demise, but I am relieved that terrible man is dead. Thank you for what you have done, Lucien. Despite the sad news, Miss Eleanor—that is Lucy's great-aunt—will be ever so grateful to learn the truth. It is dreadful to be left not knowing."

"I hope it will be some comfort. The family should be proud that Lucy was trying to prevent the rebels' attack, and in a way, she did. Without the inquiry into her death, we might not have uncovered the Harwicks and their plot in time."

"Yes, they will be proud...but not surprised. She was ever a good child." After a moment, the dowager sighed and straightened. "What are your plans now you have solved this mystery for me?"

"I still have to find Jane, if I can, and then I'm headed to the country for a week or two. I have been away from Waring too long, and my estate manager wants to show off the recent improvements to the manor and the village cottages. By the time I return to London, I'm sure Lord Rothe will have a task that requires my attention."

"Of course, he will. I believe he quite relies on you...and rightly so," she said with pride in her voice. She went on, rather tentatively now, "You were quite a while with Salcott before coming to see me. Is something amiss?"

Lucien suppressed a smile. She had certainly bided her time. She must have wanted to ask that question since he arrived. "Not at all. He had offered his assistance in locating Jane Mawbry, and we were discussing the possibilities."

"Oh, what a splendid idea." Her voice remained nonchalant, but Lucien saw the satisfied gleam in her eyes. "I hope it turns out well."

He knew she was talking about more than the fate of Jane Mawbry.

• • •

Despite Lucien and Sherry's efforts over the next few days, they learned nothing new about Jane. If she was in London, she had become invisible, swallowed up by the city. Nor did they have better success with Doctor Jay. Everyone asked, "Doctor Jay who?" And of course, Lucien had no answer. He suspected the name might be an unidentifiable alias the doctor had adopted to protect the less standard part of his practice.

Lucien was at a standstill and forced to consider he might never learn Jane's fate.

On Friday, the day of the Olivers' ball, Lucien was stepping out the front door for a morning ride in the park when a coach emblazoned with the Earl of Salcott's shield pulled up in the street. The carriage door opened, and his father called out, "Ah, Lucien, I am glad I caught you. Do you have a moment to spare?"

"As long as you want, sir. Would you care to come in?"

"No, I just came to deliver a name. Dr. Pettigrew. Dr. Noah J. Pettigrew. You will find him on Lawry Street. Two years ago, he treated a young woman from Blinker's Marsh at one of the shelters. I have not approached him as I assumed you'd prefer to do that yourself."

"Pettigrew. It sounds—oh, of course." He had met a Dr. Pettigrew before while involved in tasks for Whitehall. If it was the same man, he indeed got around.

"Your know him?" Salcott asked, surprised.

"I cannot be certain, but I might."

"All the better. I hope he can assist you in locating the missing girl."

"I shall see him straight away. Thank you, sir. I was at a loss and sincerely appreciate your efforts."

"It was nothing, my boy. A few conversations, reading a file or two."

Lucien knew it had been more than that. This kind of detail on an insignificant woman hadn't just fallen into the Earl's hands without a good deal of effort.

"You are too modest. In any event, I am grateful."

"Happy to help. I must be off to a meeting, but you will let me know how this ends, will you not?"

"I shall, sir." Lucien smiled. "I have so many similar requests to that I may have to hire a town crier."

"Can I assume one of those request is from Lady Anne Ashburn?"

Lucien grew still. "Why would you think so, sir?"

"A man in my position hears things, particularly when my heir is paying marked attention to an eligible young lady."

Unsure of Salcott's intentions, Lucien answered carefully. "It is true we have become friends. Do you disapprove?"

"How could I? She is a lovely woman."

"Yes, she is."

The Earl gave him an appraising look and chuckled before ordering his coachman to drive on.

• • •

Lucien discarded his plans for a ride in Hyde Park, called for his curricle, and headed for Lawry Street. Pulling up at Number 46, he found a rather well-appointed set of rooms functioning solely as a medical establishment. Many surgeons, not having the education or status of physicians, could hardly afford such a luxury and often practiced out of their lodgings. Dr. Pettigrew must indeed be doing well.

Handing the reins to Finn, Lucien went inside. An older man dressed in clothes suggesting he was a gardener—his hand wrapped in a bloody cloth—was seated in the outer room talking with a young man.

After a few moments, the young man broke off his conversation and hurried forward, introducing himself as James Wynn, Pettigrew's apprentice. "How may I help you, my lord? Are you in need of medical treatment? I'm afraid the doctor has not yet arrived."

"I wish to consult with him on a personal matter. Do you expect him soon?"

"I honestly don't know," Wynn admitted. "He may have received an urgent request while at home. I thought he'd be here by now."

"Perhaps I might find him still at home. Does he live nearby?"

"No, sir. Near Soho Square, and I doubt if you'd find him there. He's normally up and out early."

"I see." Pettigrew's address was a surprise. Soho Square was an expensive part of town to find a mere surgeon.

Lucien's slow response must have registered with the young

man, because James grinned and added, "It's an inherited residence, I believe."

Lucien chuckled that the lad had caught him out. So, Pettigrew came from a wealthy family, explaining his gentlemanly manners, his well-made clothes, and his attendance at the society concert last winter when Lucien had last seen him. However, it did not explain why he would be tending to runaway pregnant girls or why Lucien had first met him examining corpses for Whitehall. Those hands-on tasks were typically left to surgeons, men who gained their skills through apprenticeship or on the battlefield, rather than education.

He handed young Wynn his card. "Tell him I will call back later."

"I'll do so, sir. Oh, what luck," he said, craning his neck at the front window. "I believe that's him now."

A single-horse carriage had stopped outside, and a man in his thirties stepped down. It was indeed the medical person Lucien had met before. As on prior occasions, Pettigrew was fashionably dressed as a gentleman but without ostentation, his clothes demonstrating a certain practical reserve.

Pettigrew paused upon entering the door, looking first at the waiting patient, then turning to Lucien with a questioning frown. "Viscount Ware, is it not? The Whitehall incident."

Lucien dipped his chin. "Good memory, sir."

Pettigrew smiled. "I never forget a patient. How is the arm?"

"Good as new."

The apprentice cleared his throat. "Doctor, would you like me to put the horse away?"

"Thank you, James, but no. I have to go out again." Pettigrew turned back to Lucien. "Are you here as a patient?"

"Not this time. May we speak privately?"

"Yes, of course." He pointed at an open door. "My office is right through there. I shall join you shortly, as soon as I have seen this injured man and arranged for tea."

"Take your time," Lucien said.

The doctor's inner office carried through the same common-sense approach seen in the man's attire with a strong emphasis on comfort. Lucien settled into a well-made chair with cushioned seat and back in a subdued brown. A window overlooked a tiny, enclosed garden that was filled with growing things. He knew little of plants but assumed they were mostly herbs or medicinal vegetation.

Lucien spotted a certificate on the wall and was getting up to examine it when Pettigrew strode in, followed by James with the tea tray. Surprised, Lucien sat down again. Considering the patient's bloody hand, he had expected to wait much longer. "Your patient's injury was not serious?"

"Serious enough. A mishap with the shears, but he cut nothing major. James here will finish stitching him up." He glanced at his apprentice with approval as the young man poured two cups of tea and left. "The lad is really quite skilled."

"I confess to vulgar curiosity, but what kind of doctor are you?"

"A physician who often has blood on his hands." Pettigrew gave a wry smile. "I was educated as a physician it is true, but my practical experience as a surgeon was learned on the battlefield. Now, I find I prefer treating injuries and broken bones rather than the megrims of idleness, rich food, and too much strong drink."

An interesting man, indeed. Lucien took a polite sip of tea and set it down, waiting while Pettigrew addressed his own tea and biscuit with enthusiasm. The doctor sighed and leaned back. "It was an early call, and I missed my morning repast."

"Don't let me rush you, but I do not want to take up too much of your busy day. I know you are wondering why I am here, and I won't keep you guessing. I am looking for a young woman who may have been treated by a man known as Dr. Jay. I'm hoping Jay is one of your names, or a name you have gone by, and that you can tell me of her present whereabouts."

Pettigrew's smile faded. "I cannot give you information on a patient, and—"

"I bring you no trouble, doctor," Lucien said, leaning forward. "I understand this is an unusual request and that the treatments

Dr. Jay offers may be a delicate matter, but this young woman disappeared from her home under circumstances that have raised serious concerns for her safety. Well, I have stated that badly. If you have time, perhaps I should explain the story from the beginning."

Pettigrew appeared to relax. "By all means. My calls are not urgent, and if a young woman could be in trouble, of course I will spare the time. Please go on."

Lucien began with Lucy's murder but moved on quickly to talk about Jane, her home life, her suspected delicate condition through no fault of her own, her disappearance, and the neighbors' desperate hopes for word of her wellbeing.

"A wretched but somewhat familiar story." The doctor's solemn brown eyes studied Lucien. "I would like to relieve your mind, my lord, but I am not familiar with the name Mawbry."

Lucien's spirits slumped. He had gotten his hopes too high. "Perhaps if I describe her and explain how she might have come to your attention."

As he talked about Sadie, the Blinker's Marsh midwife, Pettigrew sat forward with a smile. "Perhaps it is time to say that indeed Miss Pratt knows me as Dr. Jay, as in Jason, and the young woman sounds like Jane Bowles. I did not know all the particulars of Jane's situation. Frankly, I didn't ask, but much of her story appears to fit."

"How certain are you?"

Pettigrew laughed at this eager response. "Not at all, but come, take a ride with me while I tell you what I know."

After a brief discussion, they took the doctor's less-conspicuous gig rather than Lucien's dashing curricle. "I have a certain outward appearance to maintain," Pettigrew said. "I've had a difficult time establishing a practice where the lower classes feel free to approach me. I'm afraid going about in such a fine carriage would set back my efforts."

"Why I believe you are a fraud, sir," Lucien said with a smile.

"I suppose I am, but what else is a second son to do?"

They rode in companionable silence until Lucien asked, "Won't you tell me where we are going?"

"Patience, my lord. It won't be long now, just enough time for me to tell you about Jane Bowles. She came to me over a year ago—maybe longer—alone, frightened, and carrying a child she did not want." Pettigrew paused while he negotiated a corner. "After we talked, she decided to place it for adoption, but as her time of confinement drew near, she changed her mind. A midwife I trust delivered a healthy child, and we found Jane employment that would allow her to support the two of them—not exactly comfortable but adequate." Pettigrew drew the gig to a halt in front of a wax and tallow merchant on Haymarket Street.

"Is this where she works?"

"Last I knew. Mr. and Mrs. Sempill run the place. Nice people, respectable."

Lucien shook his head. He found it hard to accept this could truly be Jane…and was oddly reluctant to find out.

"I never thought we would find her so well positioned. Are you sure?" Lucien knew his doubts were nearing the point of rudeness and that he should apologize, but instead of being offended, Pettigrew laughed.

"I would not drag you here, sir, if I was not convinced. But you must see for yourself and address the rest of your questions to her."

"Of course. Are you coming?" Lucien prepared to descend.

Pettigrew shook his head. "This is not my affair, and I have patients to see."

Lucien paused, arrested by the doctor's words, and slowly settled back on the seat. "Your words remind me someone else is very much involved and should be present when the truth is uncovered. I cannot thank you enough for your assistance, doctor, but I shall return at a later time."

"As you wish, Lord Ware. If you will, send a note to tell me how it went."

"Of course. I can take a hackney from here and allow you to get on with your rounds."

"No need. My first call takes me past the surgery where your groom and curricle are waiting."

As they drove back through the city streets, the two men talked about the doctor's occasional medical work with the police. "A local magistrate is a family friend," Pettigrew said, explaining how he became involved. "The first time, he needed an opinion with haste, and I did it as a favor. Now, I find it intriguing."

Lucien understood Pettigrew's love of a challenge. In fact, he quite enjoyed the man's company. After thanking the doctor again, Lucien drove to his townhouse, changed into riding clothes, and called for his saddle horse. Before arranging to take Anne to Haymarket Street, he had one other thing to do.

The frisky stallion—who hadn't had a good run in several days—covered the distance to Blinker's Marsh in excellent time. Lucien didn't stay long with Dan and Mattie Ellis, but he got what he came for, and he learned that Mrs. Mawbry had packed up and left the village to live with her recently-widowed sister nearly three hours journey away.

Satisfied with what he'd heard, Lucien returned to London in time for a light meal and a discussion with Talbot over his attire for the Olivers' ball that evening.

Chapter Twenty Six

Although Lucien was looking forward to seeing Lady Anne, he
did not want it to appear so. He had not yet decided whether
to pursue his interest in her, particularly in light of his work for
Rothe. Intelligence inquiries did not leave much time for a serious
relationship nor were the risks involved appropriate for a married
man. In fact, he wouldn't be surprised if Salcott raised objections to
Lucien's work for the War Office if he believed his son was close to
fathering an heir to perpetuate the family name. Lucien had never
thought of himself as a husband or father, certainly not for years
to come, and Lady Anne was not the woman for a casual dalliance.

As a result of these constraints, the clock in the Olivers'
hallway was close to chiming midnight when Lucien entered the
ballroom. His eyes swept the room, and he chuckled to himself
upon seeing Sherbourne dancing with Emily Selkirk, a pretty
young woman from the country near Sherbourne's family seat. He
had not realized Emily was in town. Her brown curls, green eyes,
and engaging personality had held Sherry's attention the past year,
and Lucien suspected it was turning into a serious courtship. His
partner hadn't yet mentioned the possibility of getting betrothed,
and Lucien wondered if he too was concerned about reconciling
the demands of Rothe with those of a wife.

He spotted Captain Wycliff off to one side of the room speaking
with Miss Barnett and Lord Rothe. Aha. Had Rothe successfully
recruited the captain or was he still importuning him to join
Prinny spy unit? Lucien suppressed a laugh and went to find out.

They had barely exchanged greetings before Rothe turned and
lowered his voice. "I am delighted to report you shall have further
opportunities to work with Captain Wycliff from now on."

"Is it not exciting?" Miss Barnett asked, brightly.

"Now, Margret, you must be discreet and not bandy it about," Wycliff urged.

"I know," she said in a near whisper this time. "It is still exciting."

"Excellent news," Lucien said with a nod to the captain. "I look forward to it." Neither the captain nor Miss Barnett appeared concerned about the risks involved. Of course, she might not yet perceive how dangerous his work would be, and Wycliff, being a military man, was accustomed to the perils of government service. No doubt they'd sort it out.

Having satisfied his curiosity, Lucien resumed his search for Lady Anne and found her dancing with Marquess Addington's heir. The candlelight caught the highlights in her fair locks, and she looked radiant in a gown of white and rose silk as she listened with obvious interest to her dance partner. He wonder what they had found to discuss. While the young man was popular with the ladies, Lucien found him a bit shallow, not at all likely to appeal to a young woman of intelligence.

When the dance ended, Lucien excused himself from his companions. "I see Lady Anne, and I hope to claim a dance while she is free."

"Oh, do bring her over," Miss Barnett exclaimed. "I know it's only been a few days, but it seems like forever since we've talked."

"Yes, do." Rothe said. "It would be pleasant to renew our acquaintance."

The marquess had shown an immediate spark of interest at Lady Anne's name that made Lucien sigh. Without doubt, Rothe would be repeating his attempt to recruit her.

"I shall convey your wishes," Lucien promised as he stepped away. He moved quickly to intercept Lady Anne before someone requested a dance or drew her into conversation. He bowed upon reaching her. "My lady, a pleasure to find you here tonight."

"My pleasure as well, Lord Ware." She smiled at him, a dimple showing. "Was that Miss Barnett I saw you with?"

"Yes, and the captain. And Lord Rothe. They implored me to

invite you to join them, but I must claim a few moments first. I have news of Jane."

"Have you found her? Is she alive? What of the child?"

He raised an exaggerated brow. "My lady, you are showing an unfashionable amount of enthusiasm."

"Oh, don't tease me." She met his laughing eyes. "What have you learned?"

"I believe I have found her."

"Oh, Lucien," she silently clapped her gloved hands together, then blushed, realizing how informally she'd addressed him. "Forgive my familiarity, my lord."

"Nothing to forgive," he said, rather pleased. "Jane's story only wants for confirmation, and I thought it would be appropriate to share the final step with you."

Her brow wrinkled. "What do you mean?"

Lucien related the recent events that led him to Dr. Pettigrew and eventually to Sempills' candle shop. Lady Anne listened with rapt attention.

"How could you not go in and meet her?" She looked at him wide-eyed. "I never could have waited."

"I was sorely tempted, but it would not have been fair. Without your help, I would not have found her."

"I beg to disagree, my lord. You would have found her, but I shall take credit that Margret and I helped get you there a little sooner. When can we meet her?" she asked eagerly. "Tomorrow morning?"

"Exactly what I had in mind. I leave for a long-awaited visit to my country home in Waring in the afternoon. Is eleven too early?"

"Perfect. I shall be waiting. Oh, I shall be at sixes and sevens until I know."

"Perhaps this would be a good time to join Miss Barnett so she can distract you. A word of warning—Lord Rothe has recruited Capt. Wycliff and is likely to repeat his offer to you."

She smiled and shook her head. "In vain, I assure you, but let us join them nonetheless. Do they know about Jane?"

"No, I didn't mention it."

She looked up at him. "Why not? Were you afraid of raising their hopes?"

He shrugged. "I wished to share it with you first."

Understanding filled her eyes. "I am glad you did. Sharing a private secret is rather...nice."

Intimate, he corrected silently, and then admonished himself for such indulgence when their future was so unclear to him. For now he was satisfied to remain as they were, and he needed to keep that in mind.

He looped his arm with hers, and they made their way slowly around the room until they reached Miss Barnett and her companions.

"About time," Miss Barnett said. She gave Lady Anne a sly look. "I saw you with your heads together. Is it anything you can share?"

Lady Anne looked at Lucien, he nodded, and she turned to Margret with a smile. "Fantastic news. Jane Mawbry is alive, and Lord Ware has found her."

All eyes turned to Lucien.

"Not without help," he said. "And it isn't confirmed yet but looks very promising." He went over again what led him to the wax and tallow merchant on Haymarket Street. "Lady Anne has agreed to accompany me tomorrow to meet the young woman and confirm her identity."

"You will let us all know, will you not?" Miss Barnett asked.

"To be sure." Lady Anne nodded. "If you will be at home in Barnett Park, I shall call upon you in the afternoon as soon as I have seen her."

"I'll be there."

"I congratulate you, Ware," Lord Rothe said. "I understand you were assisted once again by the lovely and resourceful Lady Anne."

"Only a small assist," Anne protested. "Miss Barnett did as much as I. Of course, I am honored to have our efforts praised, and I do enjoy working on a puzzle with Viscount Ware and Lord Sherbourne from time to time. However, I am equally delighted not to have the responsibility." She smiled at Rothe. "Do you understand?"

Rothe sighed. "All too clearly, my dear. I see that Ware has forewarned you. Very well, I shall say no more on the subject." Then he smiled. "At least not tonight. I must reluctantly take myself away from such charming company as I have business yet to attend." He bowed and moved into the crowd.

"Nicely done, Lady Anne," Lucien said with approval.

"Thanks to you I was prepared, but it sounds as though this won't be the last time."

"Count on it." Wycliff's lips lifted in a smile. "I gave in immediately and saved myself a good deal of grief."

"Yes, but you *want* to work for the War Offices," Miss Barnett said. "Anne does not."

"Enough of this serious talk." Lucien held his hand out to Lady Anne as they heard the first strains of a waltz. "May I?"

• • •

Nigh on to noon the following day, Lucien's carriage stopped in front of Sempills' shop. He assisted Lady Anne to step down in her pale green gown and nodded to Gregory, his regular coachman. "We will not be long."

They paused a moment to look at the establishment. It was in good repair, the sign recently repainted. If Lucien had to guess, he'd say the business was doing well. The second floor appeared to be a lodging, and he wondered if it was the owners' home or rental property that provided additional income.

"Shall we go in?" he asked.

Lady Anne nodded. "It appears to be a respectable workplace."

The bell above the door jangled cheerfully.

The inside was neatly arranged to display various kinds and sizes of candles, tallow and wax pieces. A woman with apple cheeks when she smiled and hazel hair showing its first touches of gray stood behind the counter.

"Good morning, my lady, sir. May I help you? If you don't see what you want, I'm sure we can make it for you. We pride ourselves on meeting every possible need of our patrons."

"Quite successfully, I am sure," Lucien said smoothly. "Are you Mrs. Sempill?"

"Yes, that's me."

"Dr. Pettigrew sent us. We are inquiring about an employee he recommended to you. Miss Jane Bowles."

"Not to be disrespectful, but what do you want with her?" Mrs. Sempill eyes narrowed. "Our workers are busy in the back until six. Perhaps you should come back then."

So, Jane still worked there, but if they came back as her employer suggested, Lucien was sure the girl would be gone. Mrs. Sempill acted quite protective.

"We do not bring trouble," he said. "May we speak to her just briefly?"

"It would mean very much to us," Lady Anne said. "I promise we shall not keep her long from her duties."

Mrs. Sempill's demeanor softened as she studied Lady Anne. "Well, I suppose a few minutes wouldn't hurt...if she wishes it. Can I give her your names?"

They introduced themselves. Although the woman's brow lifted, she didn't comment or otherwise react to her distinguished visitors other than to say, "Please wait here, and I shall inquire if she wishes to see you." She disappeared through a rear door.

"I think she likes you," Lucien whispered.

Before Lady Anne could respond, Mrs. Sempill returned, followed by a young woman with dark brown hair pinned up and held in place by a plain cap to keep it out of the waxy substances she worked with.

The young woman's gaze seemed anxious but determined. She gave a quick curtsey. "My lady, my lord. You wished to see me?"

Considering the girl's obvious unease, Lucien gave a slight nod to Lady Anne. She took the hint. "Is there someplace private we can talk?" she asked.

"It's not necessary," Jane said. "Mrs. Sempill is a friend."

"I reckon we'll be fine here," the proprietress added firmly. "Unless customers come in."

"We shall hurry to avoid that." Lady Anne turned to Jane with a soft smile. "My dear, are you Jane Mawbry from Blinker's Marsh?" When the girl's eyes rounded, Lady Anne added, "I ask because we've been looking for her to confirm she is safe. Another village girl was found dead, and well, we had concerns that Miss Mawbry might have suffered a similar fate."

"What made you come to this place?"

"Sadie Pratt told us about Dr. Jay, and the doctor brought Lord Ware to Sempills."

The girl nodded as though satisfied. "I heard about Lucy Drayton, but I don't understand why you went to all this trouble to find Jane."

Lucien stepped in to explain, beginning with the early questions about the identity of the bones. "By the time they were identified as belonging to Lucy, we were interested in Jane's story and worried about her." He smiled. "And then there were the Ellises. They are so desperate for news of her—of you—that we couldn't quit looking."

"I never meant to worry anyone. Yes, I'm Jane Mawbry. I left home because…" her voice faded.

"We know why," Lady Anne said, reaching out a hand but not touching her. "We heard part of your story from Sadie Pratt."

"And part from Dr. Jay," Lucien added, using the name she would know. "You needn't fear Mr. Ramsey. He is dead."

"Mercy, me," Jane put her fingers to her lips. "Mr. Ramsey dead. I s'pose I am not exactly happy, it would be un-Christian, but I'm not sorry either."

"Nor should you be," Lady Anne said stoutly.

Mrs. Sempill snorted. "The lady's right, Janie. Don't you worry your head over the likes of him. He does not deserve it."

Jane nodded, looking a bit perplexed. "How did he die? Has something bad happened since I left Blinker's Marsh?"

Lucien and Lady Anne related the most pertinent news—

Ramsey's treasonous activities, his death, her mother's departure from the village—and ended on a good note with Dan and Mattie Ellis's offer of a place in their home.

"They are such good people," Jane said. "I wanted to tell them everything, but I could not bear the thought they might think badly of me."

"They wouldn't have, you know."

"Mama did. I couldn't stay after the things we said to one another. So Mrs. Mattie knows about Lily, my little girl?" Her eyes lit up when she said the child's name.

"They know you have a baby but not her name." Lucien met her questioning eyes. "I spoke to them just yesterday. They want you and your child to be part of their family."

Jane's eyes misted. "I would like that too."

"Shall we help you pack and take you there?" Lady Anne asked.

"No, not yet. I'll have to think about it. I have a life here now." She glanced at her employer with a shy smile. "Mrs. Sempill befriended me when I really needed someone. She taught me the business and has helped me with Lily. I have a place of my own upstairs, and decent work. Thanks to her, I've learned to care for myself and my daughter."

"What about the Ellises?"

"Oh, I want to see them. I will go on my very next day off and take Lily. I hope to see them a lot—Lily needs a family—but I won't move back to Blinker's Marsh, not now. Eventually, who knows?"

"What about your mother?" Anne asked out of curiosity. "Will you see her?"

Jane shrugged. "I may write, but I won't live with her or let her treat Lily like she did me."

Lucien and Lady Anne left Haymarket Street a short time later. She sighed and folded her gloved hands in her lap. "What a wonderful ending. After Lucy, I was so afraid…well, you understand. But Jane has a fine job to support herself, protective friends, a new family in the Ellises, and a healthy child." She sighed again. "I am truly delighted."

"A good tale to share with Miss Barnett."

"Oh, yes. And her mother. Even Sir George. Like most men, he acts as though he doesn't care about such things, but it is just a pretense."

"Most men?"

"Well, there are exceptions." She gave him that sweet, demure smile with the peeping dimple that took his breath away. Contrasting so vividly with the intrepid adventuress he had seen in her more than once, this very feminine side only added to her charm. Lucien moved across the carriage to sit beside her. When she lifted her eyes to look into his, he folded her in his arms, and kissed her.

"I have wanted to do that for a long time," he murmured several moments later.

"Really?" Anne lifted her head to see his face, her eyes twinkling. "When did you decide I was more than just an interfering female, my lord?"

"I do not recall ever saying that."

"You did not need to."

"Well, my dear, if you're going to pin me down to a date and time, the answer is never. You *are* an interfering female. Inquisitive, meddlesome, and thoroughly charming." He cut off her protest with another kiss. When he raised his head this time, he grinned. "I think I have gotten used to you, my lady."

About the Author

After retiring from a legal career with the Juvenile Court System, J.L. Buck published sixteen urban fantasy/paranormal novels under the pen name of Ally Shields. In 2019 she decided to write mysteries set in the Regency period of history she had always enjoyed, and she began work on the Viscount Ware Mystery series.

She lives in the Midwest with Latte, a mischievous Siamese cat, who often attempts to co-author her writing by taking over the keyboard. When not writing or running two blogs, Ms Buck enjoys her eight grandchildren (and a great-grandson), reading (preferably on a sunny deck), travel (USA and abroad from Africa to Europe to the British Isles to Disney World in Florida), and binge-watching any sub-genre of mystery shows.

Ms Buck loves to hear from readers and can be contacted through her website or social media (twitter: @janetlbuck or her pen name account: @ShieldsAlly)